JUN 1 3 2022

P9-DTA-367

NAPA COUNTY LIBRARY
580 COOMBS STREET
NAPA, CA 94559

WAVE RIDERS

By Lauren St John

WOLFE AND LAMB MYSTERIES
Kat Wolfe Investigates
Kat Wolfe Takes the Case
Kat Wolfe on Thin Ice

LEGEND OF THE ANIMAL HEALER SERIES
The White Giraffe
Dolphin Song
The Last Leopard
The Elephant's Tale
Operation Rhino

LAURA MARLIN MYSTERIES
Dead Man's Cove
Kidnap in the Caribbean
Kentucky Thriller
Rendezvous in Russia
The Secret of Supernatural Creek

ONE DOLLAR HORSE SERIES
The One Dollar Horse
Race the Wind
Fire Storm

STAND-ALONE NOVELS
The Snow Angel
The Glory
Wave Riders

LAUREN ST JOHN

WAVE RIDERS

FARRAR STRAUS GIROUX

New York

Farrar Straus Giroux Books for Young Readers
An imprint of Macmillan Publishing Group, LLC
120 Broadway, New York, NY 10271 • mackids.com

Copyright © 2022 by Lauren St. John. All rights reserved.

Our books may be purchased in bulk for promotional, educational, or
business use. Please contact your local bookseller or Macmillan Corporate
and Premium Sales Department at (800) 221-7945, ext. 5442, or by email
at MacmillanSpecialMarkets@macmillan.com.

Library of Congress Cataloging-in-Publication Data

Names: St. John, Lauren, 1966– author.
Title: Wave riders / Lauren St John.
Description: First American edition. | New York : FSG Books for Young
Readers, 2022. | Originally published in Great Britain by Macmillan Children's
Books in 2021. | Audience: Ages 10–12. | Audience: Grades 4–6. | Summary:
After their guardian disappears, twelve-year-old twins Jess and Jude are
fostered by the Blakeney family, but their search for information about
their parents puts them in danger when they uncover secrets their wealthy
benefactors want to keep hidden.
Identifiers: LCCN 2021046011 | ISBN 9780374309671 (hardcover)
Subjects: CYAC: Twins—Fiction. | Brothers and sisters—Fiction. | Orphans—
Fiction. | Secrets—Fiction. | Inheritance and succession—Fiction. | Mystery
and detective stories. | LCGFT: Novels. | Detective and mystery fiction.
Classification: LCC PZ7.S77435 Wav 2022 | DDC [Fic]—dc23
LC record available at https://lccn.loc.gov/2021046011

First published in Great Britain by Macmillan Children's Books, 2021
Designed by Veronica Mang
Printed in the United States of America by Lakeside Book Company,
Harrisonburg, Virginia
First American edition, 2022

ISBN 978-0-374-30967-1 (hardcover)
1 3 5 7 9 10 8 6 4 2

For Lucia, who, like me, loved oceans
and dolphins. I'm honored and humbled
that our paths crossed on the page.

CONTENTS

I'm not afraid of storms, for
I'm learning how to sail my ship.

—*Louisa May Alcott*

We have salt in our blood, in our sweat,
in our tears. We are tied to the ocean.
And when we go back to the sea, whether
it is to sail or to watch it, we are going
back from whence we came.

—*John F. Kennedy*

WAVE RIDERS

Alone

It all began with a rogue wave.

Later, Jess would think: What if the sea had been wilder that night? What if the wave that broke ranks and ambushed their yacht had been one of those monsters sailors dread, with a glittering crest as high as a house and enough breaking pressure to crush a cruise ship or dash a helicopter from the sky?

What then? Would she have lived to tell the tale?

The freak wave that slammed into *You Gotta Friend* at five minutes to midnight on the third Saturday in November wasn't a supersize killer, but its impact was enough to hurl Jess against her cabin wall, bashing her cheek and splitting her lip.

Blood and wood varnish met on the tip of her tongue. Fear kickstarted her heart.

She snapped upright in her sleeping bag and flicked on a flashlight. Her books—just seven dog-eared copies, each more precious than gold—were wedged safely in their nook, but the small oil painting that was the sole reminder of her mother had wrenched free of its nail and fallen onto her bunk. Jess laid it carefully beside her pillow. She'd hang it up again when the crisis had passed.

Rubbing her cheek, she waited for Captain Gabriel Carter's familiar shout: *Life jackets, kids, and don't forget your safety harnesses. Jude, if I catch you on deck without yours, you'll be in trouble.*

When they'd first set sail from Bantry Creek, Florida, 154 long days ago, her twin brother had pretty much believed that their guardian could walk on water. Now, increasingly, Jude and Gabe butted heads.

But to Jess's surprise, there was no call to action from the skipper. No rustle of waterproofs or stamp of boots on the companionway steps that led to the deck. Only the whining of the wind, the clanking of the halyard and the *slap-slap* of waves against the hull. Through the salt-splattered hatch, the sky was panther black.

Were it not for her throbbing cheek and stinging lip, Jess would have wondered if she'd dreamed the wave. Whatever it was couldn't have been serious or Gabe would have yelled for them, and Sam, their Swiss shepherd dog, would be barking madly.

Jess decided that no news was good news. That was her first mistake.

Her second was switching off her flashlight and hunkering back down into the silky cocoon of her sleeping bag.

· · ✳ · ·

Next thing she knew it was 8:59 a.m. That was unheard of. Her brother was the noisiest boy alive. He was also an early riser. Dawn was his favorite time of day, and she and Gabe had no choice but to "enjoy" it with him.

"It's like living with an elephant," Jess had complained after being rudely awakened for the zillionth time by crashing pans, whistling and stomping, and exuberant bursts of song.

"Thanks for the compliment, sis," Jude shot back with a grin. "Elephants are famously quiet. They tread so lightly on the savanna, they barely leave a trace. I'm touched that you think I'm as sure-footed and silent as they are."

That was Jude: irrepressible. Life was one long joke to him. Gabe was constantly telling him that his best quality was also his worst. It was impossible to get him to take anything seriously.

Jess padded into the galley in her pajamas. It was as immaculate as she'd left it the evening before. That was odd too. By this time, there'd usually be at least two mugs in the sink, plus a smear of jam, a spill of milk, and a trail of crumbs on the teak dining table. Sleepily, Jess moved to the fridge to look for juice, almost treading on an upturned chocolate cake and twelve scattered candles. A plate had shattered too. It was only then that she remembered it was their birthday that day, hers and Jude's. They'd planned to celebrate. Now their cake was ruined.

Jude's cabin door was propped open, his neatly made bunk on display. Gabe's cabin was empty too. Usually spotless, it now resembled a scene from *Titanic*. A locker had burst open. Sailing gear and the contents of the first aid kit were strewn everywhere. Bandages and Band-Aids sagged in a spill of soda from an overturned can.

But what really made Jess's scalp prickle with unease was that their dog, Sam, didn't come racing down the steps to greet her, the way he had every morning for the past five months. He always yelped with joy and spun in circles as if he hadn't seen her in forever.

"Gabe?" she yelled. "Jude? *Sam?*" No answer.

Something was wrong.

Out of habit, she pulled a life jacket over her pajamas before climbing the companionway steps to the deck. Her brother was fast asleep in the cockpit, his tanned face squashed up against a blue-striped cushion, wheat-colored curls falling over his eyes.

Jess's relief was short-lived. Her brother didn't stir, and neither did Sam. The dog was sprawled on his side on the wet deck, unconscious, his creamy-white coat lifting in the wind.

Jess felt a bolt of pure fear. Sam was the best guard dog ever to take to the seas. The chances of him dozing through so much as a tiptoeing mouse were zero.

There was no sign of Gabe, and not a lot of places he could be. They were on a yacht, surrounded by open ocean. The lifeboat was stowed securely in its compartment. Gabe's safety line hung from its usual hook.

Jess leaned over the side, hoping that Gabe had merely gone for a swim. That's when she saw it. The anchor warp, which she'd helped Gabe put down when they'd moored near

Devil's Bay the previous night, had snapped. The yacht was adrift.

What was going on? Had she slept through some emergency? Had the rogue breaker that flung her against the cabin wall caused Jude and Sam to slip and bang their heads? Had Gabe gone for help?

But, no—the dinghy was still tied up at the stern, bouncing on the waves.

Fighting off panic, Jess shook her twin's shoulder. "Jude, wake up! Jude, come on, this is not funny. JUDE!"

His hazel eyes opened a slit before closing again. "Woz up? Tired. Lemme sleep."

She shook him harder. "Jude, I need you. You have to wake up. Where's Gabe? What happened?"

When her brother didn't stir, she turned on the hose and squirted him with a jet of cold water.

He sat up in a hurry then. "W-w-what was that for? Ow, my head hurts. Why's Sam flopped out like that? Is he ill? Where's the skipper?"

"That's what I'm trying to find out."

"What do you mean? If he's not on deck, he must be down below."

"No, Jude, he's not. He's nowhere."

A terrible coldness was creeping into Jess's bones. After checking on Sam, who was whimpering drowsily, she hurried to the bow.

To starboard, and a long way off, were the volcanic outlines of a couple of islands. Elsewhere, there was nothing but empty ocean, without another boat or seagull in sight. The expanse of blue made Jess feel claustrophobic, as if the water was closing in on her, making it hard to breathe.

Jude was doing a frantic search of the cabins. When he reappeared, his face was as pale as the sail. The twins clung to the mast together, staring into the sapphire deep, willing it to give up its secrets.

They didn't speak. There were no words. They were more than a thousand nautical miles from Bantry Creek, the only home they'd ever known. Without Gabriel, they had nothing and no one in the world.

They were alone.

CHAPTER 1

A Mysterious Encounter

One day earlier . . .

Picture yourself on a tropical island, on a beach so white it shimmers. The sand is as silky as baby powder between your toes. Doves coo and terns turn lazily in a crystalline sky. Scarlet- and purple-winged parrots flit among the palms. The water is the color of aquamarine gemstones, deepening to jade around undersea caves and indigo in places where the seabed drops away sharply. Turtles and angelfish glide through pink coral reefs.

Naturally, there are dolphins.

Your home is a sleek thirty-seven-foot Rustler yacht, and you can sail it anywhere, any time you choose. The Bahamas or Baja, California, this week; Turkey or Turks and Caicos next month. The Cape of Good Hope! Australia, even! Forget school. As for homework, that's a thing of the past. You can spend all day, every day, paddling in lagoons, barbecuing lobsters, or snoozing on a sun lounger.

Now imagine that you'll be doing this for the rest of your life. Forever and ever. Sound blissful? Remember that, even in paradise, the weather's unpredictable. Sea squalls and hurricanes can whip up out of nowhere with terrifying speed. What if you capsize? What if there are sharks? What if you're seasick? What if there are *pirates*?

And don't forget that, below deck, the living compartment's barely big enough to swing a ship's cat. Every irritating habit, frustration, fear, or flare of temper is magnified. Being with your crewmates twenty-four/seven is a true test of love, especially when one of those crewmates is your ultra-aggravating twin brother. Not everyone survives it.

"You're the most hateful boy who ever existed," spluttered Jess, spitting up seawater, after falling headfirst and fully clothed into the marina, thanks to Jude. "When I get out of here, you're dead."

As she swam strongly back to the pontoon, where her brother was doubled over with laughter, it crossed her mind that one person's idea of heaven was another's hell.

Take Jude. If it were up to him, they'd only ever put into harbor a couple of times a year. He lived and breathed sailing and the sea. When he was ashore, he rarely left the marina, preferring to hang out with Gabe and the other yachties chatting about bilge pumps, knots, and rigging.

Jess, on the other hand, counted the days, hours, and minutes until they reached their next port and the furniture stopped moving.

That day's Caribbean paradise was particularly welcome and not just because they'd spent most of the past three weeks at sea, or meandering from one uninhabited island to the next. Gabe had promised her two whole days in one place. Jess couldn't wait to enjoy a shower that wasn't a cold trickle and eat a meal that didn't start life in a tin.

But the main reason she'd cheered when Gabe guided *You Gotta Friend* into a berth at the Nanny Cay marina was because the British Virgin Island of Tortola had a bookshop. By a happy coincidence, the latest in Jess's favorite mystery series was being published that very day. As they docked, Gabe had handed Jess her birthday money and told her to treat herself to *five* books.

Jess had been so excited that she'd helped secure the yacht in record time. Convinced that every young reader within fifty nautical miles would be on a mission to snap up *Castle of Secrets* by Ellie Ellis, she'd set off at a sprint for the bookshop. She didn't notice the hose that Jude had abandoned while mooning over a Leopard superyacht until it sent her belly flopping into the marina. Sam, thinking it was a game, had jumped in too.

"I didn't leave it there on purpose," protested Jude, putting his hands up to ward off blows as his dripping sister chased after him and as the dog barked wildly from a safe distance. "Anyhow, you shouldn't be so clumsy."

"And *you* shouldn't be so careless and messy," accused Jess.

"Not again," chided Gabe from the deck of the yacht. "Beats me why y'all gotta bash heads over every doggone thing. You're twins. You're supposed to be best buddies."

"Urgh," said Jude, pulling a face at his sister.

Jess rolled her eyes. "Freak."

"Geek!"

Luckily, Gabe didn't hear them over the barking. "Sam, that's enough! Quiet! Jess, it'll take you five minutes, max, to dry off in this heat. Go get your mystery books. Jude, you're about to be twelve. It's time you took some responsibility for your actions and quit goofing around."

"It wasn't his fault," said Jess, leaping loyally to her brother's defense. "I should have been looking where I was going."

"Thanks, sis, but I can fight my own battles," muttered Jude, a scowl clouding his good-natured face. "Sorry for laughing though."

In a louder voice, he said: "Yes, sir, Captain."

"And what do you say?"

"Apologies, Captain."

"And?"

"Apologies, Jess."

Gabe jumped onto the pontoon. He ruffled Jude's hair affectionately. "That's more like it. Once we've refueled, let's hit the chandlery and get those sailing gloves you wanted for your birthday. Now, kids, a little bird told me there's a beach barbecue to die for on Tortola. If you promise not to squabble, I'll treat you both to a slap-up lunch."

· · ✳ · ·

Desert Island Books had a hot-pink storefront and a sign shaped like a palm tree. Inside, it smelled the way all good bookshops should, of remembered forests, both real and imagined, and inky dreams punctuated with peril, high-stakes adventure and dragons.

In this case, it was also fragranced with the tropical scent of its customers' sunblock.

"You're in luck." The woman behind the counter tossed her long braids over her shoulder. "We have one copy left—on the Hurricane Specials table at the back. It's so hot off the press, it's practically smoking." Out of the corner of her eye, Jess saw a girl with deep brown skin making a beeline for the Hurricane Specials. Jess flew between the shelves, but it was too late. The girl was clutching *Castle of Secrets* to her chest, face aglow. Her beaming mother was wishing her happy birthday.

Jess could not have been more crushed if an entire box of copies of *Lord of the Rings* had fallen on her head—but what could she say? A birthday today trumped a birthday tomorrow. She'd have wept if the girl hadn't looked so delighted. At least Ellie Ellis's newest bestseller was going to a deserving home.

"Don't worry—we can order you another," the bookseller consoled her. "We'd have it in by Tuesday. When do you leave Tortola?"

Jess tore off to the boatyard to find Gabe. *Surely* they could stay an extra couple of days? It's not as if they were on a schedule. Early on in their voyage, she'd asked her guardian how long they'd be at sea and he'd laughed at the question.

"That's not how sailing around the world works, girl! We're not in a race or on a timetable. We're living the dream! Best guess says it'll take two years. Depends on the wind and the tides and whether we need to stop for repairs or to earn extra cash or whatever. We're going with the flow, you know."

At the boatyard, yachts were parked on trailers or winched up high in harnesses like wounded whales. Jess spotted Gabe right away. He was talking to someone silhouetted behind a dinghy sail. She hung back, not wanting to be dragged into any dreary discussions about inboard engine diagnostics.

Suddenly, Gabe's voice rose. "Sorry, pal, you have the wrong man. Now if you'll excuse me . . ."

Through the white sailcloth, Jess saw a shadowy hand grip Gabe's shoulder and spin him around. For an instant he and the spiky-haired stranger were shadowboxing.

Jess, frozen as a shrimp on ice, thought she heard the other man snarl, "If you ever breathe a word . . . you'll live to regret it." Then a welding iron shrieked in the boatyard workshop, drowning out his angry words.

Before Jess could run for help, Gabe came striding toward her. He had a beet-colored face and his collar was crooked, yet he grinned at her as if he didn't have a care in the world.

"What happened?" cried Jess.

"What happened where? Hey, how did you get on at the bookshop? Did you find *The Castle of Adventure*, or whatever it's called?"

Jess stared at him in confusion. The book had gone from her head. "No, I mean, are you okay? That person seemed . . . upset."

The skipper kept walking. "Oh, him. We had a minor dis-agreement over the price of a new winch. Too much sun can make a man crazy. Those types are best avoided. Change of plan. Let's grab takeout, round up your brother and dog, and hop on a quad bike to Josiah's Bay. Turns out the beach barbe-cue here's a bit of a tourist trap."

Jess glanced over his shoulder. The silhouette behind the dinghy sail had vanished.

By the following morning, so had Gabe.

CHAPTER 2

Even Good People Have Secrets

"There has to be a logical explanation—something we've missed," said Jess. "He *can't* have just disappeared . . . Can he?"

For the thousandth time that morning, the twins' gazes roamed restlessly across the ocean, as though at any moment Gabe might bob up to the surface in a diving suit, lift his mask, and say, *Sorry I've been gone so long, kids, but you won't believe what I've found! A sunken galleon full of treasure!*

Or come roaring up in a speedboat, yelling, *Ta-da! Birthday surprise!*

Ordinarily, Jess's supersensible, wise-beyond-her-years approach to life made her easy to tease and was the cause of many of the twins' rows. Now Jude was grateful for it. Jess was right. She was always right. Not as often as she thought she was but quite a lot. Added to which, she'd read so many mystery novels that she practically had a degree in detection. And that's what the situation called for: a detective.

She was in private investigator mode now as she said, "Jude, tell me again what you remember about last night."

But Saturday night didn't make sense unless Jude first thought about Saturday afternoon. So that's where he started, with the trip to Josiah's Bay.

Neither of the twins had eaten since discovering Gabe was missing three hours earlier. They'd been too busy maneuvering the yacht to a mooring buoy near the Dog Islands. Consequently, Jude's stomach rumbled as he recalled the smoky aroma of flame-grilled seafood that had wafted in his direction as he'd waited with Sam near Tortola's finest beach barbecue the previous day.

On land, Jude always felt like a fish snatched from the sea. His skin became taut and itchy as if it had suddenly shrunk, and his limbs, well adapted to balancing on a bouncy, wind-blasted deck, felt weighed down by gravity.

Almost everyone who passed him had paused to admire the Swiss shepherd. Jude wouldn't have minded if they'd wanted to chat only about dogs, but sooner or later they all wanted to know which yacht he was on and who was skippering it. Inevitably, they leaped to the conclusion that he was on a sailing holiday with his family. That Gabriel Carter was his dad.

Jude always dreaded that part. Gabe was *like* a father, but he wasn't his dad. Could never be his dad. His dad was dead, and nobody would ever replace him.

Over the years, Jude had perfected the art of avoiding prying questions, but that afternoon one couple had been particularly nosy. They'd taken a shine to Sam and kept pawing him. As they fussed over the dog, they'd grilled Jude on where he'd sailed from, whether he had any siblings, and how long his father planned on staying in the Caribbean.

"What an adventurous life you must lead! Where's Dad taking you next?"

Desperate to stem the torrent of questions, Jude bluntly informed them that his parents were dead. That was a mistake, because their faces crumpled with pity.

"You poor, poor boy," said the woman with a sigh. "If you don't mind me asking, what happened to them?"

Mercifully, Jess and Gabe came into view at that moment. Jude bolted through the palms to greet them, dragging Sam behind him.

Looking back, he should have guessed that something was off as soon as he saw his sister and guardian. Jess, who'd talked of nothing but the books she planned on buying with her birthday money *for days*, hadn't bought any, and Gabe was acting weird.

Breaking the news that he wouldn't, as promised, be treating the twins to the "beach barbecue to die for" because he had a "much better plan," Gabe had exuded fake cheer.

Jude, who was starving, let out a heartfelt groan. But before he could beg Gabe to change his mind, Jess caught his eye and shook her head.

He wished now that he'd asked more questions.

Regrettably, he'd thought only of his stomach. And Gabe

had soon won him over with an industrial quantity of coconut shrimp, roti, and key lime pie, bought from a wildly expensive café. He'd also hired an ATV (all-terrain vehicle). The three of them had roared through the lush green hills to Josiah's Bay, Jude sitting in the back with the dog.

The pricey picnic and ATV were out of character too. Gabe loathed what he called "rip-off" tourist joints. But Jude hadn't dwelled on that either. He'd been too busy savoring the picnic and enjoying the kind of afternoon that always made him pinch himself.

Somewhere, far away, kids were sweating through exams, plonked in front of televisions, staring at their phones, or otherwise sealed off from nature, in dank and stifling rooms in smoggy cities. Meanwhile, he and Jess got to play Frisbee with their dog in the sunshine on a beach that looked newly laundered.

Later, Jess swam laps in the choppy bay while Jude messed about in rock pools and beachcombed for shells and starfish with Sam. A near-drowning incident at the age of seven had left him wary of swimming in rough water. He'd never have admitted it, least of all to his sister, that the fear had intensified since they'd left Florida.

"Jess, stay in the shallows where I can see you," ordered Gabe. "The rip currents here are notorious. If one grabs you, you know to just go with it, right? Don't fight it. Swim parallel to the shore, and the rip'll sweep you back in."

Jess had heard the rip-current speech a hundred times over

the years, but she dutifully promised to be careful. Gabe knew very well that she was more dolphin than girl. Under normal circumstances, her guardian would have swum with her. He loved swimming almost as much as she did. Instead, he stayed in the shade, tapping moodily at his phone.

"What's eating the skipper?" Jude asked, when Jess returned to the beach. "He's about as relaxed as a surfer in a cove full of tiger sharks."

"Who knows." She toweled off her hair. "Maybe he's still ticked off with the boatyard guy for trying to cheat him over the price of a winch. They nearly got into a fight."

Jude stared at her. "A fight? Over a winch? But we don't need a new winch. The ones we have work just fine. Are you sure that's what he said?"

"Hey, kids!" called Gabe. "I've had a flash of genius!" He came trotting over. "Jess, you asked if we could stay here longer so the bookshop could order your mystery book, but we can do better than that. If we sail to Virgin Gorda later today—maybe anchor overnight in the Baths National Park—you can buy your books at Leverick Bay on your actual birthday! How does that sound? Jude, you'll love it there too. From what I've heard, some of the superyachts in the North Sound have to be seen to be believed."

He grinned. "Before we leave Tortola, let's swing by the bakery. A birthday isn't a birthday without cake!"

· · ✳ · ·

"If anything's happened to Gabe, it's *my* fault," Jess said emotionally. "We left Tortola a day earlier than we were meant to because of my stupid book. If I hadn't made such a big deal about *Castle of Secrets*, Gabe wouldn't have decided to sail us to Virgin Gorda to buy it on my birthday."

"You don't know that," countered her brother. "If Gabe wanted to avoid the man at the boatyard, he might have used your birthday present as an excuse to leave the island sooner than he promised. And don't call books stupid. They're not stupid—not to you, anyway. When I say stuff like that, you get mad at me."

Jude closed his eyes and dug his fingers into his temples. "This headache's stupid. It's killing me."

"Maybe the takeout shrimp gave you food poisoning," fretted Jess. "If Gabe felt sick or dizzy in the middle of the night, he might have fallen overboard."

"Food poisoning? From the shrimp? No way! They were *delicious*. We felt fine afterward. Anyway, rotten shrimp wouldn't have made us sleepy. We'd have been barfing our guts up over the side."

"Eww, gross." Jess screwed up her nose. "Wait—the coconut lady! We forgot about her. What if *she* put a sleeping potion in our drinks?"

The vendor had gone from Jude's mind too, but now he pictured her clearly. She'd been selling local treats, souvenirs, and jewelry near the marina gate when they'd returned at twilight, but it was the green coconuts she seemed most intent on selling.

"Nectar of the gods, sweet as anything," she'd told Gabe, her face veiled by the long purple shadows. She'd cut the top off one and stuck a straw in it. "Buy two, get one free."

"I spilled mine and didn't taste a drop, but Sam lapped it up," recalled Jess. "If her 'nectar of the gods' was drugged, that would explain why the dog was in a virtual coma too."

Jude and Gabe had planned to enjoy drinking the coconut water once they were underway, but the Christmas Winds that swirled around the Virgin Islands just as the hurricane season drew to a close had blown in with little warning. Gabe had judged it safer to anchor near Devil's Bay than to continue on to the North Sound.

It wasn't until night closed in and they were getting ready for bed that Gabe had remembered the coconuts in the fridge.

"You've worked hard, kid. Stay hydrated," he'd told Jude, handing him one with a smile. "Go ahead and catch some Z's. I'm going to stay up and watch the stars."

A knife of fear twisted in Jude's gut. "Last thing I remember is asking Gabe if I could watch the stars with him. Everything else is a blank."

Jess, who'd gone to bed early with a book, said, "What are the chances of a rogue wave striking here, in these islands?"

Jude shrugged. "Not impossible, but a big swell, a north swell, is more likely."

The twins glanced at the ocean again, each thinking the same thing. If his drink was spiked, Gabe might have been unsteady on his feet when an extreme surge bucked the yacht.

"But why would a total stranger put a sleeping draft in our drinks?" demanded Jude. "It doesn't make sense."

"Maybe the coconut lady was in league with a gang of thieves? Say they saw the marina logbook and thought we were spending the night in Nanny Cay, they might have plotted to creep on board and rob us while we were unconscious."

Jude wasn't convinced. "I love *You Gotta Friend*, but she was the oldest, least valuable boat in the marina. Some of those superyachts are worth tens of millions of dollars. They have passengers with hundred-thousand-dollar watches and diamond rings on every finger. Anyone can see that we don't have a thing worth stealing."

"We need to find Gabe's phone," said Jess. "That way we'll know who he was messaging from the beach. If the man at the boatyard wanted revenge for some past wrong, he might have paid pirates to kidnap Gabe."

"Then why didn't the pirates take us?" scoffed Jude. "You gotta stop reading so many mysteries, sis. This is real life, not a fantasy."

"If you read the news once in a while, you'd know that real-life pirates are forever hijacking boats in the Caribbean Sea and Indian Ocean," Jess retorted huffily. "Maybe these particular pirates just didn't want to deal with an extremely annoying boy."

Her brother rubbed his sore head. "All these maybes are freaking me out. If the skipper's not back by tomorrow morning, I say we break into his secret compartment and search for clues. Agreed?"

Jess's eyes widened. Gabe had forbidden them to open the metal box hidden beneath a floorboard in his cabin unless it was a life-or-death emergency. "Don't you dare touch it unless I'm forty fathoms under the sea and swimming with the fishes," he'd warned them. "If I'm still breathing, it doesn't count."

He hadn't mentioned what to do if he vanished in unexplained circumstances.

"Agreed?" pressed Jude.

"Agreed," Jess said reluctantly. "Oh, Jude, I'm scared. I miss Gabe so much. He wasn't perfect, but he was a good man."

Jude huddled nearer to his sister and dog. Whatever had become of the skipper, he had a bad feeling that there was no way back.

"Jess, even good people have secrets."

CHAPTER 3

The Promise

That night, the twins fell asleep on deck in their clothes, listening out for engines, for the cry of a struggling swimmer, for a radio message, for anything.

They were exhausted from searching for Gabe. Fearful of moving the boat in case Gabe returned, they'd spent hours scrambling over the uninhabited Dog Islands, Jess half hoping that their guardian had gone exploring in the darkness in a moment of madness and was lying unconscious behind a boulder or in a rock pool.

In the afternoon, Jude had rowed out as far as he could in the dinghy while Jess put on a snorkel and scoured the nearby shallows. But when the sun went down without them finding so much as a thread from the orange T-shirt Gabe had been wearing when they last saw him, they'd had to admit defeat.

As they slept, the yacht swayed with the current, lines squeaking. The sea wind moaned like a discontented monster.

In the early hours, Jude was woken by light so dazzling he thought someone was shining a flashlight in his eyes. When he opened them to find himself bathed in moonlight, he felt a rush of happiness. He was at sea. Free.

It wasn't until he saw Jess in the cockpit, face puffy with crying, clutching Sam as if he were a teddy bear, that he remembered. Sorrow flooded through him.

Gabe was gone, claimed by the sea—or worse.

"He's not coming back, is he?" said Jess.

Love and rage flamed in Jude's chest. He vowed then he'd do everything in his power to protect her.

But he couldn't start by lying to her. "No, sis. I don't think he is."

She said fiercely, "Then let's not wait till sunrise. Let's open the secret compartment now."

Down in Gabe's cabin, Jude used a screwdriver to prize open the board beneath the bunk. He hesitated before lifting out the metal box. "Sure you want to do this? What if we don't like what we find?"

Jess handed him the key. "Gabe's taken care of us since we were babies. Whatever's happened, we need answers."

Jude's stomach was a cauldron of nerves and nausea. In the past twenty hours, he and Jess had eaten almost nothing. Their birthday had come and gone without being celebrated.

Gabe's words had proved eerily prophetic. *Jude, you're about to be twelve. It's time you took some responsibility for your actions and quit goofing around.*

Jude twisted the key.

If the twins had expected something dramatic—a gun, a disguise, a false identity—they were disappointed. Stuffed in the metal box was a waterproof pouch holding Gabe's passport and driver's license, his yacht registration papers, a credit card, and $200 in cash. There was also a brown envelope containing an annual statement from an American bank.

Everything seemed in order apart from the bank statement. Gabe had always insisted on paying for everything they needed, even expensive sail repairs, using cash he took out of ATM machines.

"Safer that way," he'd told them. "Cash is king if you don't want the whole world stealing your money or knowing your business."

The ATM withdrawals listed on the bank statement charted their travels: $250 in Miami, $310 in Key West, $160 in Exuma, $500 in the Cayman Islands, and so on. There was nothing unusual or unexpected.

What did get their attention was the $10,000 deposited in Gabe's account a week before they left Florida and the $1,000 deposited in it on the first day of every month since.

Jude frowned. "It's almost as if the skipper's being paid a wage. I didn't know he was working for anyone."

"Neither did I. They're international payments too." Jess

squinted at the reference. "HOPEFLI. Do you think that's a person or a company?"

Jude gave a hoot of laughter. "Could be secret agent code. Half the time he went out on those night fishing trips back in Bantry Creek, he'd come home with no fish or day-old fish. It always made me suspicious. Wouldn't it be funny if it turns out that he's an actual spy? For years, we've been his cover as he's carried out lethal missions for the FBI or CIA, only this time something's gone horribly wrong."

"No, it would not be funny," Jess said crossly. "Jude, be serious for once. Looking back, don't you think it's weird how we left Florida at night and in a hurry, as if we were bank robbers hightailing it out of town?"

"Nah, we set sail at night because of the tides. And because the skipper hates goodbyes."

"Forget tides and goodbyes, Jude. Nothing about the way we set sail five months ago was normal. What kind of guardian says, 'Pack your bags, kids! We're off to sea for a year, or maybe forever!' I mean, one minute we were sitting happily in school. Next, we were being plucked out halfway through a lesson—"

"*I* wasn't sitting happily in school," said Jude with a scowl. "School was the worst. The kids, the teachers, the lessons, the detentions. Every second was pure torture. The day we set sail was the best of my life."

Jess glared at him. "It was the worst day of *my* life, but never mind about that. Jude, don't you see, it doesn't matter if you felt good about going and I didn't, or who was right and who was wrong. It doesn't even matter how we felt yesterday. Everything's changed now that Gabe's disappeared. We have to face facts. Either he's had an accident or there's been foul play."

"This is nuts," railed Jude. "Bet you there's an innocent explanation. Any minute now, Gabe'll come stomping in and give us hell about going through his private stuff."

Sam chose that exact moment to come lolloping down the steps and burst into the cabin. The twins nearly had heart attacks.

Jess recovered first and gave the dog a cuddle. "Poor Sam. We forgot to give him dinner last night. Forgot to feed ourselves too. Let's take a breather and scramble some eggs. If we don't eat, we'll be no use to Gabe or each other."

Despite this sage advice, Jess managed only a few mouthfuls of food before pushing her plate away. The eggs and bread—picked up in Tortola when they'd stopped to buy cake—reminded her that the cupboards in the galley were almost bare. Replenishing their supplies was another thing Gabe had planned to do on the island before inexplicably changing his mind.

What had changed it? The scuffle at the boatyard?

Or something more sinister?

Jess looked again at Gabe's bank balance: $15,822.

To her, it seemed a fortune. Who was paying him and why?

"What happens to the cash if Gabe . . . doesn't show up?" mused Jude.

The yacht rolled on a wave. Jess grabbed the fold-out table to steady herself.

"Oh, I could kick myself for not being nosier. I never asked Gabe how he went from fixing boat engines and oiling decks to living the dream overnight. Never, ever questioned where he'd found the cash to walk away from everything without a backward glance."

"He'd been saving up for years!"

Jess gave her brother a look. "Oh, please. He had a jarful of coins. That was his idea of saving. One time, I overheard Anita at the Castaway Diner telling somebody that she hadn't any notion how Gabe's shipwright business stayed afloat. Anita said he had the accountancy skills of a seagull. That didn't stop somebody from handing him ten thousand dollars the week before we set sail, plus five thousand more in the time we've been gone. And five hundred dollars every month before that. I guess you're right, Jude. Even good people have secrets."

Jude said slowly, "But are they the kind of secrets that could have got him killed?"

Jess flinched at the word *killed*. It belonged to her mystery novels, where murderers and assassins were fictional. She hoped it would stay that way.

"I s'pose we have to consider every possibility. Is there anything else in the pouch?"

"*Nada.* Oh, wait—there's an inside pocket." Unzipping it, Jude tipped it upside down.

A piece of paper fluttered out. He caught it in midair and passed it to Jess.

She read aloud:

GABRIEL,

A LONG TIME AGO, YOU PROMISED THAT YOU'D GO TO THE ENDS OF THE EARTH TO KEEP THEM SAFE. CIRCUMSTANCES HAVE CHANGED, AND I'M AFRAID THAT IS NOW NECESSARY. YOU KNOW WHAT TO DO. OUR ARRANGEMENT WILL CONTINUE UNCHANGED. GOD SPEED.

"*Them?*" Jude said. "Are they talking about us?"

Jess was in shock. "What 'arrangement'? Is this about the thousands pouring into Gabe's bank account? Was Gabe being paid to protect us? To be our *bodyguard*?"

Jude studied the paper for clues. It appeared to be part of an email with the date, time, and sender snipped out. Judging by the creases, Gabe had tossed it in the trash before changing his mind.

"Jess, let's say the man at the boatyard *did* recognize the skipper, that it wasn't just a case of mistaken identity. Remind me what he said?"

"His voice was muffled by the dinghy sail. I couldn't even tell you what accent he had. All I made out was: 'If you ever breathe a word . . . you'll live to regret it.'"

Jude began to pace the small living quarters. "What if Gabe witnessed a crime on one of his night fishing trips? A smuggling operation. The smugglers might have paid him hush money to leave town in a hurry and to keep his mouth shut. Maybe they changed their minds later and decided to shut him up permanently."

Jess shivered, suddenly chilled. "Doubt it. If the letter *is* about us, it means there was nothing spontaneous about our voyage. That there was a plan all along. And when Gabe got the email, he activated that plan. We left Florida in a rush for a reason."

"So, we've been on the run and we didn't even know it?" Jude was incredulous. "Then whoever is looking for us must be deadly dangerous. Why else would the skipper go to such lengths to keep us out of their clutches?"

"They must have a long memory too. The person who wrote this message is calling on a favor from way back. If Gabe was being paid to take us to the ends of the earth to keep us safe, then somebody has been hunting us for years. Possibly our whole lives."

"*Hunting us?* But we're nobody. Who *are* they?"

"More important," said Jess, "who are *we*?"

CHAPTER 4

The Devil and the Deep Blue Sea

"*Good morning, good morning. Anyone home?*" boomed a voice on a megaphone.

Sam exploded into action, his deep bark gunshot-loud in the confined space. He bounded up the steps and continued to sound the alarm from the deck.

A thirty-foot gray inflatable patrol boat loomed in the galley porthole.

Jude ducked out of sight. "It's the marine cops! Two of them."

Jess's knees almost dissolved. "It's good news—has to be. They've saved Gabe!"

Or bad news, was her second thought, but she banished it from her mind. "Worst-case scenario, they're here to tell us which hospital he's in."

"Worst-worst-case scenario, they can help to find him," said her brother. "Worst-worst-worst-case scenario, they can help *us*."

Until that moment, the twins had refused to allow themselves to consider the grim fate that might befall them if their guardian didn't return; if the police or social services discovered two just-turned-twelve-year-olds alone at sea.

Their eyes locked in shock.

But there was no time to think about it now. The yacht seesawed on the surge as the police boat came alongside.

Jess snatched up her life jacket. "Jude, the box! If Gabe is back, he'll kill us if he finds we've been raking through his private stash. I'll hide it under the floorboard. You go stall the cops."

"No, you're better with strangers. I'll hide the box and be right up."

"GOOD MORNING, GOOD MORNING . . . PERMISSION TO STEP ABOARD."

Jess flew up to the deck, realizing too late that she looked feral, her long dark hair salt-stiffened and tangled, her T-shirt stained with ketchup and sticky tears.

In the galley below, Jude skidded on a piece of broken china as he rushed to gather the pouch's contents, nicking a toe and banging his elbow on the cabin door.

Overhead, Jess grabbed the dog's collar and leaned over the guardrail. She smiled her best, most innocent smile. "Shush, Sam! Morning, Officer—everything okay?"

"Good morning to you, young lady. All is well? We've had reports of suspicious activity in the area."

"All is excellent," said Jess, taking in the easy grins and relaxed but alert body language of the two Caribbean policemen. No Gabe.

The cops were on the lookout for trouble but not yet aware they'd found it.

"We're just chilling," added Jess for extra effect. "Another day in paradise. Nothing suspicious going on around here. How about you? Caught any criminals today? Rescued any sailors or swimmers?"

The officer at the helm laughed. "None so far. We had a fearsome north swell last night, and it musta scared off the smugglers and kept the tourists in their beds. Where's your skipper? May we talk wit' him?"

"He has a migraine; he's lying down," improvised Jess.

"Want me to check on him?" asked the cop.

Overhearing the question as he emerged on deck in two mismatched socks, one with a bloodied toe, Jude said hurriedly, "Oh, hey, good morning, Officer. Sorry, the skip's busy checking charts and making breakfast. He can't come up right now."

The lead cop cocked an eyebrow: "He's lying down or he's makin' breakfast and checking charts? Can't be all three."

"He must have made a miraculous recovery, which is great news because he promised to make us pancakes," lied Jess at the exact moment that Jude told them Gabe was also frying up hash browns 'n' eggs.

"Eggs *and* pancakes," affirmed Jess, shooting her brother a glare. "And hash browns. They're yummy fried potatoes."

"Yeah, he's cooking up a storm." Cupping an ear, Jude bent over the companionway. "What was that, Skipper?" He straightened. "Captain Carter says thanks for stopping by, Officer. Everything's fine. We're totally fine."

The policemen exchanged glances. One opened his note-book and jotted down a few details. The other reached for the yacht ladder.

"If the captain can't come to us, we'll come to him."

"No!" cried Jess. "I mean, he's at a delicate stage of cooking. The pancakes could be ruined."

The cop was still smiling, but instinct told him that all was not as it seemed. He put a determined boot on the ladder of the yacht.

The Swiss shepherd hung over the edge and snarled down at him. Jess pulled Sam away half-heartedly.

Undeterred, the policeman climbed.

Had his radio not burst into crackling life just as he put a hand on the yacht's guardrail, the fate the twins feared most might have followed as swiftly and dismally as a guillotine. But it did. Judging by the speed with which he returned to his own boat, the call was a life-and-death emergency.

Before gunning the engine, the policeman cast a final hard stare at the children and dog, as if committing their faces to memory.

"Enjoy your pancakes in paradise. Mind you take care now."

Jude watched the patrol boat go until it was a speck on the turquoise horizon. His fists were clenched.

"No way are they taking us to any orphanage or whatever they have these days. I'd rather die."

Jess was trembling. "Don't worry, ten thousand stallions couldn't drag me to one of those places, and I wouldn't let them touch you either. What if they separated us?"

The twins said together: "We need a plan."

A wedding party on a catamaran sailed into view, bass thumping.

Jude shielded his eyes from the morning glare. "First, we need to get out of here. Where should we go? Pick an island and let's sail there."

Jess was startled. "But what about Gabe? How will he find us if we move?"

"Sis, we've drifted a long way. If Gabe did fall overboard, he could be washed halfway to Puerto Rico by now."

And be fish food, Jude tried not to think, but a great white glided into his brain and filled it with images he wished he could unsee.

Jess said mutinously, "Just because we can't tell the cops that Gabe's lost at sea in case the child protective services snatch us into care doesn't mean we should give up on searching for him. He's our family. I'm not going anywhere till we agree that unless we have concrete proof that Gabriel's gone for good, we'll keep looking for him."

Jude itched to move on, to hear the snap of the sails. The thought of being imprisoned in an institution filled him with terror. He wanted to be long gone before the cops came sniffing around again, but to placate Jess he said: "Fine by me."

He pulled on his new sailing gloves.

Jess stood her ground, arms crossed. "I'm serious, Jude. I plan to get to the bottom of what has happened to Gabe—if I have to turn over every shell and pebble on every island in the BVIs—"

"Jess, there's thirty-six of them!"

"Then we have to hope we discover the truth on the first, second, or third island. So far, we have five mysteries to solve. Gabe's disappearance is only one of them."

She ticked them off on her fingers:

"One: Did Gabe have an accident, or was he the victim of foul play? Two: Who's been putting money into his bank account? Three: Who sent the email? Four: Who is hunting us? And five: Why?"

"Five mysteries? Is that all?" Jude said lightly. "No problemo. We'll be the FBI and Sherlock Holmes combined. Only, can we please get out of here before anybody else comes poking around, asking awkward questions? We can find another uninhabited island and lay low till we figure out what to do next."

He took the email out of his pocket. "Here, you can keep this."

The creased paper was cool in Jess's hand, but rereading the words galvanized her like nothing else.

A LONG TIME AGO, YOU PROMISED THAT YOU'D GO TO THE ENDS OF THE EARTH TO KEEP THEM SAFE. CIRCUMSTANCES HAVE CHANGED, AND I'M AFRAID THAT IS NOW NECESSARY. YOU KNOW WHAT TO DO...GOD SPEED.

Jess zipped the email into the pocket of her life jacket. "Basically, we're caught between the devil and the deep blue sea."

Jude looked keenly at her. "I know which I'd choose. How 'bout you?"

For an answer, Jess put on her deck shoes. "Mainsail or headsail?"

Jude didn't hesitate. "Headsail. If you slip the mooring line, I'll deploy to port. Keep on the starboard side or you'll get whacked in the head as the sail fills."

He hopped into the cockpit and began working through his predeparture safety checklist. Sam squeezed in beside him. Absentmindedly, Jude stroked the dog's ears.

Jess felt a rush of affection for her twin. He seemed both impossibly grown-up and way too young to be in charge of an oceangoing vessel. "Jude, if Gabe *has* gone forever, what then?"

He glanced up, surprised. "We carry on."

"Carry on? And go where?"

"Anywhere you fancy. Auckland, Ireland, San Diego, the Seychelles . . ."

"What about school?"

"You can teach us. We have the lesson plans. We can set a timetable and everything."

"And how do we survive?"

"We just will," Jude said simply. "Maybe I don't have a Yachtmaster Ocean certificate, but I'm a decent sailor. I'll skipper and you can crew."

"Gee, thanks," said Jess, temper flaring. "Why do you get to be the skipper?"

Jude grinned. "Because I'm the best sailor. I can read a chart, for starters. Anyhow, you're the detective in this family. Figuring out five mysteries is a full-time job."

"That's true," conceded Jess. "But what'll do we do for

cash?" Even as she spoke, a plan was formulating in her mind. "Forget it, let's worry about that later."

Jude was staring in alarm at the flotilla of charter yachts, speedboats, and dinghies sailing over the horizon. He said vaguely, "Yeah, we'll worry about that later."

He was putting on his deck boots when Jess spontaneously rushed over and hugged him. She cuddled Sam too, so he didn't feel left out.

Jude smiled and gripped the wheel. "So, we're really doing this?"

"Yes," Jess said, "we really are."

Up in the bow, she braced herself against the pulpit and leaned out over the water, poised to reach the yellow buoy.

Jude was checking the wind direction. "Ready to slip?" he called.

"Ready, Captain."

Diamond droplets of seawater speckled Jess's arms as she hauled in the mooring line. "Clear," she shouted.

Jude released the furling line, and the blue-and-orange headsail filled with a *whoosh*.

The yacht responded like a racehorse on the gallops. Jess felt the boat's power and grace as she rode the first waves.

The fresh-salted air rushed through her lungs and cleared her head. The knot in her chest loosened slightly. Jude's point, about the yacht drifting for hours after the mooring buoy snapped when the freak wave struck, was a good one. Whatever Gabe's fate, they wouldn't find answers by staying in one place.

Their only hope of learning the truth was to move on.

Keeping low, she went over to the shroud, the wire rigging that secured the mast. It was her favorite place on the boat. Sam came to sit beside her as she dangled her legs over the side. The hull made music as it sliced through the wind and water.

Anchored, Jess had felt helpless. But as they sailed, her confidence seeped back. At the helm, Jude's shoulders squared and he stood straighter too.

For better or worse, they'd taken charge of their own destiny.

It wasn't until hours later, when a pleasure cruiser packed with bronzed young people in Speedos and bikinis swerved dangerously near to them, causing Jude to take rapid evasive action, that the knot returned to Jess's chest. This time it lodged there.

Beneath her life jacket, the email seared her heart. Who had sent it? Why did they care?

Did they care, or were they also part of some strange and sinister plot?

For as long as she could remember, Jess had adored reading mysteries. She loved putting herself in the shoes of fictional detectives and trying to crack the clues and spot the villain before they did. But now that her guardian was missing and she had a starring role in her own mystery, she wasn't sure where to begin.

How do you solve a mystery when that mystery is you?

CHAPTER 5

Dolphin Dreams

Gabe had always said there were only two types of people in the world: those who believed their glass in life was half-empty, and those who were glad it was half-full.

"Not true," Anita, the Castaway Diner's smart, vivacious manager, had told the twins back in Bantry Creek, pursing her lips in that particular way of hers. "Millions of folk don't got nothing in their glass at all. Fact is, they don't even have an empty paper beaker. I prefer a different saying: 'We can complain because rosebushes have thorns, or rejoice because thorns have roses.' Your mama was more of the rejoicing kind."

On this, she and Gabe were agreed. Right from when the children were tiny, Anita and Gabe had encouraged them to honor their mother by rejoicing in the small things.

Rather than wallow in self-pity because their dad was dead and their mom had passed away one hour and twenty-three minutes after they were born, the twins had grown up believing they were blessed. An honest, good-hearted man had officially adopted them, and they had more unofficial adoptive "mothers" than anyone in America.

Eleven, to be precise. The entire female staff of the diner.

Except for Tiffany, who everyone knew was a fully-fledged child-loathing, fire-breathing dragon.

"Most kids have one soccer mom. You two got lucky and got a whole team," Anita would tell Jess and Jude with a laugh.

They also had two unofficial "fathers," if one counted Ricardo and Al—respectively kitchen hand and grill operator *extraordinaire*. The men had appointed themselves as Gabe's support crew and the twins' backup dads to "even out the numbers."

Gabe and the twins had lived about a minute's bike ride from the boatyard diner, in an airy timber rental house with a rocking chair on the porch. Since their guardian worked long and unsociable hours, the waitresses took it in turns to run Jess and Jude back and forth to school. They also supervised their homework, albeit with mixed success.

As a result, Jess and Jude ate most of their meals at the diner. In between, they hung out with Gabe at the boatyard, helping him oil decks, maintain rigging, or scrape barnacles off hulls.

While Gabe considered it his sacred duty to teach the twins sailing, barbecuing, and lifesaving skills, the Castaway "mamas and papas" competed to impart alternative snippets of wisdom to their growing charges.

From Cindy Rogers, who dreamed of making it big someday

in Nashville, Tennessee, Jess learned to sing and Jude to play the blues on a beat-up Gibson guitar.

Leonie told them how to treat a burn with tepid water, honey, and lavender, and how to stem an arterial bleed.

Ricardo showed them some karate and boxing self-defense moves.

Al gave them a dramatic education in the art of extracting an angry Burmese python from a toilet cistern. It wasn't a lesson the twins were anxious to ever repeat.

Carly taught them the names of migrating birds.

Saskia advised them what to do in the event of a frying-pan fire or a jellyfish sting.

From Lucille (tattooed, brawny, Harley-Davidson-mad, heart of gold), Jude learned motorcycle maintenance. To Jess, Lucille revealed that it took twenty-eight days to make or break a habit.

"My advice? Don't get bad habits in the first place," Lucille confided from the kitchen steps, where she sat smoking and downing chocolate Hershey's Kisses. "Eat your greens. Keep your nose clean. Stay away from ice cream."

When Jess cast a skeptical glance at Lucille's overflowing ashtray and pile of candy wrappers, wondering why she didn't take her own advice if it was so easy-peasy, the Castaway's best waitress barked: "Don't do as I do, girl. Do as I *say.*"

Before the twins were "knee-high to a turtle," Regina taught them how to cook. When Jude complained that he'd rather be out fishing or messing about on a boat, Regina set him straight on life's priorities.

"Don't you be that boy who can't cook and expects his sibling or parent to do everything for him. When that boy grows into a man who expects his partner to do the same, he shouldn't be surprised if that partner slings his sorry ass out on the street."

Jude, who was only eight at the time, was shocked. "Gabe says cussing is wicked."

Regina laughed till she cried. "*Ass* is not a cuss word, Jude. Nor's *booty*, *bum*, or *bottom*. A good behind is a gift from Almighty God. Now, taking the Lord's name in vain, *that's* cussing. So's using hating words or hurting ones. If you're having a bad day or a sad day or you're just plain mad, I'd recommend *sugar*, *godfather*, *fiddlesticks*, *gosh darn it*, *drat*, or *poo*. My own personal favorite is *sardine*."

"Sardine?"

"You got it. If I drop a brick on my toe, a stinky 'Sardine!' is the only thing that's gonna make me feel better."

Jess didn't believe her, but two days later, Regina actually did that very thing. She dropped a cast-iron skillet and almost broke her foot. True to her word, she hopped around on one leg shrieking, "Sardine, sardine, dang and blasted SARDINE!"

When she wasn't giving lessons on how to swear politely, Regina taught the twins cooking 101. "Every chef needs a repertoire. Those are the meals you can whip up on autopilot, when you're so sardine exhausted you can barely recall your own name."

Thanks to Regina, the twins left Bantry Creek, Florida, with enough cooking savvy to prepare any dish on their mentor's recommended menu:

Breakfast:

Eggs (scrambled, cheesy, over easy, and sunny-side up),
grits, hash browns, pecan pancakes, banana waffles

Lunch:

Caesar salad, grilled cheese, sweet-corn chowder

Dinner:

Mac 'n' cheese, three-bean chili, fish and chips, Mexican
burrito

So, over the years, they had learned a lot. But it was the gaps in their learning that kept the twins awake at night.

Their own history was a mystery.

In notably short supply was information about their parents.

About their real dad, they'd heard only two details: His name was Jim, and he'd given his life to save his best friend.

"Where did this happen? *How* did it happen? Who *was* his best friend?" the twins had asked Gabe and the waitresses as they grew older. Eventually, they had to accept that those questions might never be answered.

All they knew about their mom, Ana Davis, was the romantic tale Gabe had spun for them.

That Ana had blown into his life like a hurricane, on the wings of a storm. That he'd been on his way to the diner after securing the boats in the marina when a Greyhound bus had wheezed to a halt across the street.

The boatyard was at the end of a potholed road. Most

customers arrived by water. Greyhounds were rare enough that Gabe paused to watch the passengers disembark. There was only one. When the bus pulled away, there she was, so slight and ethereal he'd thought she was a trick of the light.

As he stared, the rain had swept in, hard and heavy. He'd expected her to bolt for cover or for a friend to materialize and drive her away, but she just stood there, motionless in the deluge.

"Something told me she had no place to go. Don't ask me where I found the nerve, but I headed on over and informed her that the Castaway made the best coffee and maple pecan pancakes in all of Florida. Said I'd consider it a personal favor if she let me buy her both before she was blown to Alaska by the storm.

"Her only luggage was this itty-bitty backpack that was soaked through, and we were both half-drowned, but her smile lit up the marina like sunshine. She said, 'Oh, where I come from, this is just a breeze.' I asked, 'Where's that—Outer Mongolia?' She just giggled and said, 'Maybe I'll tell you; maybe I won't.' But she never did. The nearest she ever came to it was telling Cindy that she'd traveled so much, she thought of herself as a citizen of Everywhere."

By the time Gabe had persuaded Ana to accompany him to the diner, she was turning blue with cold. From there, Anita and Cindy took over.

By the following morning, Ana Davis had a job waiting tables and a room above the diner. Both turned out to be crucial.

What no one but Anita guessed in those early days was that Ana was two months pregnant.

Before the hurricane moved on, Gabe knew two things: (a) he was besotted with her, and (b) that her heart belonged to her late husband.

What happened to him and why she'd fled her home and/or country with little but the clothes she stood up in, she refused to reveal.

"The past is past. That's all I'm going to say."

Over the years, Jess and Jude had begged Gabe and their Castaway family for even the most minuscule details the adults had gleaned about Ana's background. But, although they'd lived and worked alongside her for six and a half months, nobody seemed to have intuited anything.

The diner staff couldn't even agree on her accent. While Carly said it had been Australian, Ricardo insisted it was South African. Saskia was sure Ana had been Canadian or a New Zealander. Cindy said that it had been obvious that she was British or maybe Dutch.

Al had made up his mind that she was a posh New Yorker trying to hide her roots.

Given time, Ana might have trusted Gabe or Anita enough to tell them the truth about her past. But time ran out for her one cold November day. Gabe had rushed her to the hospital when she began bleeding heavily. The twins were born three weeks prematurely. Before they were two hours old, their mother had been cruelly taken from them.

"She lived just long enough to hold you both in her arms,

name you, and tell you she loved you," Gabe told the twins when they were old enough to understand.

At the hospital, the midwife and nurses had assumed that Gabe was Ana's partner. She'd deliberately not corrected them. As a consequence, Gabriel Carter was named as the twins' father on their birth certificate.

Afterward, when Ana's room was cleared, the waitresses found no passport or identifying papers. Her social security number had turned out to be fake. Ana's worldly goods numbered just two: a little oil painting with a chipped, gold-painted frame; and, oddly, a horseshoe. Jude was given the horseshoe for good luck, though heaven knows their poor mother hadn't had too much of that. Jess, who loved drawing, became the caretaker of the painting.

Growing up, Jess had spent hours wondering why the picture had been so special to her mother that when she'd left her old life, it and the horseshoe were the only things she'd kept. Was the painting a cherished gift from the twins' father? Was the artist a favorite? Or was the scene it depicted a special place to them?

And where had the horseshoe come from? A gift shop? Or had it belonged to a horse one of them had ridden and loved? Jess supposed they'd never know.

Gabe and the waitresses had been the best substitute family ever, but now they were a thousand nautical miles away. On

Monday night, as *You Gotta Friend* tugged at her mooring near Ginger Island, which Jude had chosen for its solitude, Jess longed for a mom or dad to comfort her and tell her everything would work out all right.

She wondered, a little desperately, if anything would be all right ever again. Whenever she tried to imagine herself and Jude wandering the oceans like lost spirits for months or years to come, despair threatened to swallow her up.

For now, *You Gotta Friend* was a sanctuary, but Jess ached to have a real home of her own, one with walls, doors and windows and, most important, bookshelves.

Home wouldn't be home for her without books. And where would that home be? Over the years, Jess had asked herself that a thousand times. The answer was always the same.

Not Miami or San Francisco or New York City.

Not Paris, Rome, Melbourne, or even Cambridge or Oxford.

Not a mansion with a swimming pool, or a gleaming glass-and-chrome penthouse.

No—home, to Jess, was the home in the painting. A simple whitewashed cottage with a gray-tiled roof and two dormer windows, overlooking a sandy beach and glistening blue bay. It had a picket fence with poppies and cornflowers out the front.

But where was it?

As with her mother's accent, opinions on the location of the cove in which the cottage was situated had been many and varied. Some were positive it was Northern Ireland, the Eastern Cape, or Scandinavia. Others were certain it was Iceland or Nova Scotia.

There was no artist's signature and only one clue. On the back of the painting, scrawled in faded ink, was written *Dolphin Dreams*.

Nestling into her sleeping bag that night, Jess willed the painting to come to life. She pictured herself walking through the front door, taking off her coat, and settling down in front of a crackling fire. Jude and Sam would be lying on the fluffy rug beside her.

A table would be spread with homemade soup or stew and local bread. An apple pie would be baking in the oven, a jug of cream or custard at the ready.

The owners of the cottage were hazy figures in Jess's imagination, but they'd be warm and welcoming. It would turn out they'd been expecting the twins all along.

Her reverie was interrupted by a yell. "*JESS! Jess, come quick. Listen to this.*"

For once, the news on the radio was free of static, relayed by a somber reader: "The body of an unidentified white male has been found by fishermen near the Cowrie Sands Resort. Police are appealing for witnesses. A postmortem will be carried out—"

Jess let out a sob. "It's Gabe, isn't it? Jude, it's Gabe."

"Sure looks that way."

Jude's voice sounded tinny and remote in his own ears. He sat down before he fell down. He'd thought he could handle it, but somehow having a stranger all but confirm the death of the only father the twins had ever known made him feel as if he were falling into an abyss with no bottom.

The smallness of him and Jess, their *aloneness* in the big, wide world, was impossible to absorb. Jess slumped down too, and the dog squeezed between them. He licked away their salty tears. This time, there was no comforting them.

CHAPTER 6

Lottery

Two days later, on November 25, the twins sailed to Virgin Gorda, the island Gabe had planned on taking them to before he disappeared.

They felt guilty for thinking about supplies and cash so soon after their guardian's passing but had no option. The food cupboard was bare, and their water reserves almost gone.

The previous evening, they'd held a memorial service for Gabe on a deserted beach. The weather had played its part too. The sun had gone down in a blaze of glory, leaving the sky streaked with violet and rose gold. There were few things that Gabe had enjoyed more than a theatrical sunset, and it made Jess smile to believe that nature had laid on a dazzling display especially for him.

That afternoon, Jude had caught some mahi-mahi, Gabe's favorite fish. While Jess laid out a picnic rug and brought paper plates and other bits and pieces from the boat, her brother built a fire in a circle of rocks. The twins barbecued the fish over the coals.

When it was ready, Jess set a place on the picnic rug for Gabe. The fish was sweet, smoky, and sharp with lime. She served it with the last of their jasmine rice.

Afterward, Jude fashioned a boat from coconut palm leaves. Jess filled it with gifts of gratitude to the man who, for twelve years, had been the best father he could to a couple of kids who were not his own. A man who might have lost his life trying to spirit the twins away to a safe harbor.

Among their offerings to him were a parrot feather, a card drawn by Jess, beeswax candles, and a photograph of Gabe's dad in his US Marines uniform. At the last minute, Jude added his precious horseshoe.

"Sure you want to part with that?" asked Jess, knowing how much it meant to him.

"Yes, because it's kind of a double gift. Mom would want to thank Gabe for everything he did for us."

"A triple gift, then," said Jess, understanding. "If the horse-shoe belonged to our dad, he'd want Gabe to have it too."

When it grew dark, they lit the candles and pushed the palm boat out to sea. As the flames twinkled bravely into the night, Jess read a poem by Mary Elizabeth Frye, which she'd found on the shelf beside Gabe's bunk. It had been tucked into the memorial sheet from his own father's funeral, so they guessed it had been special to him.

The poem was called "Do Not Stand at My Grave and Weep," but Jess found it near impossible not to break down as she read its moving lines. She'd realized that Gabe had borrowed from the poem many times over the years to help the twins come to terms with the loss of their parents. He'd always told them that when a person passed, they weren't in the ground or in an urn. Their spirit lived on in a "thousand winds," or in the "gentle autumn rain," on the wings of birds, or in the "diamond glints on snow."

Despite the poem's entreaty, Jess and Jude couldn't help crying.

At that point, they decided that Gabe would prefer them to celebrate his life, not mope about it. Jude dug out the CD player and turned up the volume on one of Gabe's beloved *Greatest Hits of the '80s.*

They danced beneath a crescent moon, with Sam barking and trying to join in, until all three of them were too exhausted to move another step. Then they fell asleep in a huddle on the beach, wrapped in the picnic rug as the fire burned low.

Now they were at Virgin Gorda on a mission to get fuel and supplies. Jess was also determined to buy the birthday books Gabe had intended her to have, and both twins needed some cold-weather sailing gear.

"Nothing too expensive," cautioned Jess as they strolled through the scarlet-roofed Leverick Bay Resort. Under different circumstances, she'd have been dazzled by the sophisticated shops and colorful markets. The heady mix of sun, sea, and glamour had earned the island a reputation as a billion-aires' playground. But she felt guilty enjoying herself when Gabe was dead and his disappearance an unsolved mystery.

It was Jude who convinced her that the best way for them to honor Gabe's memory was for them to see the places they visited through his eyes.

"He'd have been complaining that Leverick Bay was a rip-off and too flashy while secretly having the best time," said Jude. "He'd have been blown away by the superyachts and by the North Sound. I am. Admit it, Jess—you are too."

Jess confessed she was. She could see why the North Sound was considered one of the world's greatest harbors. The color of the water alone was a happy-making triumph of nature. The showers at the marina erased days of dirt, worry, and sadness. A smiling man at the laundromat promised to transform their foul bag of laundry into clean-pressed clothes just hours later.

Gabe's cash bought them a fabulous brunch. They enjoyed French toast and caramelized banana at a table overlooking the bay. Colorful Hobie Cats, paddleboarders, and kiters dotted the turquoise waters. To Jess, everyone seemed to be having the time of their lives. She wondered if she'd ever feel that way again.

The French toast was definitely a step in the right direction. By the time she'd finished, she felt a great deal more positive. Sailing round the world without Gabe started to feel possible. It might even be fun. If the New Zealand–born

Dutch sailor Laura Dekker could circumnavigate the globe alone, aged fifteen, the twins could surely manage it together.

To cover up the fact that she and Jude were dining alone, without any adults, Jess assured the waiter who took their order that they were being joined by their uncle later. Then she told the waitress who brought their bill that their uncle had been held up.

The lie was surprisingly easy. That was the thing about lying, thought Jess. It was seductively straightforward to begin with, but one fib led to another, and it became harder and harder to untangle yourself if it all went wrong.

They'd come ashore armed with Gabe's credit card.

"Feels wrong," said Jude, twisting the silver card in his hands. "Like we're stealing."

"I know what you mean, but we have to be practical. Gabe's gone, and we need money." Jess checked her watch. "Our laundry won't be ready till two. Let's go to the bookshop."

"I don't want to go to a boring bookshop," Jude snapped rudely.

"And I don't want to go to another boring sailing shop," Jess said with feeling. "How about we split up? Kill two birds. You get the cash while I go see if I can find *Castle of Secrets*. I'll meet you back here at one p.m."

She borrowed a pen from the surf shop opposite and wrote Gabe's PIN on the restaurant receipt. By chance, Gabe had given her his code in the Cayman Islands when he was dealing with the sail tear and needed quick cash from the ATM.

"It's his grandma's birthday: November tenth. Just remember that his grandma was British. Put the day before the month like they do, not the other way around like we do in the US. Easy as pie."

"Day before the month. Got it."

Jude took the scrap of paper, shoved it in his pocket, and veered off to gaze longingly at some offshore salopettes in the window of a sailing shop. "I think I might buy myself some of these. You should get a pair too. They're extra-long thermal, technical trousers. We'll need them when we head out into the open ocean."

Jess felt a twinge of dread at the thought of *You Gotta Friend* tackling the Atlantic or Southern Oceans. She'd seen the YouTube videos. Yachts riding up the faces of skyscraper waves and teetering at the top before plunging into a watery valley of doom. To Jess, the sailors who survived and even relished those conditions seemed to be another breed entirely.

On closer inspection, the salopettes were outrageously expensive.

"Jude, are you nuts? Look at the price of them. We're not here for a shopping spree. If we run out of cash, we'll be stuck."

"There's fifteen thousand dollars in Gabe's bank account," Jude reminded her. "It won't last forever, but it's a lot. And if nobody knows he's passed, whoever's giving him a thousand dollars each month might keep sending it forever."

"And what if they don't?" Jess asked heatedly. "We can't just spend it like we've won the lottery."

"How is that fair? You're getting a load of books."

In Jess's opinion, a few mystery novels did not remotely compare to splashing the cash on sailing gear that cost as much as the Castaway waitresses earned in a month, but she bit back a comment and promptly decided to treat herself to *ten* novels.

Still, her brother had a point. "Sorry, Jude. You have as much right as I do to decide how we spend Gabe's money. You're our skipper. If you think the salopettes will help us in colder waters, let's buy some."

A shadowboxing reflection flickered across the window.

Jess spun round, heart hammering. No one was there.

"What is it?" Jude stared worriedly at her. "Jess, what did you see?"

"It's nothing. Just my imagination."

But the unwelcome reminder of the boatyard incident with Gabe and the aggressive stranger had sapped the innocent delight from Jess's day. Even the bookshop had lost its appeal. She debated whether to go with Jude to the bank for safety's sake but told herself she was being silly.

Her twin hesitated. "Come with me. I don't like leaving you alone."

"Jude, relax. I'm fine. Just get the most cash possible out of the ATM. I don't want to come here again."

On his own, Jude became increasingly agitated. It was unlike Jess to be so jumpy. Something, or someone, had scared her.

It didn't help that, minutes after leaving her, he glimpsed the couple who'd grilled him on his life story on Tortola. They recognized him and waved. Jude pretended not to see them and shot through a beachwear shop and out the other side.

The quicker he and Jess left Leverick Bay, the better. He'd run to the ATM, then join Jess in the bookshop. That way, at least he'd know she was safe.

He didn't count on eighteen cruise-ship passengers also needing the ATM.

Jude was tempted to give up, but then he and Jess would only have to return another day. *It's not as if ATMs grow on palm trees*, he chided himself.

As he itched and sweated in line, some instinct made him glance up. On a hotel balcony high above, a man in mirror shades was staring down at him, talking into his phone. Slung over his shoulder was a long-lens camera.

Hunter was the word that flashed into Jude's brain. He and Jess had dropped their guard. They'd forgotten they were being hunted and that the same person who might have brought about Gabe's demise could have tracked them to Leverick Bay.

"Your turn," prompted a woman in a billowing cerise shirt.

"Thanks, sorry." Jude fumbled for the receipt with the PIN on in his pocket. It wasn't there. He turned his pocket inside out, but there was nothing but tissue fluff.

"We haven't got all day, son," said a man clutching the hand of a child with a dripping ice cream.

Math was Jude's best subject. Normally, numbers were his strength. But the pressure of everyone staring at him had sucked the PIN code right out of his head.

At the last second, he recalled Jess talking about Gabe's grandma's birthday: Relieved, he tapped in *1101*.

The card was declined.

Jude was livid with himself. He'd forgotten that the day part of the number came *before* the month: *0111*. As he reentered the code, someone's phone burst into song, making him jump and hit the *2* on the keypad. Involuntarily, he glanced up at the balcony. Mirror-glasses man was gone.

The ATM beeped. The card had been refused again. Jude made a third attempt—*0111*. As he pressed Enter, he remembered that Gabe's grandmother's birthday was on the tenth of November, not the first. He should have put in *1011*.

It was too late. The machine burped like a hungry toad and swallowed Gabe's card. Jude tried to grab it but it was gone. He stared at the card slot in numb disbelief.

"What a pain," said the woman behind him. "You must have entered the wrong PIN too many times. I've done it myself. Nightmare if you're island-hopping."

"What do you mean? How do I get it back?"

"You don't. Your bank will have to issue a new credit card and PIN. Those get posted to the address where the card's registered. If your house is on the other side of the world, someone you trust will have to courier it to you. Hey, don't look so anxious. Mistakes happen. Your parents will sort it out."

"Any chance you can review your banking arrangements someplace else?" grumbled the man with the ice-cream-coated child. "Some of us want to get on with our day."

It was 1:12 p.m. now, and Jess would be waiting for him, but Jude couldn't face her. Not yet. He sat on the pavement with his head in his hands. Without cash, his hopes of avoiding being put into care crumbled to pieces. What would he and Jess do? What would his sister *say*?

"You're late," said Jess, although she didn't seem too bothered. She was already three chapters into *Castle of Secrets* and had the contented glow of an avid reader in the grip of a page-turner. "Everything all right? Did you get the cash?"

"No," admitted Jude. "Had second thoughts."

Which was true. He'd had second, third, fourth, and fifth thoughts, none of which altered the fact that he'd basically thrown away $15,822. No bank on earth would hand a new credit card to a couple of kids who weren't Gabriel Henry Carter. Jude's forgetfulness had destroyed any chance they'd had of sailing around the world.

He'd have to break the news to Jess sooner or later, but now didn't seem the best time.

Hey, sis, that lottery you mentioned? Guess what—I blew it.

Jess set down her backpack. "Jude, we need extra cash. Until we know who's after us, any time we anchor in a crowded place, we're taking a risk. It's hard to hide when you haven't a clue who you're hiding from."

"Yeah, but think about this. If we withdraw a stack of cash so soon after Gabe's passing, and the police somehow link the body they've found with our yacht, it'll look deeply suspicious. The cops could accuse us of murder."

"Omigod, Jude. That hadn't even occurred to me. And if we use Gabe's credit card to buy clothes or food when we haven't reported him missing, that might look dodgy too. We could end up somewhere *worse* than an orphanage. We could be sent to a youth detention center or one of those boot camps for out-of-control kids."

"It's a minefield," agreed Jude. "Let's grab our laundry and get some supplies with the cash we already have, then head for the nearest uninhabited island. I cannot wait to get out of here."

CHAPTER 7

Horseshoe Reef

Afterward, Jess would always wonder if the real reason they decided to sail to Horseshoe Reef was because it was forbidden to amateur sailors. It was a test. If she and Jude could make it there and back in one piece, it would be proof that they were the skilled young yachtsmen their guardian had trained them to be. They'd be ready to take on the world.

Failure was not an option.

The week before he died, Gabe had shown them Instagram photos of butterfly fish and turtles gliding through the eighteen miles of pristine coral that ringed the island of Anegada.

"You'll love it there, Jess," he'd said. "It's a true snorkelers' paradise. And, Jude, you'll learn some new navigational techniques getting there too. It might seem like plain sailing, but beneath the surface, there's a world of trouble. Whole forests of branch coral that'll put a hole in your hull before you can say 'baloney.' Only licensed skippers are allowed there."

Jess had been entranced. "It's so beautiful; it doesn't look real."

"Uh-huh. And over the centuries, the captains of more than three hundred warships, galleons, and trawlers have thought the same thing—right up until their boat got smashed into splinters on that lovely white reef."

He'd clicked through to a couple of eerie shots of greening anchors, clown fish, and groupers weaving through shipwrecks.

"Back then, few mariners knew that in the Anegada Passage, the ocean drops off a cliff. Sailors call it the 'O-My-God-A-Passage.' Imagine. You're cruising along in seventy feet of clear water, watching the pretty pink flamingos. Then—*boom*—the bottom of the planet drops into oblivion. Where the Caribbean Sea meets the Atlantic Ocean in the Puerto Rico Trench, it's over five miles—that's twenty-seven thousand feet—deep."

Jude had leaned in. "Five *miles*? That's wild."

"Yep, it is, and it makes for a real maelstrom of currents. But that's not your only challenge. The seabed around there is an underwater mountain range of shelves, caves, coral, fault lines, and tectonic plates, all shifting about like a DJ at a mixing desk. Earthquakes happen fairly regularly. Toss weather into the equation, and you can understand why Anegada's a ship graveyard to rival the Cape of Good Hope."

"Yeah, but most of those ships went down in the olden days," said Jude. "Wouldn't happen now because we have modern charts and digital depth sounders. It's not the Bermuda Triangle."

Gabe had shaken his head. "You have a lot to learn if you think a depth sounder and a few gadgets are all it takes to save you if things go bad, Jude. That's where experience comes in."

"So, can we go there?" asked Jude, eyes shining. "Can we sail to Horseshoe Reef?"

"Try stopping us," Gabe had said with a grin.

Jess had been unable to believe her ears. "Why would we go there when there's a chance we might sink our yacht?"

"For the thrill of it!" Gabe laughed. "Kidding—just kidding. Don't fret, Jess. Anegada's a spectacular place. I hear there are dolphins too. If we're lucky, we might get a chance to swim with them."

From that moment on, the idea of swimming with dolphins had lodged in Jess's head and become an obsession.

But the main reason the twins decided to sail on their own to Anegada was because they were grieving and bored.

Nine days had gone by since they'd had brunch at the fancy café in Leverick Bay. Nine formless days of perfect sunshine, perfect sea, perfect beaches, and perfect families enjoying themselves.

Perfect was not going out of style in the Virgin Islands any time soon.

Less than perfect was life on *You Gotta Friend*.

Jess had always adored swimming, reading, and walking Sam on beaches as much as Jude lived to fish and tinker with boats. But without Gabe, life at sea got real boring, real fast.

Gabe, they were discovering, had lent their days shape.

It wasn't that he was a stickler for discipline or structure. Nor did he have much in the way of ambition or goals. Quite the reverse.

But nobody could deny that he'd had an unstoppable zest for life. He had been passionate about nature, sailing and experiencing the world far from their shores, and he'd encouraged the twins to be the same. The loss of his big, loud, warm presence had left an emptiness that was impossible to fill.

Most evenings, he and Jude had practiced knots or planned the next day's route. Quite often, Jess would read aloud to the two of them before they all turned in for the night. As far as Jess could tell, Gabe had last opened a novel in high school. But both he and Jude relished a good tale if they were read to.

The twins hadn't realized how much they'd enjoyed these times until they were gone.

They even missed the things they'd complained bitterly about when Gabe was around. How bossy he was about keeping the boat shipshape. How some days it seemed that he was on their case twenty-four/seven, lecturing them about finishing their homework and chivvying them to tidy lines, put on life jackets, clean the galley, and scrub the deck and toilet.

In short, he'd given their lives purpose.

Purpose, Jess was learning, was vital. Purpose meant moving forward.

Growing up in the frenetic, chaotic diner had had its charms, but Jess had always yearned for a normal life. She'd dreamed of going to a first-class school with a wide range of subjects. She would have liked to take lessons from teachers who knew more than she did. She'd wanted school friends, and routine, and an actual bedroom with space for more than a handful of books.

She'd wanted to one day go to university.

In this, she'd been encouraged by Victoria, a law student who'd spent a summer flipping burgers at the diner.

"Jess, you're smart. You have a fine brain. Use it, don't lose it. If I were you, soon as I turned eighteen, I'd smoke outta here so fast, I'd leave tire tracks. Places like the Castaway and Bantry Creek, they're like superglue. Not because they aren't nice, but because they *are*. They're as comforting and familiar as a squashy feather duvet. You snuggle up in that thing and you think, 'It's cold and nasty outside. Maybe I'll stay cozy today and leave tomorrow or the next day or the month after that.' It's easy enough to let half a lifetime go by.

"My advice: fix your sights on University of California, Berkeley, or Oxford or Cambridge across the pond, even the Sorbonne in Paris. Fly far and fly free, little bird. You won't regret it."

Jess had taken that advice to heart. She'd always studied hard and tried her very best on even the tiniest spelling bee. But with Gabe gone, her interest in lesson plans and homework had waned drastically. Her brother refused to even open a schoolbook.

"What's the use when I'll probably end up crewing a yacht or working in a boatyard like Gabe?" he told his sister.

Increasingly, Jess found it difficult to motivate herself. Given the choice between algebra and rereading a mystery, she'd choose the mystery every time.

Tomorrow, she promised herself each day. *I'll start on that history project tomorrow.*

She was telling herself this very thing when Jude stumbled, yawning, from his cabin in boxer shorts and a torn vest. It was 10:15 a.m. on December 4. Always an early riser, he'd started sleeping in late—once or twice until lunchtime.

He opened the food cupboard. "Where are the Cheerios?"

"We finished them yesterday. Bread's all gone too. I've told you ten times that we need to get more supplies."

"Actually, I'm not that hungry," said Jude, although his grumbling stomach was audible from the other side of the living quarters.

Jess was worried sick about him, and not just because he was noticeably thinner. His spark had gone. Something was bothering him, and yet the brother who'd always talked to her about everything was withdrawn and closed off to her now, when it mattered most.

Jess would have given anything to have the old Jude back. To be woken at the crack of dawn by him crashing and banging about in the galley, accompanied by his irrepressibly cheerful whistling. The strained silence on the boat was becoming too much to bear.

"What do you fancy doing today?" asked Jess with forced

enthusiasm. "It's your turn to choose. Pick any island on the chart and we'll sail there."

"Anywhere?"

"Anywhere."

Jude fetched a chart and laid it on the counter. "What I'd really like to do is sail to Anegada."

Jess followed his finger. It was on the tip of her tongue to say, *Have you lost your mind? After all Gabe told us about it being a wrecking yard of Spanish galleons and sailors' ambitions?*

But then she remembered the dolphins, and how snorkeling Horseshoe Reef had been at the very top of their guardian's wish list.

"Why not?" she said.

"Is that a yes?" Jude looked brighter than he had in weeks.

Jess laughed. "Yes, yes, yes. We'd be doing it for Gabe. It was the number one wish on his bucket list."

"Absolutely," agreed Jude. "We'd be doing it for Gabe."

"Swim with me, Jude," pleaded Jess that afternoon at Anegada.

Ever since Gabe's disappearance twelve days earlier, Jude's fear of deep water had been intensifying. The way he saw it, if a yachtsman with thirty years' experience could be washed overboard by a single wave, it proved that the smallest slip or miscalculation could result in the same happening to Jude.

What would happen to Jess then?

Jude knew he had to get over his ocean phobia, just as he knew he had to tell his sister about the lost bank card.

What use was a penniless sailor who couldn't swim?

For the past five and a half months, he'd avoided swimming whenever possible. However, this afternoon, his confidence had roared back. He was buzzing with the success of their outbound voyage. He felt elated. As skipper, he'd safely and effortlessly guided *You Gotta Friend* to Anegada. Jess had also done a first-rate job of crewing. The twins agreed that the trip had been well worth the risk.

Once anchored, they'd spent an enjoyable morning exploring the coral and limestone island. There were flamingos on the salt flats and iguanas scrambling over the rocks. Fragrant frangipani and feathery sea lavender grew around beaches with names like Flash of Beauty and Windlass Bight.

To Jude, who was starving, almost the best bit was when Jess produced a bonus seventeen dollars she'd found in Gabe's backpack. He didn't say a word when she blew it all on takeout tacos and soda from a cute beach hut on Cow Wreck Beach.

After their lunch went down, Jess took out her snorkel. "Swim with me," she begged, wading into the aquamarine shallows.

"Yes, yes, yes," said Jude with a grin, surprising even himself.

Her face lit up, and he immediately felt guilty. He knew he'd been a bear with a sore head around the boat. He also knew it couldn't go on. He owed it to Jess to tell the truth and to live up to his promise to himself to do everything in his power to protect her and make her happy.

The swim was as blissful as everything else on Anegada. The water felt like satin on Jude's skin. For the first time in a long time, he remembered why he'd once loved swimming nearly as much as Jess did.

It's all going to be okay, he told himself. *My phobia's all in my mind. Once I've built up my sea-swimming fitness, it'll go away altogether.*

· · ✷ · ·

They were under sail and watching Anegada recede in their wake when Jude plucked up the courage to tell his sister about the lost bank card.

"Jess, I've been thinking. Maybe we should head back to Florida. Tomorrow even. It'll be the easiest thing. The safest too. Who's gonna hunt us or hurt us if we're at the diner? If anyone tries anything, Lucille will get her biker friends to have a word with them."

He paused nervously. "Why are you looking at me like that? I thought you'd be pleased. You seemed mighty wary about tackling far-flung oceans. This'll be the easiest thing. We can return to Florida till we're eighteen. Anita and the waitresses will look after us. We can live in a room above the diner, like Mom did. I'll quit school and do odd jobs around the boatyard and—"

Jess cut him off. "I'm never going back to Bantry Creek," she said with quiet determination. "It's a cul-de-sac."

"What's a cul-de-sac?"

"If you read books, you'd know," Jess retorted cruelly. "It means we'd be stuck there for the rest of our lives and never escape."

Jude was stung. "Your problem is you read *too many* books."

"And yours is that you don't read any. You haven't even opened the one I bought you in Leverick Bay. Gabe was the same."

Jude glared at her. "Why are you always making me feel stupid?"

"Same reason you make me feel like a dunce when I don't know some sailing term," retorted Jess. "If you're such a sailing genius, why do you want to go to back to Florida? We have over fifteen grand. Why don't we sail to Cannes or to Sydney, like you promised?"

"It's complicated," Jude said defensively. "There are hurricanes and dangerous tides. Stuff you know nothing about."

"What I do know is that our food stores are empty and Sam's starving hungry. I thought we had one last can of dog food, but I was wrong."

The Swiss shepherd was barking at the waves. Jess watched him distractedly.

"We're down to two cans of carrots. I'm with you on avoiding crowds, but we need supplies."

"There is no fifteen grand," shouted Jude at last. "I lost it."

Jess went still. "What do you mean, you lost it? That's impossible. The ATM only lets you withdraw three hundred dollars at a time."

"I forgot the PIN and the machine ate the card. Happy now? You can call me an idiot all you like. I deserve it."

Sam was whining anxiously, which made Jude feel even worse.

There were tears in Jess's eyes. "Jude, why didn't you tell me? What are we going to do? Without cash, we won't even make it out of the Caribbean."

"This is both of our faults, not just mine," Jude said in furious despair. "Because of your books, we left Tortola a day early and Gabe was washed overboard. And in Leverick Bay, you sent me to get cash on my own because you just had to go get your mysteries. Your books have cost us *everything*."

"I hate you," Jess said coldly.

"Not as much as I hate you." He swung round. "Sam, will you *stop barking*? Just shut up!"

Jess cried, "Jude, look! What *is* that?"

A vast anvil-shaped black cloud with smokelike streaks issuing from its flat lower edge filled the horizon.

Jude's heart rate tripled. Blood pounded in his ears. It was a sight he'd hoped he'd never witness. It was a sea squall.

CHAPTER 8

Sea Squall

Jude lunged for a safety line and threw it to Jess. "Clip this on to your life jacket *now* and fetch your deck boots! Get ready to do what I say when I say it. Every second counts. We need to reef the sails before they overpower the boat."

The expression on Jude's face as he ran to take the helm while tightening the straps on his own life jacket frightened Jess more than the approaching squall. There was not a scrap of boyishness in it. He reminded her of the sailors who tackled the mountainous waves of the Southern Ocean. All he cared about was survival.

Theirs.

That's when Jess knew they were in trouble.

Sam, who hated storms, knew it too. He skittered down the steps and onto Jess's bunk, where he covered his eyes with his paws.

The pace at which the anemometer flipped to thirty-five miles per hour and day turned to night blew Jess's mind.

When the black wall of rain came driving in, it hit the yacht like a freight train. *You Gotta Friend* gave an almost animal shudder and groan.

Crouched on the aft deck, Jess gasped at the physical force of it. Within seconds, she was soaked through.

At the helm, Jude had to cling to the wheel with all his might to avoid being blown off the stern. He turned the boat downwind as the mainsail filled, the roar of it merging with the gale and sea. Overhead, the rigging clanged and screeched.

"Jess, furl away the jib, quick as you can," yelled Jude, struggling to make himself heard above the din. For one paralyzing moment, Jess couldn't remember where the furling line was or what it did, though she'd used it only that morning. She could barely recall her own name.

But as the yacht tipped dramatically, giving her a premonition of what lay ahead, she snapped into urgent life. The furling line was in the cockpit. Her job was to reduce the headsail and slow the boat.

While she worked the line, Jude battled to steer a safe course. Gale-powered, *You Gotta Friend* was already at racing pace. Any faster and he feared she'd take flight. Angry waves came at them from every angle. If the boat was caught side-on by a breaker, she'd capsize.

"Hurry, Jess," he shouted, desperately trying to get a read of their position. "Keep a steady pull on the furling line or it'll snag. No, no, not like that! You're doing it all wrong. Oh, where's Gabe when I need him?"

"I'm trying, I'm trying," cried Jess, nearly in tears.

"Sorry, sis—you're doing great," called Jude, contrite as the line released. "I need to get the boat under control is all. It would help if we could ease out the main . . . Well done. You did good. Now lock it down—"

The yacht heeled dangerously. Her sails skimmed the waves. An instant of lost concentration and Jude had turned the boat too close to the wind.

Before he could right her, disaster struck.

The jib caught the wind and ballooned again. Thrown off-balance when the yacht powered forward, Jess was helpless as the furling line burned through her hands. The pain was ferocious.

Struggling to scale the sloping deck, she slipped and fell against the guardrail. A plume of salty spray smacked her in the face. Spitting seawater, Jess got an up-close-and-personal glimpse of greedy gray waves, waiting to swallow her, before her safety line pulled tight.

Jude gripped her arm and hauled her into the relative safety of the cockpit. "Stay strong, sis. We can do this," he shouted into her ear.

The twins clung to each other briefly before returning to the fight.

What happened next happened at warp speed; Jess's brain had trouble processing it.

Unsure which way to steer, Jude overcorrected. The boat jibed. The boom swung wildly.

Jess blinked. The Jude-shaped space at the helm was empty.

"No!" she screamed.

Rushing to the stern, she looked back. Jude and his red life jacket were in the sea, already shrinking into the distance. She was alone on an out-of-control yacht, with no way of saving him.

Just when it seemed impossible that the situation could get any worse, it did.

A blur of pink coral was the only warning Jess got before the yacht hit the reef, splintering with a ghastly crunch and catapulting Jess high into the air. As she crash-landed on the deck, she heard china and other breakables smashing down below. In the living quarters, Sam was barking hysterically.

Jess didn't need Ellen MacArthur to tell her that *You Gotta Friend*, the twins' only home, was wrecked beyond repair.

Jess lay winded on the deck. Rain needled her cheeks. Seawater spilled across the deck and lapped at her ankles.

She sat up suddenly and painfully. Now, more than ever, every second counted. With the yacht stopped, she had a chance of saving her brother.

Hope lent Jess strength. Grimacing, she staggered to the stern, salt spray biting into her raw hands.

She spotted him almost at once. That was a miracle, but her heart froze at the sight of him. He wasn't waving or yelling for help. He hung lifeless in his red life jacket, blood streaming from his head. Jess clung to the rigging, unsure what to do first.

She needed at least two crew to help her: one person to watch Jude; another to send out a distress call; and a third to try to save Jude. With no one to assist, it was hard to decide which to do first.

The sound of gushing water got her moving. Pushing back the companionway cover, she rushed down the steps. Sam was beside himself with gratefulness to see her. She gave him a reassuring cuddle before tuning the VHF radio to channel sixteen.

She'd been practicing emergency drills since she was five, but it was bizarre to be doing it in real life. Clutching the receiver with shaking hands, she called: "Mayday, Mayday, Mayday. This is sailing vessel *You Gotta Friend*. We have a man overboard and we're taking on water. We're sinking."

"Copy that, sailing vessel *You Gotta Friend*. This is the United States Coast Guard. State your position."

"I'm not sure. We're in the Anegada Passage, I think, south of Horseshoe Reef. Everything happened so fast."

Water was swilling around Jess's ankles. Sam was shivering and whimpering. She put a comforting hand on his head and wished someone would do the same for her.

"How many souls on board?" the operator was asking.

"Three if you count Sam, my dog. I'm Jess Carter. Oh, please come as fast you can. My brother, Jude, is in the water and bleeding. I think he has a head wound."

"Is he wearing a life jacket?"

"Yes and, uh, blue sailing shorts and a white T-shirt."

"How long has he been in the water?"

"Five minutes. No—more like seven. I have to go look for him. Please come quickly."

"Don't worry, Jess. I've already notified Virgin Island Search and Rescue. VISAR, they're called. They're on their way. Best thing you can do for your brother is to stay calm and keep a close watch over him. Do not let him out of your sight. And *do not*, under any circumstances, enter the water yourself. The VISAR crew will rescue Jude for you."

· • ✳ • ·

If it hadn't been for the dolphin, she'd never have found Jude, of that Jess was certain.

When she returned to the deck, there was no hint of his red life jacket amid an endless vista of gray. The wind had eased, but the waves were still wild. Tears mingled with the rain on Jess's cheeks. She'd made the wrong decision in calling for help before trying to save him. Her brother had been swept away.

Just as she was fearing the worst, a flash of silver split the gloom.

A dolphin arced above the waves.

Beneath it, Jude's head and shoulders rose briefly before sinking beneath the turbulent sea. His life jacket should have been keeping him afloat, but it wasn't. He was tangled in something and being dragged under.

Jess didn't think twice. She went against the advice of the US Coast Guard and everything Gabe had ever told her about ocean rescues, namely, to stay put and watch the struggling swimmer until help arrives. Acting purely on instinct, she tied the lightest of the lines to her wrist and jumped into the ocean.

In Florida, Jess had swum the length of the nearby bay

most days with Gabe and a couple of the Castaway staff. She'd been doing it since she was seven and was one of the fittest, most fearless swimmers in Bantry Creek. Even so, the violence of the current shocked her. For every ten strokes she took, it forced her back five.

She dived deep to try to escape the waves. Once or twice, she thought she glimpsed the dolphin again. She never doubted she would reach Jude. They were twins—half of the same whole. They belonged to each other.

As she tired, Jess became possessed by the conviction that the dolphin had been sent by Gabe, or even her mom, who'd left them the *Dolphin Dreams* painting. It was the dolphin that gave her the will to keep going until she got to Jude. Somehow, she was able to hold her breath underwater long enough to use her safety-lock knife to cut the old fishing net that now entangled him, dragging him down.

Belief in the dolphin lent her the endurance to pull her unconscious brother to the destroyed yacht using a line.

Sam, in a life jacket of his own, was barking on the deck. Jess heaved her aching body onto the transom. She tied Jude, still in the water, to a rail. With her last ounce of strength, she dragged herself down into the cabin to rescue their mother's painting, twisting her ankle on the return journey. Pain exploded through her. She collapsed on the deck, and there she stayed.

When the thirty-foot orange inflatable VISAR boat arrived, the four rescuers found her dazed and incoherent, her limbs a patchwork of bruises and bleeding scratches.

As the crew eased Jude onto a backboard and began to assess his condition, Jess was dimly aware of their growing consternation.

"Where's Mom and Dad?" asked one of the volunteers, after first wrapping Jess in towels and checking her blood oxygen levels with a pulse oximeter. "Where are the *adults*?"

"Good question," Jess mumbled in response.

Placing a warm hand on her forehead, the woman said softly, "Sweetie, were Mom and Dad below deck when you crashed? Are they in the water?"

Her voice seemed to come from outer space, on an otherworldly receiver. Jess tried to answer, but no words came out.

A flashlight beam burned the back of her eyes.

"The girl might have concussion too," the woman told her crewmate. "Jess, are you in pain? Where does it hurt? Can you hear me? Where are the grown-ups?"

Jess felt herself zooming out from the scene and circling high above, like a sea eagle on a thermal. She saw Jude on a stretcher being lifted onto the lifeboat. Another man gripped Sam's collar.

Lastly, Jess saw herself, colorless and limp, being stretchered onto the boat.

"We have no one," Jess whispered to her rescuers. "Nothing."

The woman bent nearer. "What did you say?"

"Save Jude. I can't live without him."

And then she passed out.

CHAPTER 9

Double Helix

Jess returned to consciousness the way a ghost passes through a wall. She crossed the line in one fluid step and lay alert, listening to the soft, insistent beep of hospital monitors.

Jude was asleep in the next bed, his head bandaged up like Tutankhamun. An intravenous drip dispensed droplets of life into his right arm. His left wrist was in a plaster cast. His bare chest was an art exhibit of bruises, iodine, coral grazes, and cardiac electrodes sending readings to a bank of machines.

Most important, he was alive.

Jess wanted to rush right over and throw her arms around him, but her limbs refused to cooperate. It was as if her blood had been replaced with syrup.

Every cell in her body ached. Myriad coral scratches itched and stung her skin. Bruises throbbed on muscles she didn't know existed. Mittens covered her rope-burned hands. A nerve jangled in her thickly bandaged left foot, propped up on a plump pillow.

Two nurses sat with their backs to her in vinyl armchairs, watching TV. The news was starting. A breezy anchor delivered the usual mixed tidings. Corrupt officials. A fight over taxes. A luxury resort with the promise of hundreds of jobs.

Out of the blue, a helicopter view of Anegada flashed up, along with a scrolling headline: COPS PROBE CASTAWAY TWINS LINK TO JOHN DOE.

"Who's John Doe?" Jess heard one nurse ask.

"That's what they call unidentified bodies," the other answered.

Jess stared in disbelief as shaky aerial footage of police divers inspecting the wreckage of *You Gotta Friend* filled the screen.

Squall gone, Horseshoe Reef was once again a tranquil turquoise idyll. However, the sight of it triggered a near-panic attack in Jess.

Her heart rate began to climb on the monitor as she relived the violent waves pulling her under and bashing her against the reef. Coral raked her skin like a cheese grater as she tried to hold her breath long enough to free Jude from the fishing net ensnaring him.

The TV gave a static pop as a nurse unmuted it, snapping Jess back to the present.

"The mystery surrounding the dramatic rescue of twin children from a sinking yacht on Horseshoe Reef yesterday deepened this morning. A police spokesperson confirmed that DNA found on the boat proves beyond a doubt that its skipper, Gabriel Carter, was the mysterious John Doe found dead on a Cowrie Sands beach on November twenty-third.

"Tonight, Star News can exclusively reveal that Carter, a forty-five-year-old shipwright from Bantry Creek, Florida, adopted the twin boy and girl after their mom died. The family left the US last summer to live the dream of sailing around the world.

"What happened to turn that dream into a nightmare?

"As detectives wait to speak to the children, who are recovering from their ordeal in a Tortola hospital, they'll be seeking answers to these urgent questions: How did two twelve-year-olds end up alone on a yacht near Horseshoe Reef, Anegada, in seas so lethal that three hundred vessels have gone to their graves there?

"Police believe that Carter drowned a couple of weeks ago. Why didn't the twins report him missing at the time?"

The TV camera zoomed in on a colorful beach hut. An overtanned reporter said, "At the Taco Shack on Cow Wreck Beach, owner Suzy Long recalls serving the twins shortly before the squall blew in."

The reporter held her mic out to Suzy, who leaned in.

"They stuck in my mind because they weren't like the usual tourist kids we see around here," said Suzy. "They were thin and kinda scruffy and paid with a bagful of change. Not an adult in sight. I'd have been concerned if I hadn't seen them laughing with their dog on the beach. They looked happy. Now I feel guilty I didn't warn them about the storm, but only a lunatic would let two kids sail these deadly seas on their own."

The reporter nodded fervently. He turned an earnest gaze on the viewers. "Few people know the twins better than Anita

Williams, owner of the Castaway Diner in Bantry Creek, Florida. For years, her diner was their second home, and her staff their backup 'mamas and papas.' They cooked for the children, drove them to school, and helped them with home-work while Gabe Carter, their guardian, worked long hours at the boatyard next door. Star News goes live to Castaway Diner in Bantry Creek to find out more."

Tears sprang into Jess's eyes at the sight of the diner, with its cheerful blue-and-yellow tablecloths and DISH OF THE DAY—peach cobbler!—menu board. Regina was plating up waffles in the kitchen while Ricardo washed dishes in the background.

Leaning on the counter was Anita.

"Ms. Williams, how did you feel when you heard that the twins were at the center of a high-seas drama? According to the Virgin Island Search and Rescue crew, it was only the quick thinking and heroism of young Jess that saved them both from certain doom at Horseshoe Reef."

"Gabe's death has hit us hard," said Anita. "He was family to all of us at the Castaway. As for Jess's heroics, she always was part dolphin. She could swim before she could crawl. Sharp as a whip too. And Jude was always either on a boat or fixing 'em. But they were just regular kids. Sweet kids. Jude could be hyper and goofy one minute and shy as anything the next. Jess was quiet and mostly lost in a book. Whatever went wrong on those islands must have forced them to grow up real fast."

She looked directly into the camera lens. "Jess and Jude, if

you ever need us, your Castaway mamas and papas will always
be here for you."

The bulletin ended. A chair scraped back. Jess pretended
she was asleep.

One nurse fussed over Jude. The other sighed as she
straightened Jess's sheet.

"Oh, Nurse Rolle, my heart breaks for these kids. If I were
them, I'd keep slumbering too. Why is fate so cruel to some
children while giving others so much more than they need?
What do these twins have to look forward to? No mom or
dad, no guardian, and they've lost the boat, which was their
only home. No way of sugarcoating that. Any which way you
look at it, they have a rocky road ahead."

"Jude, I can tell by your breathing that you're awake," said Jess.
"It's been two days now. You can't give me the silent treatment
forever. We have to talk."

Her brother didn't stir. He just lay there, stubbornly facing
the wall.

"I know you hate me," said Jess, "but I'm surprised you
don't care whether Sam's dead or alive."

That got to him.

He rolled over with difficulty, wincing in pain. Too weak to
sit up on his own, he pressed a button and let the bed do it for
him. His eyes were half hidden by bandages.

"Jess, don't you understand? I hate myself. Not you or Gabe

or the boat or the freaking storm. *Me.* Gabe always said that most times it's not the ocean or the weather that kills sailors; it's arrogance and ego. Not bothering with safety lines. Thinking you're a better sailor than you are. Being too cool for school. My ego could have gotten you killed. Could have killed Sam too. Where is he? Is he . . . ?"

"Alive? Yes, he is. And having loads more fun than we are. A dog-obsessed woman who heard our story on the news offered to walk Sam and take care of him. She runs some animal charity here. When we're a bit better, Barbara will bring him to the hospital garden so we can pet him."

"I'm glad Sam's okay," Jude said miserably, "but I wish you hadn't saved me. Apart from anything, it's embarrassing— being saved by your sister."

"You're saying that if I was knocked overboard in a storm, you wouldn't have jumped in to rescue me?" accused Jess.

"You know I would! I'd give my life to save yours."

"You mean you wouldn't just leave me to drown because it would be *embarrassing* for me to be saved by my own brother?"

"Point taken."

"Jude, Gabe would have struggled to get us out of that squall in one piece. You were magnificent. I know we wrecked the boat, but I was impressed with us. We made a good team. Sorry for being a beast before the storm."

"Me too," said Jude, shame-faced but smiling. "Thanks for saving me, sis."

"Any time, bro. Now, if we're done feeling sorry for ourselves, we need to put our heads together. The police are champing at the bit, desperate to question us. We need to get our story straight or our darkest fears about being taken into care and separated will come true."

"Have the police learned anything more about what happened to Gabe?" asked Jude. "What if there really *was* foul play, and now whoever spiked our drinks wants us gone too? If we're on the news and stuck in the hospital, it wouldn't be hard for them to track us down."

The same thought had crossed Jess's mind, but she hoped that both of them were being melodramatic. She and Jude had assumed that the email they'd found was about them, but maybe Gabe's promise to take "them" to the ends of the earth had been about a string of pearls or some rare gold coins or something else of enormous value. Not a couple of scruffy orphans.

Even so, until they knew what shape any possible threat might take, it was best to err on the side of extreme caution.

"Wait until you meet Nurse Rolle," she told Jude. "It would take a brave assassin to get past her!"

"I see," said Detective Jack Trenton when they were done telling him their story the next day. "Yes, I see."

Jess found it impossible to tell what he was thinking. His thin face gave nothing away. Yet there was something about his hopeful, expectant expression that invited confession. He had hardly sat down before the twins found themselves willing and eager to tell him all the secrets they'd ever had. He was like a human truth serum.

For the past forty-five minutes, the policeman's tall, lanky frame had occupied a chair in the twins' hospital room. He talked less and listened more than any adult they'd ever met.

It was only later that Jess worked out that the way he got results was by only ever asking half questions. It left her with an uncontrollable urge to fill in the blanks.

"And you felt it best to keep that to yourselves because . . . ?" he inquired softly.

"And your thinking on that was . . . ?

"You suspected foul play because . . . ?

"And your plan was . . . ?

"So you decided to visit Horseshoe Reef because . . . ?"

Finally, he said: "Is that everything? You've left nothing out?"

Jess fought the urge to tell him about the crumpled note they'd found in Gabe's locked box, which she and Jude had agreed was their secret.

Thankfully, Nurse Rolle came by to check on them, distracting the detective long enough for Jude to whisper, "Jess, should we say anything?"

Jess put a finger to her lips.

The detective turned suddenly but gave no sign of having noticed. He picked up his hat and turned it over in his hands.

"So, to sum up, after Gabriel disappeared, you decided not to report him missing and to continue sailing around the world for as long as you could because you were afraid that the authorities—people like myself—would lock you up in an institution, perhaps even separate you?"

"Yes," said Jude. "And now because I messed up—"

"*We* messed up by deciding to go to Horseshoe Reef," Jess reminded him.

"Our worst nightmare is going to happen."

Detective Trenton considered them gravely. "You do know that modern residential institutions for children are a far cry from the orphanages in books and films? There are caring places, even inspiring places. We'd do our best to place you in one of those."

"What if turns out that, behind closed doors, they feed us gruel and are mean and cruel after all?" demanded Jess. "We'd be far from here. You'll be busy solving crimes. You'll have forgotten about us. You don't understand what it's like to be all alone in the world. To have no one."

"I understand better than you might imagine. I was in care myself."

Jess swallowed. "You were?"

"Believe it or not, cops can be orphans too," he told her. "I was raised in a group home for kids without families in Boston."

"Then you *do* understand," cried Jess. "Detective Trenton, promise you won't let them separate us or drag us away somewhere awful. Jude, maybe you're right. We should go and live at the Castaway Diner. Anita and the waitresses will take care of us."

The policeman looked uncomfortable. "I'm afraid it's not quite so simple. It seems that your US citizenship is in question. No one doubts that you were born in Florida, but there are irregularities on your birth certificates. Your mom was using a fake social security number, and Gabe lied about being your father. He did what he did out of the goodness of his heart, but the law sees it differently. Until the situation's resolved, you're wards of the court and . . . stateless."

Thinking about the lost bank card, Jess asked, "Did Gabe leave us any money in his will? Maybe we could buy another boat to live on."

"No will has been found," replied Detective Trenton. "To be honest, even if one turns up, it'll be invalid, because Gabe didn't adopt you legally. Any money he had is likely to pass to his half brother, who lives in Alaska."

Jude was in a state of shock. "You're telling us that me and Jess are stateless, homeless, motherless, fatherless, guardian-less, *and* penniless? Wow. That's a lot of-less."

"Yes, it is," admitted Jack Trenton. "I don't suppose Gabe ever discovered where your mom was born, or whether you had any distant relatives?"

"We drove him crazy asking and asking," said Jess. "Trust me, he was as in the dark about Mom's background as we were."

"There is one thing we can try. Ever heard of DNA?"

Jess had to stop herself from rolling her eyes. Why did people assume that just because she lived on a boat she was half idiot? As a mystery reader and aspiring detective herself, she'd known about DNA for years. She couldn't resist showing off her expertise to the detective: "Deoxyribonucleic acid? Of course we've heard of it."

The detective smiled. "Then you'll know that DNA is basically a genetic fingerprint. Everyone's is unique."

"Forensic scientists use it to link murderers to crime scenes," said Jude.

"Indeed, they do. But people have also traced long-lost family members using DNA profiling. We could try that in this case."

"Yes, please!" cried Jess, her mind leaping to possible long-lost royal cousins or kindly uncles residing on lavender farms in Provence or amid the dreaming spires of Oxford.

Jude was wondering what would happen if their long-lost cousins turned out to be bank robbers or child-loathing bullies living in isolated rural hamlets. What then?

But he agreed with Jess. For good or for bad, they had to know.

"Try not to get your hopes up too high," cautioned Jack Trenton. "Despite what you see on TV detective shows, there's only a one-in-a-billion chance of a match."

CHAPTER 10

Blues and Royals

Ten days after they were shipwrecked, Detective Trenton returned with some of the answers the twins had been seeking their entire lives.

Answers to questions such as where had their mother been born and raised, and where had she journeyed from before she blew into Bantry Creek on the hurricane's wild wings?

They knew even less about their dad. They didn't know his full name or his occupation. Would Jack Trenton tell them how and why he came to save the life of his best friend?

Jess and Jude were in the hospital garden when the detective turned up. After much begging, they'd persuaded Nurse Rolle to allow Jude out of bed for an hour so he could see Sam.

"Yes, on condition that Jess keeps that hairy mutt on a leash. I don't want it jumping up and knocking you flat. Jude, you'll need to sit in a wheelchair in the shade."

"Jess's the one with the sprained ankle, not me," protested Jude. "Nothing wrong with my legs apart from a few scratches."

"And what happens if you have a fainting spell and hit your foolish head on the concrete?" demanded Nurse Rolle. "Do you really want a cracked skull to add to your dramas? Are you angling to spend another month on the ward under my care?"

"No, ma'am, I am not."

"My care not good enough for you, boy?"

"Your care's the best, Nurse Rolle," Jude said hastily.

She laughed. "Well, then. The wheelchair it is. Any case, the sea air'll give you a boost. Better than any medicine. I'll give you a portable alarm too. You feel dizzy, you press it and I'll come a-walking."

"You mean, you'll come running?"

"No, boy—I'll be walking. If any Usain Bolt stuff is needed, I'll leave it to Nurse Jones."

It was Nurse Jones who pushed Jude's wheelchair out to the garden at midday. Jess swung beside them on crutches. The nurse sat them in the shadows of a late-flowering flamboyant tree while she talked to Barbara, Sam's foster carer, nearby.

Jess was lolling on the bench and Jude was about to throw a Frisbee for his beloved dog when Detective Trenton strode up the path. After a brief word with the nurse, he came over.

He took off his hat but stayed standing. "I have news."

Jess noted that he didn't say whether the news was good or bad.

"We have a match."

An electric thrill ran through Jess. Jude gulped. He reached for his sister's hand and gripped it painfully. Detective Trenton looked nervous. "Truthfully, when I suggested we try the DNA route, I thought we had very little chance of finding your parents. I confess to being astounded by the result. I hesitate to describe it as a miracle, but it's difficult to see it any other way."

He took a notebook from his pocket and consulted it before continuing. "Ready?"

"Ready," the twins said together.

"Your father was British . . ."

"*British?*" cried Jess. "Like Miss Marple, Sherlock Holmes, and the Famous Five!"

"Like them, yes. Your dad was born in Shoreditch, East London. His name was Jim Gray."

"Gray?" Jude said in wonder.

Jess turned the words over in her mind. Gray was a fine name. Humble and kind. She'd never heard a better one. Jim Gray of Shoreditch, London. Did that mean she was Jess Gray now?

"He started his career in the Blues and Royals . . ."

"*Royals?*"

"Yes, but before you go thinking you're some top secret royal cousin, that's the nickname for the queen's horse guards. For five years, Jim Gray was in Her Majesty's cavalry regiment at Buckingham Palace."

Jess was overwhelmed. It seemed so fantastical.

Her dad had guarded Queen Elizabeth II!

"I thought you might like to see a picture of him."

And just like that, a huge piece of the puzzle of them, of who they were, slotted into place.

The soldier in the photo was the spitting image of Jude, albeit without the sun-bleached curls. Beneath his polished brass-and-steel helmet, with its magnificent scarlet plume, he had a military buzz cut. But he had Jude's laughing eyes and square jaw. Both twins had inherited his smile and his neat, straight nose with a tiny kink on the bridge.

He was holding the reins of a towering black horse. Seeing their dad for the first time was equal parts devastating and the best thing ever. If only they'd had a chance to get to know him.

"Next, Jim took a job as head groom in Gloucester-shire . . . ," Jack Trenton was saying.

"Wait—why did he leave the queen's cavalry?" asked Jude.

"From what I could glean, he'd married your mother, Joanna—"

"Our mom's name was Joanna?" This from Jess. "I thought it was Ana."

"Jo—Ana, Joanna?" said Jude.

"—and they were looking to leave the city and start a family. She was a New Zealander who'd come to the UK to work as a nanny. An opportunity arose for Jim and Joanna to work together as a couple at Blakeney Park, a stately home on a three-hundred-acre estate. Jim took care of the horses, and your mother was a personal assistant and—later—carer to

Robert Blakeney, a newspaper owner in poor health. There they stayed until your father's unfortunate accident."

Jess was still thinking about her mom being from New Zealand and about Blakeney Park. As she absently threw a ball for Sam, she wondered if the stately home was anything like Downton Abbey. Was it terribly grand and romantic, or was it a Gothic mansion with castlelike turrets and spider-filled attics?

"Our dad died saving his best friend," Jude informed the policeman, not without pride.

Detective Trenton said carefully, "Jude, it may be that not everything your guardian told you was strictly . . . accurate. The fact that your mom left no ID or personal belongings suggests she wanted to erase her past."

He paused a beat before continuing.

"I did manage to find a newspaper report from that time. There was an accident near the estate in heavy rain. Part of a bridge collapsed. That much I can confirm. As you already know, your father sadly passed away, and his employer, Robert Blakeney, also lost his life. The coroner ruled it an accidental death. If your mom says your dad died a hero, I'm sure he did."

If the detective was concerned that this news might distress them, he needn't have been. After a lifetime of being kept in the dark about anything to do with their parents' past, each precious gem of new information—even the painful bits—lit up their universe like a star.

The twins were reeling. It was incomprehensible to Jess that the birds kept on singing. Didn't they realize how momentous it was for the twins to finally learn their dad's name and know where he and their mom had been born?

"Apologies for interrupting, Detective," said Nurse Jones, walking over. "I need to get these children back to the ward. Jess, Jude, say goodbye to your dog."

"Forgive me, Nurse Jones, but there is one more thing I have to discuss with the twins. The most important thing. Would you give us five more minutes?"

"There's more?" Jess couldn't believe it.

"The current owner of Blakeney Park, Clifford, is the son of your dad's former employer, Robbie. He inherited his father's newspaper business after Robbie's death. When Clifford and his wife, Allegra, learned of your plight and the connection to their estate from my Metropolitan Police contact, they were moved to tears. They have three children of their own, you see. Within twenty-four hours they'd contacted us. They wish to offer you a home . . ."

"A home?" Jude was stunned.

"At Blakeney Park?" Jess said faintly, picturing anew the Gothic mansion. Why would total strangers offer to take them in? It seemed too good to be true. Did they like dogs? Would they consider offering Sam a home too? What if they didn't?

Detective Trenton was studying them for a reaction. "Obviously, child protective services will have to run stringent checks on the family. And you'll have to meet Clifford and Allegra to see if you like them and would get along. But if you're amenable to the idea of moving to a country estate in the United Kingdom, the Blakeneys have promised to foster you and take care of you until you come of age."

He smiled. "Look, this is a lot to absorb all at once. I'll let you mull it over for a day or two before we speak again. Meanwhile, I printed out an Instagram photo of Blakeney Park. Thought you might like a glimpse of the estate where your parents worked—and your potential new home."

The following morning, a bodyguard was posted at the door of the twins' hospital room.

"Courtesy of the Blakeneys," the head of the hospital explained to Nurse Rolle. "The family are concerned that if news gets out that they might foster Jess and Jude, there'll be a media storm. I agree. I'll thank you to make Ivan welcome, Nurse Rolle. He's here for your benefit, as well as that of your patients."

From then on, the twins were never alone. Ivan even accompanied Jess down to the garden. He watched from a distance as she chatted to Barbara and threw a ball for Sam.

In the pocket of her pajamas was the picture of Blakeney Park. Jess couldn't stop thinking about it. Bathed in sunshine, the stately home was built in honey-colored stone. It gazed out across rose gardens, lawns mown in stripes, and paddocks full of glossy horses.

"A little bird told me your news," said Barbara, beaming at Jess. "Oh, don't worry, I'm sworn to secrecy. What a fairy-tale ending for you and Jude.

"You'll have heard of Clifford Blakeney, no doubt. He's a media mogul like Rupert Murdoch, only not quite so fabulously wealthy. Millions not billions."

Jess had never heard of the Blakeneys in her life, and Clifford being a media mogul was the least of her concerns. "But are they kind—Mr. and Mrs. Blakeney?" To Jess, kindness was a quality infinitely more essential in a prospective foster family than any number of newspaper empires or millions and billions.

"Clifford's one of a kind, sure!" Barbara laughed. "And Allegra is a famous beauty. From what I've read, they have a gorgeous stately home and the best of everything. Cars, horses, wall-to-wall luxury. You'll want for nothing."

She cast an admiring glance at Jess, as if Jess had personally engineered the quirk of destiny that might catapult them to Blakeney Park.

"From orphans to fortunes. You'll be the luckiest children in the world!"

CHAPTER 11

The Luckiest Children in the World

In Florida, Jude's best friend had been a boy who didn't believe in magic.

"No such thing, dude," Aaron had informed him. "When Houdini vanished an elephant, or David Copperfield made the Statue of Liberty disappear, d'you think they had some invisibility superpower? Or when Dynamo walks on water or fully levitates above a tower, d'you think he's channeling Jesus? No—that's some next-level trick engineering or special effects. It's smoke and mirrors, man."

The way Aaron explained it, illusionists were like sneaky politicians. His father had worked in the mayor's office, so he considered himself a semi authority on the subject.

"Corrupt politicians, their whole gig is distracting you. They start a dumpster fire on one side of town and get every-body freaking out, blaming each other and trying to round up a fire hose. Meantime, the politician's long gone. They're off nuking innocent civilians or gifting a polar-bear wilderness to a bunch of fossil-fuel cowboys. Same deal with magicians. If we can get you focused on this shiny gold watch here, you won't notice us leading an elephant onstage over there."

Aaron's ambition was to be the creative whiz behind a famous illusionist. To this end, he spent hours studying Houdini's great escapes. He'd given Jude a blow-by-blow account of how the great magician—handcuffed and in leg irons—had escaped an underwater crate in New York's East River. Jude, who had a fear of being trapped underwater, had had nightmares for days.

When he was seven, he'd disobeyed Gabe and sneaked off to the beach alone with his new bodyboard. A barrel wave had blasted him off his feet and treated him to a white-knuckle ride on an underwater roller coaster. Jude had been out of fight and nearly out of air by the time he was saved by a surfer.

Gabe had been apoplectic.

"Respect the sea or she'll disrespect you to death," he'd ranted. "I'm glad you're okay, and I love you, kid, but I need you to promise me that you'll remember this."

Five years on, disrespecting the sea again—being overconfident that he could sail a yacht safely to Anegada when thousands of experienced sailors had failed—had almost cost Jude his life.

Worse, he'd almost killed his sister and dog too.

Not surprisingly, his nightmares had returned with a vengeance in the hospital. Night after night, inky water closed over him and fishing net bound him as effectively as Houdini's manacles.

But on the morning of December 17, he was woken from a bad dream by a bright light. Once, twice, three times, it flashed.

Jude blinked. A monstrous eye glowered down at him. He let out a yelp and retreated into the pillows.

The cyclops tilted to one side, revealing a rumple-haired, stubble-faced photographer behind it.

Unabashed, the man adjusted his settings and fired off another couple of shots.

"Nurse!" yelled Jude. "Nurse, help!"

"Don't worry, I have permission—you and Jessica being minors and all," said the photographer. "The nurse was going to chaperone, but she's had to step away to take a call. Some emergency. Don't stress. Ivan is watching over you." He nodded at the bodyguard filling the doorway, inscrutable behind his dark glasses.

Why Ivan needed sunglasses in a dimly lit hospital room was anyone's guess. Jude doubted anyone was bold enough to ask.

The photographer extended a hand before realizing that Jude was unable to shake it. "Adam Buckley, *Daily Gazette*, London. Great to meet you, Jude. I'll be covering you and your sister's story on an exclusive basis for our paper."

"Our *story*?"

Jude wondered if he was in a twilight zone between dreaming and waking.

"Surely you know that you and your sister are about to become one of the biggest stories anywhere. Twelve-year-old twins found abandoned on the high seas being taken under the wings of one of the most famous families in Great Britain. From desert-island rags to glamorous Gloucestershire estate. Trust me, you're the luckiest children on earth to have the Blakeneys looking out for you. Stop the vultures circling. Wait till you clap eyes on your new home."

Adam switched on a lamp and flooded the room with glaring light. "Mind if I take a few more snaps?"

Jude minded a great deal but didn't know how to say so. He wished the nurse and Jess would return.

"Sure. Whatever," he mumbled. "Uh, why don't you wait till my sister comes back? She's probably out walking our dog, Sam. Maybe he can be in the picture too. He can't come into the hospital, but, you know, in the garden somewhere."

"Whatever you say," said the photographer, training a wide-angle lens on Jude's bed and clicking three times. "You're in charge. Just trying to get on top of my game before the big guns arrive. Mrs. Blakeney's already on her way."

Jude's head was still fuzzy. He wasn't sure what the man was talking about. The twins had been told that Clifford and Allegra were planning to fly out from the UK to visit them, but he hadn't expected it to happen quite so soon.

"I hope Mrs. Blakeney doesn't arrive before the doctor takes off my bandages and I get a chance to take a shower. He told me he'd remove them yesterday, but I guess he forgot."

Adam gave a dry laugh. "Donations from the Blakeneys tend to play tricks with people's memories."

"Excuse me?"

The photographer was over by the window, adding a filter to his lens. "Like I said, we definitely want the 'before' photos, if you catch my drift. Nothing says 'survivor' like a head bandage with a smear of blood on it. Push up your left pajama sleeve. How did you get that epic bruise?"

To Jude's immense relief, footsteps squeaked on the corridor linoleum.

"Lord have mercy, *what* is going on here?" demanded Nurse Rolle. "Ivan, I thought you were here to protect these vulnerable children. Why haven't you put a stop to this?"

She swooped on the light switch and killed the glare. "Didn't I tell you *no pictures* and to sit motionless in a chair and keep your camera locked in its case till I could supervise, Mr., err . . . What was your name again?"

"Buckley, Nurse. Adam Buckley," groveled the photographer. "As I explained, I'm from the *Daily Gazette*. Apologies if there's been a misunderstanding. I thought you told me I could start setting up my equipment in preparation for—"

"That 'emergency' call was a hoax," interrupted the nurse. "Don't s'pose you'd know anything about that, Mr. Adam Buckley?"

A young receptionist dashed in, steering Jess before her. "Mrs. Blakeney's on the way! Doctor said to have the twins ready, make the hospital proud."

The photographer and bodyguard snapped to attention as if they were in a military parade. Nurse Rolle moved smoothly to conjure order out of chaos, straightening Jude's pajamas and sheets with one hand and restoring pristine order to the room with the other.

Attempts had been made to brush Jess's hair, but it had resisted taming. A hospital gown disguised Sam's muddy paw prints on her freshly laundered pajamas.

Jude watched his sister wriggle into her hospital bed and sit up primly. She looked both petrified and hopeful.

He felt as if they were on a runaway train with no driver. Up ahead, there was a promising light, but the tracks were loose and threatening to derail them at any moment.

Final destination? Unknown.

CHAPTER 12

Trick of the Light

The sterile air of the hospital room parted with a sigh, giving way to a scent as exotic as the gardens of the Taj Mahal at midnight.

Allegra Blakeney entered in a swirl of azure silk shirt and white linen trousers. An eager assistant scampered after her. A harried doctor hovered in the doorway.

At the sight of Jude, his head swathed in bandages, she cried, "Oh, my dear boy. You look like a wounded young soldier from the First World War. And, Jess, my goodness. What you've both been through. So courageous. It's a wonder you're still alive. But I'm getting ahead of myself, as usual. I'm Allegra Blakeney. It's my great honor to finally meet you. My husband and I have been captivated by your adventures. We're a little in awe of you—well, us and half the planet."

She laughed, and the twins—who were overawed themselves—laughed nervously with her.

"May I sit here?" she asked, perching on Jess's bed without waiting for a reply.

Tenderly, she took Jess's left hand between her cool, satiny palms. Up close, her auburn mane glowed like an autumn fire. Combined with flawless skin and mesmerizing lilac eyes, the effect was quite dazzling.

"What pretty hair you have, Jessica."

"It's Jess," Jess mumbled shyly. "So do you, Mrs. Blakeney. Have lovely hair, I mean. Yours is stunning."

"Why, thank you, Jessica . . . *Jess*." Allegra seemed enchanted, as if she only rarely received compliments. "My husband, Clifford, sends his regrets that he wasn't able to accompany me. He's *dying* to get to know you both but was held up by some business crisis or other. The media world is so *relentless*. Everybody wants a piece of him. He has a million staff, but, honestly, some executives are as helpless as newborn lambs."

She looked absently at the plum-colored nails on her free hand before turning another radiant smile on the twins.

"Thankfully, Clifford came up with a solution—as he always does. He begs your permission to record our first meeting. He wants to feel as if he's here with us. Our readers would love that too. *Very* informal. Adam, who you've met, will take a few snaps and jot down a couple of quotes. Astrid, my assistant, will do her best with the video camera. Would you mind terribly, Jess and Jude?"

Jess heard herself gush: "No, of course we don't mind, do we, Jude? We're so grateful to you for offering us a home."

Jude nodded dumbly from the next bed. "We were worried we might end up in a home for unwanted kids."

Allegra was moved. "My dear boy, how could we *not* offer you a home? When Scotland Yard contacted Clifford to tell him that the DNA of two children saved from a sinking yacht in the Caribbean matched that of a former head groom at our estate—a man who died more than twelve years ago—we could hardly take it in. It was like something out of a movie."

"Sure is," said Nurse Rolle.

Mrs. Blakeney glanced sharply at her, but the nurse was absorbed in checking notes on a clipboard. Allegra returned her warm gaze to the twins. "My husband places a high value on loyalty, as did his father, Robert, before him. In the years that Jim Gray was employed on the estate, Clifford was in London full-time, working flat out to build the business. He only met your dad once or twice in passing before his, uh, unfortunate, accident. But, by all accounts, he was an outstanding groom. Devoted to horses. He especially liked the difficult beasts. Personally, I consider that a most admirable quality."

She smiled up at Astrid, who was videoing the conversation.

"But I digress. To cut a long story short, our hearts went out to you when we heard of your plight. That you were homeless and penniless. We're fortunate enough to have a comfortable house with ample room. We wanted to welcome you into our home, give you hope and opportunity. Send you to excellent schools, if that's acceptable to you both."

"I'd love that." Jess glowed at the mere thought. "Wouldn't you, Jude?"

"So much," Jude said insincerely, adding belatedly: "Thank you, Mrs. Blakeney."

"Call me Allegra. Of course, our motives aren't entirely unselfish. We were thinking of Caspian, our son."

Jess was confused. "I thought you had three kids?"

"We do, but Mark and Racine, my husband's children from his first marriage, are grown up and work in our media business. Caspian is thirteen, close to your own age. He cannot wait to have some kid company and ready-made friends at Blakeney Park. 'Make a welcome change from all the old farts around here,' is what he told me."

Jude snorted. Jess stifled a gasp.

Neither of the twins could imagine talking to an adult that way.

Allegra didn't seem offended in the least. She laughed gaily. "He's such a character, Caspian. Full of mischief and fun. Exactly like Clifford when he was a boy, from what I'm told."

The photographer said, "Any chance you could sit on the chair next to Jude, Mrs. Blakeney? It would be fab to shoot you from a different angle."

Allegra did as he asked, smoothing her metallic-blue silk shirt and turning her attention to Jude.

Jess had to stifle a giggle. Her brother looked as if he were basking in his own personal sun.

"After everything you've endured, I want to spoil you a little,"

Allegra was saying. "Even with my husband's contacts, we're unlikely to get you home for Christmas, but when you do arrive, we'd love to have one or two welcome gifts waiting in your rooms. Naturally, we'd like those to be gifts you'd choose yourselves, not random baubles chosen by me or Clifford's PA. Would you mind giving us some pointers? Jess, what treat would bring a big smile to your face?"

"I—I, thank you. You're too kind. A home is the only gift we need."

Jude answered for her. "Jess really, really enjoys books, Mrs. Blakeney. Adventures and mysteries."

Allegra laughed. "How sweet! Adventures and mysteries we can do. Clothes too. We don't want to waste money on things you'd never wear. I've had Astrid bring along some fashion catalogs. Make a note of whatever your heart desires, and it'll be waiting in your room when you get home."

Home. She said it so easily, as if it were written in the stars that, in their twelfth year, Jess and Jude Carter would find themselves living at Blakeney Park.

Jess stared at Allegra in wonder. A room of her own. Books. Clothes from a catalog. If she was dreaming, she hoped she'd never wake up.

"How about you, Jude?" Allegra said. "If you could have anything you wished for, what would it be?"

"I'd wish for *You Gotta Friend*," Jude answered without thinking. Then, because she was regarding him in puzzlement: "She was our yacht."

Allegra gave an incredulous laugh. "We have a bit of money, my husband and I, but I'm not sure we can stretch to a yacht. What are we talking about? Half a million bucks? A million?"

Beneath his bandages, Jude was crimson with embarrassment. "I didn't . . . I wasn't . . . I just . . ."

She was staring at him with interest. "You still want to sail? After your yacht nearly *killed* you? After you were *shipwrecked*?"

"Yes, but that was my fault, not the boat's," Jude admitted. He added hurriedly, "But not for a long time. Years and years. When I grow up, I mean."

"Interesting. Is there anything else you'd like? Something safer and"—Allegra laughed—"about half a million dollars cheaper. Any hobbies?"

Jude had a splitting headache. His mind was a blank. He couldn't think of a single thing he wanted or needed, apart from Jess and Sam.

Jess replied on his behalf. "Jude's always wanted a bike."

"A bike? Astrid, am I clairvoyant or what!" Allegra said with delight. "A bike you shall have, Jude, and it'll be the best bike you've ever seen."

She didn't quite click her fingers but not far from it. Astrid set down the video camera and summoned up a glossy sports-equipment catalog, which she gave to Jude. On the cover, a grinning boy on a tricked-out red-and-black mountain bike was hurtling down a rocky trail, a shining sea in the distance.

Astrid put a fat pile of fashion brochures on the end of Jess's bed, earning a frown of disapproval from Nurse Rolle. "Make a note of everything you'd like and I'll have someone collect them later. Like Allegra said, you'll miss Christmas, but we'll do everything we can to have at least a few of your choices waiting when you arrive at Blakeney Park."

She looked inquiringly at Allegra. "It's almost eleven a.m., Mrs. Blakeney. We need to leave soon if we're going to make our reservation."

Allegra pressed her hands to her heart. "This has been such a joy, Jess and Jude. Unforgettable. I can't bear to say goodbye, but it isn't goodbye really. Just au revoir. We'll meet again soon."

She turned to her assistant and the photographer. "Astrid and Adam, do you have everything you need, picture- and film-wise?"

"I feel as if we're missing drama in some of the shots," said Adam. "These kids have been to hell and back. It would be good if we can show that with, like, life-support machines and whatnot."

"You're so right," said Allegra. "I should have spotted that myself. Dr. Martinez, why aren't the machines blinking?"

"I'm not sure I understand."

"In films, there are usually drips dripping and a monitor with a squiggly life-and-death line that invariably goes flat."

"A cardiac monitor?"

"Exactly. The cardiac monitor starts beeping manically, and

a nurse screams for a crash cart. Then someone races in with paddles that look like boxing pads. What's that thing that electrocutes people and starts their hearts working again?"

"A defibrillator. But, Mrs. Blakeney, that tends to happen in the ICU. Jude was critical and on fluids and a cardiac monitor when the search-and-rescue guys first brought him in, but the twins are in fine shape now. I'll be taking Jude's bandages off later today."

Allegra was silent, but her disappointment was evident.

"I have an idea," Dr. Martinez said hurriedly. "Nurse Rolle can tape an IV tube to the top of Jude's hand and get the cardiac monitor going again. Mr. Buckley, if the background's out of focus in the shot, you won't be able to read the boy's heart rate and blood-oxygen levels, but you'll still get that life-and-death effect."

"Marvelous," said Adam. "And, perhaps, Jude could be propped up on the pillows with his eyes closed, as if he's in agony but bearing up with courage and fortitude. Jude, would you do that for me?"

Jude looked at if he'd rather saw off his own leg with a rusty penknife. "I guess."

"You're *such* a brave boy, Jude," Allegra praised.

She blew both the twins air-kisses and beamed at the bodyguard as she and Astrid prepared to leave.

"Until we meet again. I'll look forward to it."

· • ✳ • ·

"Ooh, you're *such* a brave boy," mimicked Jess when they'd gone.

Jude was mooning over a mountain bike in the catalog. "Don't say that. She was nice. Better than nice."

But he felt oddly empty, as if the hospital room had been the setting for some grand illusion and he'd missed it because he'd been charmed into looking the other way. He told himself off for being ridiculous. He and Jess were fortunate beyond their wildest wishes. Everybody kept telling them so.

He wondered what the boy would be like. Caspian, Allegra's son. Would they be best buddies? Play cricket together? Build dens on the grounds?

All Jess could think about was the room with a view that would be waiting for her at Blakeney Park. She was determined not to dwell on the ethics of her would-be foster mom bringing a news photographer into their hospital room.

She was on her way to the bathroom when she heard Allegra and Astrid chatting as they waited for the elevator behind an extravagant tropical display. Their voices were remarkably similar. Jess had no intention of eavesdropping, but she couldn't help overhearing when one of them said, in a tone steeped in disdain: "Fancy the horse boy's son thinking he could have a yacht. The cheek of it!"

CHAPTER 13

Star Guests

"Ever imagine you'd be flying first class to the life of your dreams?" asked Astrid, as she helped Jess transform her seat on British Airways' exclusive upper deck into a crisp, comfortable bed.

The hard knot had returned to Jess's stomach. She wanted to burst out: *Which part of our guardian is dead and Jude and I are about to cross the Atlantic to live with strangers in a strange land do you not understand?*

But she knew that Mrs. Blakeney's assistant was only trying to be kind.

"We're very lucky and extremely grateful," she said for the hundredth time.

In the lay-flat bed beside her, Jude was watching an action movie. He took off his headphones. "Excuse me?"

"I said, 'We're very lucky and extremely grateful,'" intoned Jess.

Jude grinned. "Yes, we are. Thanks, Astrid."

Jess had never told him about the "horse boy's son" comment, partly because he'd been over the moon about his new bike, and partly because she'd become convinced that she must have misheard.

After all, Astrid was sweeter than Halloween candy, and the Blakeneys hadn't put a foot wrong since Allegra's hospital visit nine days earlier.

They'd passed every social services check with flying colors.

They'd sent small, thoughtful Christmas gifts and cake to the twins and their nurses, and donated money to a local children's cancer fund.

They'd insisted on flying Jess and Jude first class to London on December 26. Sam had gone on ahead.

The twins had been braced for a fight over their dog. "We're not going to England without him," they'd told Detective Trenton. "He's our family."

That had come as news to the Blakeneys. Yet, within hours, the Swiss shepherd dilemma had been smoothed over too. The twins' worries about their beautiful dog spending Christmas alone in an airport quarantine facility had been offset by their relief that the British family had opened their hearts to Sam too. He'd be joining the twins at Blakeney Park soon after their arrival.

All things considered, there was no earthly reason for Jess's sense of impending doom. Yet she couldn't shake it.

"Try to remember how many people are wishing you bless- ings and happiness in your new life," Nurse Rolle had coun- seled the twins. "Your friends at the diner. Me and Nurse Jones. Detective Jack Trenton. The readers of the *Daily Gazette* . . ."

The nurse was careful not to look at the newspaper on Jess's bedside table, with its banner headline: SAVED BY DOL- PHINS: THE INSIDE STORY OF THE TWELVE-YEAR-OLDS WHO SURVIVED THE WORLD'S DEADLIEST REEF—ALONE!

The double-page spread was full of eye-catching quotes such as: "I knew there might be sharks, but all I could think about was saving Jude."

Jess couldn't recall mentioning sharks in her phone inter- view with a *Daily Gazette* reporter, but she *had* said the bit about saving Jude, so she supposed it was possible.

She wondered who at the diner had given the *Daily Gazette* childhood photos of the two of them. Jess suspected Tiffany, the waitress Anita had sacked years before.

There were four pictures: one photo of the twins sharing birthday pancakes with Gabe; one of Jess surfing; one of her and Jude clinging to a couple of the naughty beach ponies; and one of a grinning Jude high in the crow's nest of a visiting Dutch ship.

This last was captioned: *The boy who could sail before he could walk.*

"Jude reminds me of myself at that age," Ethan Lathe, Jude's Australian sailing hero, had told the paper. "He has that raw passion for sailing, that fearlessness. Sea squalls can be deadly, no matter how experienced you are. Those guys just happened to be in the wrong place at the wrong time. I say, good luck to them. Keep sailing, keep dreaming."

Overall, it was a flattering story, but Jess supposed it had to be. Like Star News, the *Daily Gazette* was owned by Clifford Blakeney.

"They call Clifford 'the Godfather,'" Barbara, the dog caretaker, had informed her. "Don't be alarmed. Not *that* kind of godfather—not a Mafia boss. It's only because he bears a close resemblance to Marlon Brando, the actor who starred in the *Godfather* films."

Jess had found it difficult not to think of Clifford as the Godfather ever since. She kept reminding herself that he must have a heart of gold to offer a home to the children of a long-forgotten groom he'd hardly known.

In the overhead locker was Jess's precious painting. It was odd to be returning it to the English estate where her mother had once lived. Odd, but comforting. Jess planned to hang it in her new room. If her mom's picture was with her, she'd feel at home.

"How are you doing, Jess?" asked Astrid when the seat belt sign went off. "There's a ton of entertainment on your screen. I need to go speak to Ivan about something, but I'll be back shortly."

Jess put on headphones and scrolled through the *A* to *Z* of movies and shows. The choice was overwhelming. She'd never heard of most of them. Gabe hadn't let the twins watch much TV.

She was only on the *B* section when a title caught her eye: *The Boy Who Scooped the World: How Robbie Blakeney went from Miner's Son to Media Mogul.*

Jess pressed Play and was soon absorbed in the story of "Little Robbie," the sickly Welsh boy who'd started a village newsletter at age fourteen to give a voice to local miners—some younger than himself. Many miners suffered from black lung disease and were forced to slave for pennies in cramped, dangerous conditions.

When Robbie was just sixteen, his hand-printed *Daily Gazette* exposed the villains behind a mining disaster that killed his father and twenty-one other men. He beat Britain's biggest newspapers to the story and used the money to launch Daybreak Media. The same company now owned by his son, Clifford Blakeney, the twins' new guardian.

Jess flicked through the boring bits of the film. She was interested in the part about Blakeney Park, which Robbie had bought as a crumbling ruin. According to a friend, the main reason he'd purchased the stately home was to save the estate's forest—home to rare owls and woodpeckers—from loggers and developers. He'd married soon afterward and had a glamorous society wedding. A son, Clifford, had followed within a year.

Jess fast-forwarded again and was catapulted seventeen years ahead. A teenage Clifford, handsome as a prince in Eton College top hat and tails, was now heir apparent to his father's media empire.

He had a sulky, discontented air, which Jess put down to his mother running off with a concrete tycoon when he was just nine. His father was now in a wheelchair, after suffering a printing-press accident. The narrator said: "It was when Robbie Blakeney broke his promise to buy Clifford a Rolls-Royce for his eighteenth birthday that the trouble—"

The volume died. The headphone cord was plucked from its socket.

"Jess, what are you doing?" Astrid bristled with disappointment. "I thought you'd watch something fun like your brother, not a dull documentary packed with lies. I really think that you and Jude should get some sleep now. You have a big day tomorrow."

Jude pressed his face to the window of the helicopter. He wanted to be the first to spot Blakeney Park. He'd studied the aerial photo Detective Trenton had given them. He was sure he'd recognize it.

Since daybreak, their eagle's-eye view of the United Kingdom had been uninspiring.

Even before Astrid had surprised the twins with the chopper flight from London to Gloucestershire, Jude had been certain he'd see a few iconic landmarks from the plane. The English Channel! The Houses of Parliament and Big Ben! The Tower of London! Even Buckingham Palace!

But, for hour upon hour, his view had been nothing but unending dirty cloud without a chink of light in sight. Fog too. They'd been delayed for ages at Heathrow.

While they'd waited for the helicopter, Astrid had insisted they freshen up and change into their new clothes. "Allegra's having a small gathering to greet you. She'll want you to look smart."

Jude, who'd worn nothing but board shorts and surf T-shirts for years, was taken aback to discover that Allegra's version of smart was a dark blue suit and pale blue shirt. And Jess, who'd refused to wear a dress since she was six, looked equally uncomfortable in a matching blue dress, plus black tights and boots. She was biting her nails and looked a little green.

She'd put her detective hat away until they were settled.

They'd probably never know the truth about how Gabe died, but she was hoping that the Blakeneys would lend them smartphones or laptops. Soon as she had access to the web, she'd start investigating their other mysteries. If she could discover who sent Gabe that email, they'd know who'd been putting money into his account. Then all they needed to do was figure out who was hunting them and why.

As Jude gazed out at the smothering clouds, the words of the email kept running through his head:

A long time ago, you promised that you'd go to the ends of the earth to keep them safe. Circumstances have changed, and I'm afraid that is now necessary.

Jude wondered if a change in identity would help them evade whoever was hunting them. The twins were no longer Jess and Jude Carter, wards of Gabriel Carter and American citizens of no fixed address. They were Jess and Jude Gray, British citizens and wards of Clifford and Allegra Blakeney. New address: Blakeney Park, Gloucestershire, United Kingdom.

Was Blakeney Park the ends of the earth? Would they be safe there?

"Jude, look!" Jess tugged at his coat sleeve. A tear in the clouds revealed a snowy forest on the edge of a misty river.

The helicopter swooped lower.

The clouds rolled back; the sun blazed through.

A sparkling wonderland of white unfurled below them. A Christmas-card scene of snow-covered stone walls and fields dotted with sheep, Highland cattle, and horses passed beneath them as they raced toward a regal house in honey-colored Cotswold stone.

On the top tier of a terraced garden was a candy-striped tent. As the helicopter approached, people began streaming out into the snow, squinting up at the patch of peacock sky.

"A circus!" marveled Jude.

Astrid, who was in the seat beside the pilot, spoke into her headset: "Not exactly. That's your welcoming committee."

"But we don't know anyone in the UK," said Jess.

Astrid laughed. "No, but thanks to the *Daily Gazette*, a few million folk know you. You're the star guests."

The twins exchanged anxious looks. Madly waving hands and smiling faces sharpened into focus below.

Jude's chest clamped tight at the thought of being among them. He tried to will the helicopter to keep flying until it reached some desert island or mountain wilderness where he and Jess could live in peace with their dog—just the three of them.

At the same time, he was taking in the high stone walls, razor wire, CCTV cameras, and run of rottweilers. The dogs barked soundlessly, hackles raised. He couldn't hear them above the machine-gun rattle of the helicopter, but they appeared ready to tear any intruder (or twin) limb from limb.

The landscape seemed so alien. It was hard to believe that he and Jess belonged to it. That their parents had lived and worked in these fields, hills, and forests.

"A million years," Jack Trenton had told them. "That's how long DNA lasts. If you're wondering whether there'll be traces of your mom and dad at Blakeney Park, the answer is yes. In a way, you're going home."

Home came at them fast. With a bump.

As the *whoop-whoop* of the engine powered down, Jude unbuckled his seat belt and removed his earmuffs and headset.

The pilot helped them out of the helicopter. Astrid put an arm around Jess, and Ivan the bodyguard protected Jude as they ducked under the slicing blades. Snow whirled in the updraft.

We'll be safe here, Jude told himself as they crunched across the landing pad. *I hope.*

CHAPTER 14

The Godfather

"You're late."

Mrs. Blakeney was smiling, but her tone was cross. The lights of the hallway chandelier gave her teeth an iridescent sparkle, as if an oyster bed had been stripped bare in the creation of them.

"Sorry, Allegra," simpered Astrid. "Air traffic control refused to allow the pilot to take off in the fog."

"Health and safety gone bananas," Allegra said dismissively. "Never mind. It can't be helped."

She turned her attention to the twins, as if noticing them for the first time. "So great to see you, Jess and Ju—"

A spasm flickered across her face. She swayed in her high heels, clutching Astrid for support.

The housekeeper started forward. "Madam, are you unwell? What did I tell you about overdoing it?"

"Nonsense, Mary. Rush of blood to the head, that's all. Don't fuss."

Recovering, she took the twins' hands. "My dears, welcome to Blakeney Park. I hope it won't displease you to hear that I have invited a few friends for afternoon tea to celebrate your arrival. Everyone was so excited to meet you. Caspian can't wait. Lizette, where's Caspian? I told him to be here."

A young woman with a short blond bob hurried over. "He'll be down any minute, Mrs. Blakeney. He was finishing an important project."

Allegra frowned. "What could be more important than meeting our new arrivals? Kindly fetch him. Before you go, Lizette, allow me to introduce you to your newest charges. Jess and Jude, this is our fabulous au pair. She's from South Africa. She'll keep an eye on you and be your guide to the house and estate."

Jess was secretly relieved that Lizette seemed both normal and friendly.

"Astrid, I have a stylist waiting in the powder room," Allegra was saying. "Carlos works miracles with helicopter hair, and his steam iron will banish the wrinkles from the kids' clothes."

"Should we put our backpacks away first?" asked Jess, glancing at the wide marble staircase. She was dying to see her new room.

"Heavens, there's no time for that. We have fifty-three guests waiting. Lord and Lady Asher are here."

She said it as though Jess had the first clue who the Ashers were.

Seventeen minutes later, the twins were steamed, cleaned, combed, and talking to Lord and Lady Asher under a fake palm tree. The striped tent, which thronged with guests, had been transformed into a Caribbean paradise, only with a truck-load of glitter.

The aristocrats looked precisely as Jess had imagined lords and ladies to look: cherry-cheeked, crepey, and jovial.

"We've been gripped by your adventures, haven't we, Harold?" said Lady Asher.

Harold beamed benevolently. "Fascinating stuff."

"Your timber-cabin Florida home! Alligators in every creek—"

"Burmese pythons in every cistern!"

"How could I have forgotten the python?" cried Lady Asher. "So adorable. And I'm told that you were raised by waitresses and dishwashers in a hurricane zone. You survived that—and the Burmese python—only to have your high-seas escapade interrupted by tragedy and shipwreck. One couldn't make it up!"

"That's Clifford, for you," Lord Asher said approvingly. "Has a knack for predicting what'll sell papers."

Jess had a prediction of her own: Jude was on the verge of a panic attack. The tent was everything he hated. Crowded, stifling, loud, and windowless.

"Jude, we need a code word or signal for when it all gets too scary and too much," she'd whispered to him when they were briefly alone. "How about 'you gotta friend'?"

He'd grinned and agreed.

She was about to use that code now when a ripple went through the tent.

"The Blakeney brothers . . ." murmured Lady Asher.

The crowd parted before Mark and Caspian. Though they were half brothers, they were uncannily alike. They had identical haircuts and silver-gray suits.

Lizette materialized at the twins' side. "Apologies, Lord and Lady Asher. I have to borrow these two for a photo op."

She steered them through the crowd to meet Mark and Caspian. Up close, the half brothers had something else in common: a superciliousness disguised by fine manners.

"A pleasure to meet you," said Caspian, shaking their hands and flashing a professional smile at the photographer. "I told Mummy that all I wanted for Christmas was some pals to hang out with, and here you are."

"Caspian, you're such a card!" Mark laughed. "Don't mind my little brother, kids. We're delighted to meet you."

Jude's cheeks reddened with shyness. "Nice to meet you too," he managed.

Jess added: "Thanks for having us. It's an honor to be here." She'd rehearsed the words on the plane, but they sounded imbecilic spoken out loud.

"Sorry to interrupt, Mark," said the photographer. "Any chance we could get some shots of the four of you under the lights? Once we have you arranged, we'll switch the display on."

He positioned the twins in the middle with the Blakeney half brothers on either side. "Lights, camera, action!"

There was a crackle as the wire sign arched over their heads lit up:

WELCOME, TWIN

"Which one?" asked a joker in the crowd. There was an outbreak of giggles before the photographer rushed on the stage full of apologies. The *S* fizzled into life.

Caspian's shoulders shook with laughter. He noticed Jess staring at him and pretended to be coughing.

"Mark, how do you feel about Clifford and Allegra inviting a couple of children you've never met before to live at Blakeney Park?" called one of the guests.

"Long as they don't plan on muscling in on our inheritance, it's fine with me," said Mark, to more merriment.

"Yeah, long as they're not after our inheritance," agreed Caspian with a grin.

"And how about you, Jess and Jude?" asked the photographer. "How does it feel to know that you're going to be living at the legendary Blakeney Park?"

"We feel very lucky and extremely grateful," the twins answered together. They'd been repeating the same line for weeks because everyone seemed to expect it of them.

"What charming children," someone said.

"Here comes the cake," Lizette told the twins.

A waiter was wheeling in a cart laden with a spectacular island-themed creation. Dolphins somersaulted, flamingos flapped, crabs danced, mermaids frolicked, and a pirate dozed beneath a palm tree.

Jess couldn't take her eyes off the message printed on the icing beach:

Welcome, Twin

"Perhaps this is the welcome for the other twin," someone stage-whispered.

"Once could be carelessness. Twice is no coincidence," another guest observed slyly.

The waiter was having a meltdown. "The *S* was there when I left the kitchen. I know it was. Oh, look, here it is. It's slipped down the side. I've fixed it now."

"Ladies and gentlemen," Astrid said into the microphone. "I give you: Mr. and Mrs. Blakeney."

Allegra, dazzling in a silk dress, came through the crowd holding the arm of Clifford Blakeney. He was tall and balding and wearing a tuxedo and bow tie.

"The Godfather" moved slowly through the smiling guests, murmuring and nodding to acquaintances. He exuded a powerful charisma. It surged through the tent like a rogue wave.

As her new guardian approached, Jess fought the urge to flee. What if there was more to his nickname than a passing resemblance to a Mafia don in a movie?

The guests fell silent.

Lizette pushed the twins forward. Clifford's fingers were stubby and clammy when he shook hands with them. To cover her unease, Jess gabbled about being honored and grateful again. It seemed to please him, which was just as well because Jude had been struck dumb.

Clifford's voice was so low and husky that the twins had to strain to hear him.

"You like cake?"

"We love cake," enthused Jess.

Clifford addressed the room at large. "You heard the girl! What are you waiting for? Let's eat cake."

The rest of the day went by in a blur, marked only by a conversation Jess overheard in the bathroom.

"I shouldn't think Caspian will take kindly to having his thunder stolen—not after being Prince of Blakeney Park for thirteen years," said a woman's voice. "Those twins might need to watch their backs."

"Oh, I shouldn't worry about the twins," responded her friend. "They can handle themselves. If I were Allegra, I'd be more concerned about Caspian. The new boy looks as if he was raised by pirates."

"Ha ha! Maybe the boys *do* have something in common after all."

* * * * *

By the time the last guest left, the twins were dizzy with jet lag. Climbing the marble staircase felt like ascending the summit of Everest without oxygen. As Jess followed Allegra past gilded oil paintings of aristocrats and huntsmen, she felt judged. Their imperious gazes made her feel small and poor.

"Good night, twins!" Caspian said with the violent enthusiasm of a boy who's eaten too much sugar. He bowed theatrically. "I hope you sleep very, very, very well."

"That boy!" His mother laughed as she watched him dash up to the next level with Lizette in patient pursuit. "I wish I had half his energy."

Leading them along a red-carpeted corridor, Allegra opened the second door.

All the cares and worries of that long, strange day lifted from Jess's shoulders when she walked into her new room. There was a four-poster bed and a bookshelf that took up half a wall. The books' spines were turned inward so Jess couldn't see their titles, but what mattered was that they were books. A pile of brand-new mystery and adventure novels awaited her on the bedside table.

The wardrobe was open, displaying the lovely clothes she'd chosen. A basket of goodies—bubble bath, soaps, and creams—occupied a shelf. A second basket containing fruit was on a table beside an armchair.

A wide bay window offered a moonlit vista of the snowy

garden and fields. The window seat was occupied by creepy wide-eyed dolls. Jess decided she would hide them in a drawer at the first opportunity. "Is this all for me?" she said in amazement. "It's better than a five-star hotel. Not that I've stayed in one, but I've seen photos."

Allegra laughed a tinkly laugh. "All for you. I'm thrilled that you like it."

"It's beautiful. I love it so much." Jess blinked back tired, happy tears. "Where's Jude going to be? Through there?" She looked hopefully at the connecting door.

"We've had a slight problem with your brother's room," said the housekeeper. She'd come in unnoticed. "The decorator had a family emergency and left us in the lurch."

"Honestly, these workmen are impossible." Allegra sighed. "If it's not one excuse, it's ten others. What Mary's trying to explain is that the man slunk off without finishing the job. We did consider putting Jude in there anyway—"

"I'm sure it's totally fine," said Jude. "I can sleep anywhere. Hammocks, floors, boat decks, that fluffy rug over there."

"I'm glad you said that, because one of the maids tripped over a paint pot as she moved the decorator's ladder and cloths." Allegra gave a pained smile. "The room's unusable for the foreseeable future. We came up with what we hope is an excellent solution. You're to have your father's old room, Jude."

"Is that nearby?" Jess asked hopefully. "On this corridor?"

"Well, of course not." The housekeeper was indignant. "Myself and the au pair are the only staff who live in the hall itself. The rest of the help live on the estate, as your parents did when they worked here. The room we've put you in was good enough for your dad, Jude, so I trust it will be good enough for you, at least until the decorator returns. We've done everything possible to make it comfortable. Eddie, the groundskeeper, will show you the way."

CHAPTER 15

Horse Boy

Jude followed Eddie through the dark gardens. The air was Siberian, but beneath his new parka, he was boiling. Hot drops of humiliation trickled down his spine.

Half of him was glad that each step carried him farther away from Blakeney Park. The other half felt as rejected and cast aside as a stray dog.

Eddie said nothing, just leaned into the buffeting cold wind like a soldier on a night march.

"Where are we going?" asked Jude, slipping in the snow as he hurried to keep up.

"You'll see."

Eddie stopped at an arched gateway in an ivy-covered wall. Ice coated the padlock. He had to hold it between his palms to melt it enough to insert the key. The iron gate squealed open. Beyond it was a track leading to a snow-covered barn.

Jude knew where they were heading now. He should have guessed. Should have known that if his father had lived anywhere on the estate, it would have been close to the creatures he loved.

The barn door was crusty with snow. As Eddie wrestled it aside, the heady smell of horse and sweet hay came at Jude in a warm wave. There were twelve dimly lit stalls. Most horses stayed in the shadows, but a couple whickered in the hope of a late-evening treat. Unexpectedly, the bay in the last stall brushed Jude's arm with its velvet muzzle.

Eddie didn't slow. He passed the stable manager's office, where a night-light lent a blue cast to the grain bins, bridles, rosettes, and a whiteboard of feeding instructions, then ducked beneath a low beam and trotted up some steep steps.

More keys than a prison warden, thought Jude, watching Eddie trying to find the one that unlocked the middle of the three doors. It opened on to a plainly furnished room. A biting blast of wind nearly froze Jude as he entered. There were cozier igloos.

Eddie cursed beneath his breath. "Sorry, Jude—I thought they'd have had the sense to close the window."

Slamming it shut, he turned the dial up on a feeble-looking radiator. The narrow bed had been made up with a duvet patterned with yachts. Someone had made an effort with that, at least.

Jude's new clothes hung on a rail, his suitcase beside them. His backpack shared a chair with a saddle. There was a jute mat on the floor and a jug of water and a lamp on a rickety bedside table.

"Best we could do at short notice," said Eddie, reading

Jude's mind. "The grooms only use this place if a horse is sick or about to foal. Seth, our equestrian manager, heard that your dad did the same. Jim and your mum apparently lived in a cottage on the grounds. It was knocked down before my time and replaced with staff apartments. That's where I'm off to now."

He looked around. "What else? Uh, there's a shower and loo through there and a storeroom beyond that. We've put Mrs. Blakeney's gift in there for you. Hope you like it. Before I go, two rules. One: Don't be tempted to go walkabout on the grounds between ten p.m. and five a.m.—not if you don't want a chunk chomped out of your behind. Mr. B's rottweilers take their guard-dog duties seriously. Two: If you get night terrors or need help, you can reach me any time by dialing twelve on the dinosaur line."

He tapped a phone on the wall. "For the hall, dial zero. Mary, the housekeeper, will pick up. Breakfast's at eight. Don't be late."

After Eddie had fetched him an extra rug for the bed, Jude glanced toward the house. It glowed golden and enchanted through the snowy trees.

"Might not feel that way now, but trust me, you have the better deal," said Eddie, following his gaze. "Cooped up with them lot like an orchid in a hothouse—well, it's not natural. I'd choose the horses every time. But maybe that's just me."

As soon as Eddie had gone, Jude went to the storeroom. His new red-and-black bike was hanging on a rack on the wall. As Allegra had promised, it was the best bike he'd ever seen. He was about to lift it down when he saw the tires were flat. Worse, the rear one had a visible nick, as if it has been pierced with a blade.

"Of course," Jude muttered. Everything else had been ruined, why not the bike. He was so cold and exhausted, he couldn't bring himself to care.

Climbing into bed fully dressed, he sat hugging his knees. Loneliness swamped him. Try as he might, he couldn't imagine his father in this place. It was a room without personality. An icy shell. Everything about it felt wrong. The floor was too still, for a start. He missed the soothing rocking of the yacht. Missed Jess, who'd looked stricken as he was evicted from the house. Missed Gabe. Missed the mom and dad he'd never known.

Then he remembered Sam, alone and scared in some sterile airport quarantine facility. In three or four days, the dog would be joining them. Would he be allowed to share Jude's stable room? That would make it more bearable.

Despite the extra rug, which smelled strongly of horse, Jude couldn't stop shivering. Eventually, he sourced a chilly draft coming through the wooden floor near his bed. When he pulled back the mat, a board was missing. He had a clear view of the stall below.

Jude lay on his front to get a better look. Beneath him, the bay mare stood dozing. Her eyelids drooped. He fancied he could hear her breathing.

Jude breathed back. The horse's ears pricked. She looked up, and he saw shining black eyes.

A spark of hope kindled in him. Having the mare within breathing distance made him feel less alone. "G'night, girl," he called.

The horse reminded him of the saddle on the back of the chair. It was worn but well-loved, its leather buttery with polish. Why was it here? Had it belonged to his father?

Detective Trenton had told the twins that ancient DNA was often found in hidden places. "At Blakeney Park, your dad's DNA might linger in the crease of a saddle he once polished. Your mom's might be in the woodgrain of her favorite bench on the estate. Traces of it are always there, just waiting to be discovered."

Jude lifted the saddle flap. He found he could quite easily picture his dad's strong hands tightening the girth or rubbing the brass buckles till they shone. Out of the corner of his eye, he saw a light flicker.

He rushed to the window.

Through the spiny branches of the trees, a flashlight beam flashed intermittently from a window at Blakeney Park. Someone was sending a Morse code signal. Was it Jess? Could she be in trouble?

Jude was about to call the housekeeper for help when he realized that the signal wasn't the one used for emergencies. The Morse code SOS was unmistakable: three short flashes, three long, and three more short. Over the years, Gabe had spent hours teaching the twins the Morse code alphabet. Jude forced his tired brain to remember it now. With the aid of the notepad and pencil he found by the phone, he decoded the pattern of flashes.

-.-- --. ..-.

Y-G-F? What did that mean?

Seconds later, he burst out laughing. "'You gotta friend!' I *do* have a friend. And so do you, Jess!"

What he didn't have was a flashlight. Lifting the lamp on to the windowsill, he used a T-shirt to cover the light for long and short pauses.

-.-- --. ..-.

A volley of red flashes showed him that his message had been received. Jess's window went dark. Jude didn't mind. He felt better just knowing that she was okay.

As long as they had each other, they could survive anything.

Tiredness hit him like a sledgehammer. He was asleep, still smiling, before his head hit the pillow.

Jess couldn't sleep. Harsh moonlight streamed onto her bed and lent an eerie gleam to the eyes of the dolls on the window seat. She'd been so aghast to learn that Jude would be sleeping in the snow-plastered horse barn, she'd forgotten to hide them from sight. The minute Allegra and the housekeeper had left her room, Jess had dug her flashlight out of her suitcase. She'd watched the distant barn until she saw Eddie's burly figure emerge. He'd set off down the lane and been swallowed by the night.

Only then did Jess begin trying to signal Jude. When at last a light in the distant barn flashed back, she'd wept with relief.

Now it was 11:05 p.m. Somewhere, a dog kept howling. It made her think of Sam. Were the quarantine staff giving him cuddles? Would he like Blakeney Park? Would Blakeney Park like him?

Going on tonight's performance, there was no guarantee that Blakeney Park or its occupants would even like her and Jude.

Watching her brother being marched from the grand house as if he were a bread-stealing orphan from Victorian times had left Jess feeing wretched. The joy of her new room had evaporated at a stroke. She didn't buy the story about the unreliable decorator. Every wrong or accidental thing that had happened since they'd arrived had felt deliberate and designed to unsettle them.

But the room situation seemed especially mean. What could Jude have done to upset anyone? For hour upon hour, he'd been as polite and good-natured as it was possible for any boy to be.

If it were true that his own room wasn't ready, why hadn't they put him in a spare one in the actual house? There had to be at least ten of them. Blakeney Park probably had more four-poster beds than Buckingham Palace.

Jess sat up. She had to investigate. If there was a perfectly good vacant room close by, she'd know that there was something weird going on.

She padded across the fluffy rug and peered into the corridor. The lights were low and the house silent. Presumably the Blakeneys had retired to their quarters.

Jess crept along the red carpet, listening at doors.

The first one she tried was locked. The second revealed a broom closet. She was listening at a third when she heard footsteps. To avoid being discovered, she ran down the stairs opposite.

The footsteps kept coming, descending the marble steps. Jess sprinted along the first-floor passage and darted through the first open door. She found herself in a drawing room with a Steinway piano and a great many Persian rugs. Dying embers in the fireplace sent copper lights chasing across the artwork and vases.

To her dismay, voices sounded in the corridor and continued right into the room. Jess dived behind a sofa, bumping a stool against the piano.

"What was that?" she heard Allegra Blakeney ask sharply.

"Only the wind in the chimney," replied her husband. "You know what these old houses are like. No wonder there are so many ghost stories written about them."

He switched on a lamp. "See? No restless spirits here."

"I could use a gin and tonic," said Allegra, plonking herself down on the very sofa Jess was hiding behind. "What a day it's been. My nerves are shredded."

Jess's nose wrinkled. The sofa was dusty, and she had to fight back a sneeze. She had a worm's-eye view of Clifford's black shoes as he walked over to an antique cabinet and poured two drinks, adding ice from a silver bucket.

Jess couldn't believe her ill luck. The couple seemed to be settling in for a leisurely fireside chat. Her nose itched and itched. What if she sneezed? She tried tickling the roof of her mouth with her tongue. She'd read somewhere that it could stop a sneezing fit in its tracks. Thankfully, it seemed to work.

"What *are* we going to do with the castaways—now that they're here?" asked Allegra.

"We'll do what we promised," Clifford told her. "We give them a home and the finest education money can buy until they come of age. I'm a man of my word, my dear."

"Sure you are." Her tone was as brittle as a cuttlefish. "When it sells papers."

"Nobody's asking you to be the twins' second mother, Allegra. Most of the time they'll be at school, and when they are here, you'll hardly see them. Give them the run of the estate and they'll be off tobogganing or building snowmen. They're accustomed to fending for themselves. Gabriel Carter seems to have been a hands-off father, to put it generously."

"Speaking of fathers, I got a big shock when I saw the boy without his bandages. Didn't you?"

"Anyone would." Clifford's husky voice was impatient. "He's been through a lot. They both have."

"That's not what I meant, and you know it."

"My darling, I think you're overtired. You're seeing ghosts everywhere. I have just the cure. Did I tell you that I picked up a little something for you on my travels?"

Allegra said kittenishly, "No, you didn't."

"Couldn't resist. Emerald suits you so well. Shall we go upstairs? I'll collect it from the safe."

Jess's heart was pounding out of her chest by the time their voices faded. She counted to fifty before daring to venture back out. As she scooted up the stairs, Lizette appeared at the top.

"Jess, what on earth are you doing out of bed? You'll catch your death of cold in bare feet."

"I got lost looking for the bathroom," was Jess's lame excuse.

Lizette's disbelief showed, but she said gently, "I expect you're missing your brother, aren't you? Whatever you do, don't go sneaking into the grounds at night. Clifford's security guys use these *Hound of the Baskervilles* guard dogs. Trust me, they're not pets."

She smiled warmly. "Come, Jess, let's get you tucked up in bed. I'll make you some hot chocolate to help you sleep. Everything will seem better in the morning."

CHAPTER 16

Trust No One

"I feel as if I haven't seen you in a month," said Jess, laughing, then almost crying as she and Jude were reunited at breakfast the next morning.

Jude hugged her tightly. "Me too, sis. Hey, thanks for the Morse code. It helped."

"Helped me too. But, Jude, you won't believe what happened after . . ."

Lowering her voice, she described the sequence of events leading up to the drawing room escapade. "Then I overheard Allegra and Cliff—"

Jess stopped mid word. A maid with a tray was hovering behind the silk screen that concealed the scullery and kitchen. Was she eavesdropping? How long had she been there?

"Cook made you pancakes to help you feel at home," the woman said, entering the room with an air of defiance. As she set down a tray, the windows began rattling loudly.

"Don't worry, it's not an earthquake. Just the helicopter taking Mr. Blakeney to his London office," announced the maid. She watched the chopper rise over the snowfields. "The newspaper business hardly stops for the holidays. He'll be gone for the next week."

She didn't exactly sound disappointed.

Lizette came rushing in, apologizing for not being there to greet them on their first morning. Something about Caspian needing something. She seemed harassed.

Once she'd had a steadying sip of coffee, Lizette explained that, while the family took their meals in the main dining room, the twins would eat with her. Jude couldn't hide his relief. He'd been worried that he'd have to be on his best behavior, wearing his best clothes and trying to make conversation with Caspian, three times a day.

Over breakfast, the twins got to grips with British terminology. According to Lizette, what Americans called "biscuits" were scones in the UK, while "cookies" were biscuits. And what Americans knew as flapjacks were called "Scotch pancakes" or "drop scones" by the Brits, even though they looked nothing like scones or pancakes. At the same time, British flapjacks were basically oat, honey, and seed breakfast bars!

In the UK, fries were known as "chips"; chips were "crisps"; a zucchini was a "courgette"; and arugula was "rocket." And drinks were not often served with ice. When Jess asked for ice with her orange juice, it was as if she had requested a rare, hard-to-extract gem, not mere frozen tap water.

"Don't look so worried! You'll get the hang of it soon enough," Lizette told the twins with a smile.

Jess and Jude had their doubts. It was going to take time to adjust to stately home life.

There was no one around when the twins left the tearoom. Lizette had gone to find Caspian. Jude, who'd left his boots at the entrance, tried an experimental slide along the polished wooden floor in his socks.

"How about a speed-skating duel?" he said to his sister. "These slippery corridors are better than ice rinks."

Jess giggled. "Jude, we can't ... *Can we?*"

They were battling it out for the Sock-Skating World Championships, laughing wildly, when Allegra stepped in via a side door. Absorbed in checking her phone, she didn't see the children until they were one sock slide away from a head-on collision.

The twins swerved, skidded like cartoon characters, and went down in a tangled heap, still laughing.

"I'm glad you find Blakeney Park so entertaining," said Allegra with a chilly smile, "although I'd thank you to remember that there are artworks in this house worth more than your yacht. In fact, now might be a good time to acquaint you with one or two rules."

The twins listened with growing dismay as the number of house rules swelled to seventeen.

No running, sock-skating, or ball games anywhere in the hall.

No loud music. No cell phones. No internet. No unsupervised phone calls.

No backchat, discourtesy, or swearing.

No fraternizing with the help or chatting to visitors unless expressly invited to do so.

No touching of art, ornaments, or sporting trophies.

No visiting the Blakeney Park library and no borrowing of books.

"But why?" cried Jess, before she could stop herself.

"Our library is not for children," Allegra informed her. "It's stacked to the ceiling with first editions and other irreplaceable books. How do I make this simple? Spend all the time you like in your bedrooms and bathrooms, the game room and the tearoom. The rest of the house is off-limits to you. Don't take it personally. If we lived in the suburbs, I'd give you free rein, but our stately home is a museum. I hope you understand. Please be aware that the entire top story of the house is our family living quarters. That, especially, is out of bounds."

"What about Sam?" Jude asked nervously.

"Who's Sam?"

"Our dog. He's arriving on Wednesday. He's not used to the cold. If he can't come in the house, can he hang out with us at the stables and stay in my room at night?"

Allegra laughed. "Oh, wait, you're serious? Absolutely not. Some of our horses cost a king's ransom. If they were to be bitten . . ." She shuddered. "Doesn't bear thinking about. Don't worry, Jude—Eddie's prepared a great kennel for Sam. He'll have plenty of blankets and be as snug as a bug. If you do take him for a walk, please keep him on a lead at all times. We have sheep to protect."

The valet sidled in with a silver platter. "Your post, Mrs. Blakeney."

"Thanks, Terence."

Allegra flicked through the letters, frowning at a pale blue envelope with a curlew bird stamp. She tucked it into her back pocket and flashed a pearly smile.

"Goodness, for a couple of lucky children, you look awfully glum, Jess and Jude. After the carefree life you've led, I imagine that having rules and responsibility will take some getting used to. But you'll adjust. Trust me, Clifford and I only have your best interests at heart."

"Yes, ma'am. Thank you, ma'am," chorused the twins.

"Excellent. This afternoon, Lizette will go through your lesson plans for the next couple of weeks. As far as I can make out, you've spent the last year on vacation. You have a lot of catching up to do."

"We have to keep reminding ourselves how lucky we are," Jess said, through chattering teeth. Collars turned up against the teeming rain, the twins were sloshing through dirty snow with Sam. "If it wasn't for the Blakeneys, we'd never have seen

Sam again." The Swiss shepherd was shivering too, but his tail wagged continually. Being outside in the rain with his beloved master and mistress beat the alternative: freezing alone in his small, scary kennel next to the larger runs of the guard dogs.

Three long days had passed since he'd been delivered by a pet courier, yet his separation anxiety seemed to be getting worse. He couldn't bear to be parted from the twins. His quarantine experience had left him fearful that he'd never see them again. He loathed and detested his tiny run. For hour upon hour, he'd whined and howled and tried to claw his way out. Some mornings, his paws bled.

"Nothing I can do about it," said Eddie, when the twins begged to be allowed to let Sam off his lead in the garden, or have him sleep in Jude's stable room at night. "It pains me to say it, but you're guests here. The Blakeneys have already gone above and beyond flying your mutt over from the Caribbean and paying for his quarantine. Why should he get more pampering than the guard dogs? My advice? Don't go making waves. It'll end in a tsunami."

Jess didn't doubt it.

That's not to say that life at Blakeney Park was all rules and gloom. There was much to enjoy. Jess found, to her surprise, that she loved the infamous English weather and the beautiful countryside. It made her feel like a character from *Castle of Secrets*.

In between rainy dog walks and homework, she spent hours

curled up in a rocking chair beside the woodburning AGA in the kitchen—the warmest place in the house—before the cook banished her for offering unsolicited recipe advice.

Jude was in his element helping Seth, the stable manager. He'd even been allowed to groom Autumn, the bay mare, a fifteen-year-old ex-racehorse.

"She's the most placid, sweet-natured Thoroughbred I've ever met, but she has an independent streak and doesn't usually take to strangers," Seth had told Jude. "She liked you from day one though. She'd have been around in your dad's time. Maybe there's something in your voice or the way you walk that reminds her of him."

Recalling how the mare had leaned over her stall door to brush his arm with her velvet muzzle on that first dreadful night, Jude swelled with pride at the possibility that he'd reminded her of his dad.

All the same, the comment had got him thinking. He and Jess had hoped to learn more about their parents from any estate staff who'd worked with Jim and Joanna twelve years before. Oddly, it turned out that there were none.

"After his father passed away, Clifford wanted a clean sweep of staff," explained Seth. "Fresh start. No reminders. When you're grief-stricken, that's the kind of thing you do. And most of the original help had been with Robbie Blakeney from the beginning. They were more like family, to hear the housekeeper tell it. That's not Clifford's way, I can tell you. Mary's sister, Gladys, worked with your dad, but she died years ago. I doubt you'd get anything out of Mary though. She's a closed book."

With so much going on, the mishaps at the welcome party and the mysterious events of their first night at Blakeney Park had been pushed to the back of the twins' minds. But they were not forgotten. Not at all. No matter how many times Jess replayed Clifford and Allegra's conversation in her head, she still couldn't make any sense of it. If the couple had no interest in fostering her and Jude—the horse boy's "castaway" kids— why had they volunteered to do it?

And why had they been so shocked to see Jude without his bandages?

She kept thinking about Caspian and Mark kidding around about the twins' being after their inheritance, and about the welcome-party guest she'd overheard referring to Caspian as the "Prince of Blakeney Park."

"Do you think she could have been right—that Caspian actually *is* jealous about us sharing his limelight?" Jess asked Jude as they thawed out in her room after their dog walk.

"Doubt it. I'd say, whatever Caspian wants, Caspian gets. He's spoiled rotten by the looks of things. Doesn't seem interested in being friends with us either. Or if he is, he has a funny way of showing it. It wouldn't surprise me if he's the one who tampered with the 'Twins' light display. He was standing right beside it. It would only have taken him a couple of seconds to unplug the connector."

Caspian was Jess's chief suspect for that particular incident too. She was reluctant to investigate further in case her suspicions were confirmed.

"We have to give the Blakeneys a chance, Jude. They've done so much for us. Like it or not, we're here till we're eighteen. We need to get along with them."

She hung her rain jacket on a hook and shrugged on a thick sweater. "Have you noticed that there's not a single photo of Clifford's father anywhere in the house? Well, the bits that we've seen anyway. Not one."

"There's a massive picture of him at the top of the stairs," Jude pointed out.

"Yeah, but that's an official portrait of him in his study looking like a newspaper baron. Where are the photos of him and his son blowing out candles on a birthday cake? Where are the shots of them out on the estate having fun?"

A floorboard creaked in the corridor. Jess ran to the door and flung it open. A maid was standing there with fresh towels, hand raised to knock.

"She was listening at the door again," fumed Jess when she'd gone. "It's creepy how every time we try to have a private conversation, someone starts dusting a shelf or polishing a vase or saddle within eavesdropping distance. I feel like we're being spied on."

"They're probably worried we'll steal the silver," said Jude, only half joking.

Jess wished it could be explained away so easily. There was a peculiar atmosphere at Blakeney Park. It was real but unreal at the same time, almost as if the twins had woken up on the set of *Downton Abbey*. From the Blakeneys to the tearoom maid, everyone seemed to be playing a part.

Jess joined Jude on the window seat, staring out at the rain and fast-melting snow. "Until we know more, we trust no one."

Jude was in full agreement. "We trust no one."

CHAPTER 17

Tempest

"How would you like to go horse riding with Caspian?" asked Allegra, gliding into the tearoom on Sunday morning, one week after the twins had landed in London. "You do ride, don't you? There were photos of you on ponies in Florida."

"Those were beach ponies," explained Jess. "When the tourist season was over, the owner used to let us swim them in the waves for exercise."

She didn't mention the ponies' habit of bolting home along the beach, totally out of control, with the twins clinging to their salty wet necks like barnacles. "We've never had any proper lessons."

Allegra gave an airy wave. "You're too modest, Jess. Your father was a talented horseman. Riding's in your genes. Once one's mastered the basics, there's nothing to it, really. Lizette will find you some breeches and boots, and Seth will sort out a couple of helmets. See you at the barn."

A short while later, the twins, looking ready to compete at the Badminton Horse Trials, were on their way to the stables with Lizette.

A dapple-gray pony was being led out of the barn when they arrived. She was strikingly pretty but full of beans, spooking at invisible monsters.

"That's Tempest, Caspian's Connemara-Thoroughbred cross," said the au pair. "According to Seth, she's more trouble than all the other horses put together."

A grinning Caspian called them over. "Isn't she great? Cost Dad a fortune, but she's worth it. Pure fire."

He made no effort to help as Seth struggled to tack her up, just leaned against the mounting block and watched with an amused smile.

Lizette's horse, Fred, a clipped hunter, was hitched to a rail nearby.

The barn door slid open and a stable hand emerged with two saddled horses: a piebald pony called Jigsaw, and Autumn, the bay mare.

A broad grin spread across Jude's face. He'd been hoping that Seth might let him ride her. Despite Autumn's racing past, she had a reputation for being a calm, dependable ride.

"Doesn't mean she's a robot," Seth had told him. "Horses are prey animals. If they get a fright, they take flight. They run first and ask questions later."

Caspian smirked at the twins. "I see Seth's given you the beginner horses."

"That's fine by me," said Jess. "I want the most bomb-proof horse in the barn."

"Good to know your level, I suppose. I prefer—"

Behind him, Tempest gave a jealous squeal and booted Jigsaw in the shoulder.

Pandemonium erupted.

Fred reared and snapped his reins. Jigsaw rounded on Autumn with gnashing teeth. The mare leaped away with a whinny, nearly knocking down Lizette.

Caspian was caught in the crossfire. Jess glimpsed his frightened face as he reeled between biting, fighting horses and yelling humans.

Seth moved quickly to get the situation under control, but he couldn't undo the swelling on Jigsaw's shoulder.

"Jigsaw's a bit lame," he said bitterly. "Sorry, everyone, there'll be a delay while we fetch Jess another horse and get Fred a new bridle. Caspian, could you hold Tempest while—?"

"Ow!" Caspian clutched at his stomach and bent double.

Allegra was at her son's side in an instant. "Sweetie, what's wrong? Were you kicked?"

"No, Mummy—I have cramps. My tummy—*owww*—hurts so bad."

"Did you eat the smoked salmon at breakfast?" demanded his mother. "It tasted as if it had died of old age. I could throttle that cook. I've told her a thousand times to check the use-by dates."

"I dunno, maybe . . . *oww* . . . Mummy, can you take me back to the house? I don't feel well."

Groaning again for effect, he looked sideways at Jess. "Would *you* mind riding Tempest? She's longing to stretch her legs."

Jess was startled. She couldn't tell if he was challenging her or pleading with her. "I, umm—"

"Caspian, Tempest's fresh as anything," cut in Seth. "If she gets wind of the hunt—"

"What hunt?" asked Jude.

"The local trail hunt might pass through the north fields this morning. These days, foxhunting is against the law but"— Seth's eyes met Allegra's—"every now and then, friends help friends to get rid of pests. Caspian was planning to join them after he'd ridden out with you. Then this happened."

Allegra put an arm around her son. "Darling, it's generous of you to offer Jess your horse, but Tempest seems a little flighty this morning. Jess is not an experienced rider like you."

"A toddler could ride Tempest," Caspian said stubbornly. "Once she's away from the barn, she's as good as gold. 'Course, if Jess is afraid . . ."

"Jess, don't let him get under your skin," Jude said under his breath. "That pony's an accident waiting to happen."

Jess thought the same thing but wasn't about to admit that she was scared. "Thanks, Caspian. I'd love to ride her," she said with a big smile, and had the satisfaction of realizing that it was the last answer the boy had expected.

After the Blakeneys had gone, Seth helped her into the saddle. His face was maroon with suppressed fury. Jess got the sense that he strongly disapproved of Caspian and Allegra all but insisting that a beginner ride the spoiled boy's tempestuous horse.

Nevertheless, he tried to make the best of a bad situation.

"Don't worry, Jess, Tempest's well-schooled," he said. "She'll take her energy from you. If you stay peaceful, even if you're only faking it, she'll be peaceful too. Lizette, take it slow with these kids. Don't go faster than a trot. Maybe stick to walking. Whatever you do, stay away from the north fields."

CHAPTER 18

Spy in the Sky

After days of drizzling rain, the bright blue sky was a tonic. Lacy scraps of snow lingered on the hills, but the going was good. The horses moved easily along the tracks between the fields.

Too easily, in Jess's opinion. She was riddled with anxiety. Tempest shied at every second leaf. Jess's legs and arms were like jelly from the effort of holding on.

"Your pony's getting stressed-out vibes from you," counseled Lizette. "Remember what Seth told you. Stay in the moment. Focus on your breathing."

Jess had no faith in Seth's strategy but decided it was worth a shot. The gray's neck was foamy with nervous sweat.

Breathing, Jess could just about manage. Quieting her racing thoughts was harder. At the Castaway Diner, Leonie had taught her a mindfulness technique called body-scanning to help Jess with exam nerves. She tried it now. First, she focused on banishing tension from her toes in the stirrups. Then she moved on up through her knees, hips, hands on the reins, shoulders, and neck.

When she reached her brain, she worked on emptying it. She quit trying to fathom why Caspian had pushed his fancy, fiery pony on to a girl who'd requested the "most bomb-proof horse in the barn."

She also quit wondering why Caspian had pretended to have stomach cramps. She and Jude were convinced that the boy's sudden illness was invented.

"If there was an Oscar for the World's Worst Actor, he'd have won it," Jude had scoffed as they rode out of the yard. "He basically forced you to take his horse. Why? That's what I wanna know. Too lazy to ride, too chicken, or just messing with us?"

As Tempest flounced away from yet another twig, Jess shoved Caspian out of her mind. She needed to do some acting of her own if she was going to de-stress his pony. She took Seth's advice and faked peacefulness. Faked being a confident rider. Faked enjoying her day.

Before she knew it, she was actually enjoying herself for real. So was Tempest, who gave a great, shuddering sigh and visibly let go. Soon, the gray and the bay were walking side by side, matching strides.

The scenery was spectacular. It was like riding through a painting.

A distant church spire pierced a wandering cloud. A robin sang its heart out at the top of a hawthorn tree. Shaggy Highland cattle hung their heads over a stone wall to breathe misty *moo* bubbles at the passing horses.

And on the horizon, the river shone like a silver lining.

"That's the River Severn," said Lizette, twisting in the saddle. "It flows out into the Bristol Channel. From there, you can sail north to Scotland, south to Cornwall, or west across the Irish Sea and Atlantic. You guys must miss the ocean? I'm from Cape Town, and I do."

"Mainly I miss swimming," Jess told her. "All my life, I've been in the sea every day. I don't miss being on a cramped boat."

Jude kept quiet. Since moving into the stable room, his drowning nightmares had stopped. He missed sailing but not as much as he thought he would. Since wrecking the yacht, he'd lost confidence that he was a good yachtsman. What if he fell overboard again? For the time being, he was quite content to be away from deep water.

Lizette steered Fred onto a bridleway lined with gorse, bracken, and purple clumps of heather. Approaching the forest that the twins had seen from the helicopter the day they arrived, Jess felt a strong sense of déjà vu. It was as if she'd ridden this track and breathed in the green woods in another life.

She remembered the documentary she'd watched on the plane. How Robbie Blakeney had saved the forest from loggers and developers. She wondered if it was still home to woodpeckers and rare owls.

The thought of the rare owls made her smile. Given time, maybe life at Blakeney Park *would* be everything they'd dreamed of. Jude's room would finally be decorated, and he'd move into the main house. In spite of first appearances, Caspian would turn out to be a good egg. In the summertime, she and Jude would be like the Famous Five or the kids in *Swallows and Amazons.*

They'd cycle, build dens, and climb trees on the estate. They'd swim in the lake with Sam. They'd beg picnics off the cook and spend whole days exploring the estate. Whole nights, if Allegra permitted them to camp out in the forest.

Too late, Jess realized that an unidentified buzzing noise was spooking Tempest. The pony surged into a canter. Jess had to grab the pommel to stop herself falling off backward.

"What *is* that?" asked Jude, catching up to Jess.

Autumn was starting to fuss and fret at the strange sound too.

"Guys, you need to slow down," called Lizette. "Pull up your horses."

"I'm trying." Jess tugged on the reins. Tempest obeyed with reluctance. She was jumpier than a cat on a hot tin roof.

The buzzing grew louder.

"Is that a plane or a chain saw?" Lizette asked in agitation as she battled to rein in Fred.

A high-pitched baying drowned out Jude's response. Two fields away, the hunt streamed over a rise. The hounds were in full throat, on the scent of a fox. A red-coated huntsman led the charge.

"Oh no!" cried Lizette. "They're not supposed to be there. Seth told me they'd be on the other side of the estate, in the north fields."

Before she could do anything about it, Fred began to snatch at the bit and spin in circles. Tempest's eyes were out on stalks, fixed on the hunt. Her whole body quivered. Jess tried vainly to get her attention. Jude, bringing up the rear, was the only one who noticed the black speck high above them. A speck that was growing closer by the second. It was a drone.

Suddenly, it dived like a hawk on the kill.

Dumbstruck, Jude watched helplessly as it zoned in on Tempest, brushed the pony's rump, then was gone, banking over the trees and dropping out of sight.

Jude tried to warn Jess, but Tempest was already erupting. When the pony unleashed her inner bronco, Jess didn't stand a chance. Fortunately, she landed on her feet.

Tempest never even glanced her way. With a gleeful whinny, she took off. Clearing a stone wall with room to spare, she streaked after the hunt.

Jude jumped off his horse and ran to his sister, tugging Autumn along behind him.

Jess was unhurt but in tears of despair. "Why, why, *why* did Caspian trust me with his horse? Allegra will kill me if their precious pony breaks a leg. Oh, Jude, what am I going to do?"

"What you're *not* going to do is fret about Caspian," said Lizette, dismounting in case any first aid was required. She insisted that Jess eat a hard candy to stave off any possible shock.

"This is not your fault, Jess. Nor is it your responsibility. Don't stress about Tempest either. She's the best, most careful jumper I know. Unfortunately, loose horses are a menace to any hunt. She could cause a terrible accident. If you're sure you're all right, Jess, I need to go after her. Jude, will you take care of your sister? Promise me you'll both stay glued to this spot till I'm back."

"I'm really fine," said Jess. "We'll stay here, we promise."

As Lizette galloped away, Jude told Jess about the drone. "It went for Tempest like a fighter jet. It's like it had singled her out as a target. What kind of monster would do that?"

"Whoever was flying it must have lost control," said Jess. "It's the only explanation. Nobody would terrify a horse on purpose, would they? Unless . . . Jude, what if it was spying on us, like that maid who was listening at our door? I don't trust Terence the valet either."

"It's back!" shouted Jude.

The drone buzzed over the trees and headed straight for them, performing another reckless fly-by.

For Autumn, it was the final straw. She decided to run first and ask questions later. Wrenching the reins away from Jude, she bolted into the forest like a Derby winner.

"Gosh, this is so fun," said Jess, collapsing on the cold, prickly ground. "Who knew that English horse riding—horse *losing*—could be such a blast."

Across the fields, the baying hounds were milling around a copse of silver birch. Had they lost the fox or found it? Jess prayed it was the former. From a distance, it was impossible to tell if Lizette and Fred, or naughty Tempest, were among the horses and riders heading that way.

"*Now* what do we do?" fretted Jess.

Jude looked at the dark forest. "What choice do we have? We need to go after Autumn."

CHAPTER 19

Sirius

After weeks of being controlled and sometimes smothered by grown-ups, wandering through the wintery woods was pure freedom.

One breath of the pines and ancient oaks, and Jude felt better than he had since he and Jess had flown into smoky-gray London a week earlier. For the first time since they'd set sail to Anegada, he felt connected to nature. He liked the way his boots crunched on the frosty leaves and twigs. Liked the quiet and the dappling of the light through the trees.

"What's the penalty for losing two entire horses?" he asked Jess. "D'you reckon we'll have to spend a month on the naughty step, or will we be put to work in the fields until we've earned enough to pay for them?"

"Neither," said his sister as the muffled drumbeat of hooves carried through the trees. "Autumn's coming this way on her own."

Jess began to jog along the trail in hope of catching the

horse before she changed direction, but Jude pulled her back roughly. He shook his head in silent warning.

From behind a spruce, they watched the racehorse canter into view. Jess saw the problem for herself.

Autumn had a new rider. A near-invisible one.

His waist-length dreadlocks and clothes blended into the forest surroundings as if he belonged to them.

Jess sneezed before she could stop herself, and the bay mare skidded to a stop, almost throwing the rider. Recovering, he settled back into the saddle, reins held loosely in one hand. He was youngish. Twenty at most, Jude guessed. A bulging backpack hung from his shoulders.

"Hello," he said pleasantly.

Incredulous, Jude stepped from behind the tree. "Where do you think you're going on our horse?" he said. "Give her back or we'll call security."

The stranger laughed. "Don't worry, I'm not stealing her. I'm just borrowing her for a bit. There's a difference. If you wait here, I'll return her in a wee while."

He squinted through the gloom. "Hey, you're those American kids, right? I read about you. How's it working out with Clifford and Allegra? Which do you prefer: stately-home luxury or your old yacht? Me, I'd choose the ocean, but if four-poster beds and oil paintings of stuck-up ancestors are your thing, that's cool too."

"You don't know anything," Jess said angrily. "Blakeney Park is *stunning*. We're very lucky and extremely grateful."

"Yeah, but are you happy?"

"None of your business," snapped Jude. "Give us our horse, please. This is your last warning before we call the guards."

"Finders keepers," the stranger said with a grin. "Anyway, she's not *your* horse, is she? If the Blakeneys want her, let them come claim her. I'll tell them that you lost their horse and I rescued her. No doubt, they'll hand me a huge reward. Or maybe not. From what I hear, they're as tight as a submarine hatch. Now, if you'll excuse me, I'm dealing with an emergency."

"What emergency?" Jess said in disbelief.

"A fox emergency." He tilted his head. "Hear that?"

Beyond the woods, a hunting horn blew. The bloodthirsty hounds resumed their chase with a cacophony of barking.

Jess flushed with anger. "I hear the sound of hunters hounding some innocent creature to its death."

He regarded her with new respect. "So we're singing from the same song sheet."

"What do you mean?"

"I'm a hunt sab. That hunting horn you just heard was blown by one of my mates. He's doing that to divert the hounds away from the fox. It's worked twice. But it probably won't work again."

"What's a hunt sab?" Jude asked with suspicion.

He didn't trust the man an inch.

"A hunt saboteur. We're on the side of the animals. If our undercover teams learn that a hunt's taking place—foxes, deer, hares, or whatever—we try to disrupt it." He patted his backpack. "That's what's in here—disruptors."

The twins shrank away from him.

"What's a disruptor?" demanded Jude. "Are you carrying *explosives*? Was it you flying that drone? Spying on the hunters? On *us*? It frightened our horses. Jess's pony threw her. She could have been killed."

The stranger looked aghast. "Do I *look* like some kind of deranged dweeb who'd terrify horses with a drone?" He smiled wryly. "Don't answer that. For what it's worth, I had nothing to do with any drone. Can't stand the things. As for the disruptors, I have two, neither of which is an explosive. Fox poo and—"

"*Fox poo?*"

Jess knew that she and Jude should definitely, positively *not* be chatting to a stranger wearing camouflage in a forest, especially since nobody had any idea they were there. Yet she found it hard to be afraid of this curious Robin Hood figure. She could tell that Jude felt the same way.

"That's why I was late this morning," the saboteur was saying. "I had to swing by a fox sanctuary to collect fox bedding." He climbed off Autumn and took a strong-smelling sack out of his backpack. "If the hounds get a whiff of this, they'll go berserk. My other weapon is citronella." He took out a spray bottle. "It's made from an Asian grass plant. Smells a bit like orange skin and lemongrass. Confuses the hounds, puts them off the scent . . ."

He cocked an ear. "Oh no. That's not good."

Jude tensed. "What's not good?"

"The hounds have gone quiet. Means they're hunting

again. Right, kids, things are about to get serious. I'm Sirius, like the star. It's been a trip chatting with you, but it's make-your-mind-up time now. Are you with the foxes or against them?"

"What do you mean?"

"He *means*, whose side are we on—the foxes or the hunters?" said Jess.

"I'll make you a deal," Sirius suggested. "A favor for a favor."

"Are you kidding?" Jude's patience had run out. "No favors and no deals. We just want our horse back."

"The favor's not for me. It's for the foxes. A vixen and a dog. We think the vixen is pregnant with cubs."

"*Cubs?*" breathed Jess. "I've never seen a fox cub."

"They're heart-meltingly cute—or at least they will be if we can save their mum. If I'd been able to get here before dawn, like I planned to, I'd have dragged the poo sack around or sprayed the stiles and fences myself. Now it's too late. If I go out there, I'll be arrested by hunt security or the Blakeneys' estate guards. But if the two of you scatter the poo or spray the fences, you'll have endless excuses. You can say you got lost, or your horse ran away with you. And keep in mind that *you're* not the ones breaking the law. They are. Killing innocent foxes is a criminal offense."

"I'll take the spray," said Jess, suddenly deciding.

"And I'll drag the sack." Jude reached for Autumn's reins. "*Now* will you give me back my horse?"

· · ✳ · ·

And so it was that, seven days after arriving at Blakeney Park, the twins foiled a foxhunt.

Jude trotted across the fields on Autumn, dragging the sack behind the horse to lure the hounds in the wrong direction. Guided by Sirius, Jess ran on foot to spray the fence posts and tree trunks around the "earth"—the fox's den—to disguise its smell.

By the time the hounds came tearing down the fence line, Jess was hidden behind the stone wall, close to where Lizette had left them. She watched through a gap in the rocks as the hounds rushed about in bewilderment.

A terrier picked up the trail Jude had left for them and the "whips," who directed the dogs, sent them chasing after the fresh scent. The baying hounds faded into the distance. Eventually, there was no sound but the birdsong.

Riding across the field to meet Jess, Jude was spotted by a farmworker. As instructed by Sirius, he'd already ditched the smelly sack, so he had no trouble explaining that he was a hapless beginner who'd lost control of a racehorse.

The Blakeneys' security guards were rather more threatening. They came roaring up in a Jeep with blacked-out windows. The snout of a slavering rottweiler poked around the door as one man leaped out. The other yanked the dog back.

The man came bounding up to them in combat boots, with no regard for Autumn. Her nostrils flared in fear as he barked, "Seen anyone acting suspiciously?"

Jude reacted with comic befuddlement. "Like who?"

"Like any fox-hugging, tree-worshipping nutters out to ruin the huntsmen's day."

"Definitely not," Jess said mildly. "If we'd seen someone hugging a fox or praying to a tree, we'd remember it, wouldn't we, Jude?"

The man glowered at her, trying to decide if she was making fun of him. "If you do see any of those hunt-saboteur characters, run for your life. They're nutjobs, vagrants, and trespassers. Leave it to us to deal with them. Gnasher will sort 'em out."

He gestured toward the vehicle, from which snarling and snuffling emanated.

After the Jeep had roared away, the twins went to say good-bye to their new friend. He was waiting beneath a pine tree on the edge of the forest.

"You've saved many lives today," Sirius told them.

"Don't you mean two?" said Jess.

"Two adult foxes, yes—but also a family of cubs-to-be. Vixens can have as many as six babies. But it wasn't only the foxes you helped. You and Autumn saved me, too. The Blakeneys' guards are notorious. I owe you. A favor for a favor."

"It was nothing," said Jude. "We were happy to help. You rescued our horse. We scattered a bit of poo. It was a fair exchange."

"Jude, we'd better go," Jess interrupted, pointing anxiously at Lizette, who was riding across the field on Fred, leading Tempest. "Sirius, how will you get off the estate without the guards catching you? There are alarms and CCTV cameras all around the perimeter."

"Same way I got here. By kayak." He grinned. "No point in investing in a fancy security system and thug guards if you forget to monitor the waterways. We Water Rats are invisible. As far as I'm concerned, that's a great thing."

Jude stared at him. "Water Rats?"

"Boat dwellers, like you. Your home was a yacht. Mine's a beat-up old narrowboat on the River Severn. The way I see it, Water Rats everywhere are kin."

"Sirius, Lizette is almost here," panicked Jess. "Go, go, go. Wait—will we see you again?"

"Maybe you will; maybe you won't. Either way, I owe you big-time for today. Thanks, guys." He looked toward the distant hall, perched on a crown of green. "If I can ever return the favor, call on me."

"We don't have phones and we don't know England," said Jude. "How would we ever find you?"

Sirius unzipped his backpack and reverently removed a photocopied map.

"You trusted me. This is me trusting you. You're smart kids. You'll figure out what the symbols mean and how it works. As for my narrowboat, the clue's in the name. If you ever need my help, *X* marks the spot."

CHAPTER 20

Dragon Ridge

The trouble started the day after the hunt. The farmhand who'd spotted Jude "riding eccentrically and possibly up to no good" right before the hounds were thrown off the scent, had reported the encounter to his manager, Rex, a man with a face like a soggy weekend.

Eager to find a scapegoat for the hunt disaster, T. Rex, as the twins had nicknamed him, told Clifford.

Hours later, the master of the hunt called Allegra to complain that a skinny girl with long dark hair had been witnessed flitting from the copse where a pregnant vixen was thought to have an earth. Did Mrs. Blakeney have any idea who it could have been? Confronted, the twins stuck to their story. A drone had frightened Autumn. They'd gone in search of her. Jude had ridden the racehorse back to the forest's edge, where they'd agreed to meet Lizette.

"It was our first-ever tour of your estate, and we're clueless about foxhunting," Jess had pointed out reasonably. "I've never in my life even seen a vixen."

Allegra's violet gaze bored into her. "Logically, I know that's true. And yet you just happened to be in the wrong place at the right time, or the right place at the wrong time, and the foxes escaped."

"Maybe it was the drone's fault," suggested Jess. "Whoever was flying it was out to cause mischief that day. I could have broken an arm. Did you tell the police about that?"

"I've apologized twice for the pony's bad behavior," snapped Allegra, "but I refuse to waste police time with a drone that exists only in the imagination of you and your brother."

"Lizette heard it too."

"Heard it, yes. In her opinion, it was a plane or a chain saw. Even if it *were* a drone, I'm told they have a range of ten kilometers. It could have been dispatched from London or Glasgow, for all we know, and launched from a nearby field. It wasn't a drone that scattered fox bedding and sprayed citronella all over the fields. That's the work of a sab. Do you have those in America? They're unhinged eco warriors on a mission to save foxes and other vermin. Thanks to their efforts, the reputation of Blakeney Park as a haven for hunters is in jeopardy."

Jude said innocently, "I'm confused. Seth told us foxhunting was against the law."

"It's complicated," snarled Allegra. "Fine. Let's draw a line under this incident. We can't expect you to know how the estate runs overnight. A word of caution. Be very careful. You're not in Bantry Creek now."

. • ✳ • .

Two days later, the twins were in trouble again. After waking to find Blakeney Park once more carpeted in white, they'd rushed out to make snow angels with Sam.

Soon they were embroiled in an epic snowball fight. Round and round the topiary bears they went, dodging icy missiles and shrieking and laughing. In the excitement, Jude dropped the Swiss shepherd's lead. Sam joined in the chase, barking joyfully.

The sound of breaking glass stopped them in their tracks.

Mary came barreling out. "Which of you smashed that window?"

"We were nowhere near it," protested Jude. "Even if we had been, the snow's too powdery to crack glass."

"Nobody likes a liar," accused the housekeeper, prodding Jude's chest with a finger.

Sam took exception to Mary's aggressive manner.

Leaping up, he knocked her flat in the snow.

While Jess helped Mary to her feet, apologizing profusely, Jude rushed to clip on the dog's lead. As he hauled Sam away, something made him glance up. Caspian was laughing at them from an upstairs window.

The boy thumbed his nose at Jude, then ducked out of sight.

"That little weasel," Jude said furiously to Jess after they'd been marched back inside, lectured all over again by Allegra, and told they'd be paying for a new window out of any future pocket money. "Caspian smashed the glass so that we'd get the blame. What's his problem?"

"*We're* his problem," said his sister. "Don't ask me why when he has everything and we have nothing. We're going to have to appeal to his better nature, if he has one. Find out what's bothering him. Build bridges. Otherwise, he could make our lives hell."

An opportunity presented itself that evening when Clifford and Allegra, dressed like royalty, left the house in a limousine.

After dinner, Lizette went upstairs to make a call. The twins were about to start piecing together a sailing ship puzzle in the game room when Caspian wandered past the open door. When his eyes met theirs, a guilty look flashed across his face. He hurried away.

The twins dashed after him.

"Hey, Caspian," called Jess. "Any chance we could have a word?"

"I've got nothing to say to you," came the haughty response.

"Please, Caspian—it's important."

Caspian took the stairs like a stumpy gazelle and slammed the door of the family living quarters shut behind him.

Disastrously, the twins decided to follow.

Any hope they had of trying to befriend the thirteen-year-old evaporated when they burst into his room and discovered a box containing a drone among Caspian's expensive gadgets and toys.

A huge fight broke out.

Jude lost his temper and accused Caspian of trying to kill Jess twice: first, by insisting she ride his unruly pony; then, by terrorizing that pony with a drone.

"Why would I scare my own horse?" sneered Caspian. "That drone doesn't even work. I only hoped that Tempest would scare you. If she'd dumped you in the mud, I'd have laughed, just like I did when Mary yelled at you for breaking the window. It would have served you right."

"But why?" Jess said in bewilderment. "What have we done to make you hate us? Why are you so jealous?"

"Jealous? You're joking, right?" Caspian laughed rudely. "I don't want you here, that's all. Your mum was a thief, and your dad drove a car off a bridge and killed my grandfather. There, I've said it. No one else will. I don't understand why my parents fostered you."

For eleven seconds, time stopped.

Then Jude punched him. He would have hit him again had Lizette not run in and dragged him away.

· · ✳ · ·

The memory of the hours and days that followed returned to Jude now like flickering outtakes from an old movie as he gazed out of the car window.

Allegra, arriving home in a floor-length silver dress, confirming that, yes, a ruby ring had disappeared around the same time that the twins' mother had left Blakeney Park. "But it was wrong of Caspian to suggest that we believed she was the thief."

Allegra had cooled down. She was almost apologetic. "Even if Joanna *did* take the ring, it's important to remember that she was grieving for your dad and not in her right mind. It really doesn't matter now. It's so long in the past that all is forgotten and forgiven."

"What about our dad?" demanded Jess. Jude had never seen her so furious. Throughout the entire fight, her eyes had remained bone-dry. "Is it true that our father was driving on the night of Caspian's grandfather's accident?"

"I'm afraid so," said Allegra. "I'm sorry you had to find out this way, Jess. Do remember that it was an accident and that Jim redeemed himself by trying to save Robbie after the vehicle went into the river. In doing so, he lost his own life. It was a double tragedy because Clifford's father died of pneumonia not long afterward. He was frail and in poor health. The icy river was too much for him. We don't hold it against your dad, or we'd never have offered you a home here."

Clifford had remained standing throughout, staring moodily at the drawing room fire. Glancing covertly at him, Jude had noticed a dab of Caspian's blood on the white bib of the Godfather's tuxedo. "I believe it would be in everyone's best interests if Jess were to accompany me to London tomorrow," Clifford had said in his mumbled, husky way. "She can stay with my aunt until she starts school next week. Have Astrid make the arrangements."

"London?" Jess had burst out. "But I thought we'd be going to local schools. And what about Jude? If I'm going to London, is he coming too?"

"You wanted to go to the best schools," Allegra reminded her. "That was your dream. As a result, we're sending you, Jess, to one of the finest girls' boarding schools in the country, and you, Jude, to one of the most expensive boys' boarding schools. They're in London and Wales, respectively."

Panic-stricken at the thought of being torn away from his sister and dispatched to a strange school on the other side of the country, Jude had found it hard to form a coherent thought. "But w-what about Sam? Do either of these schools take dogs? How often will we be coming—?"

The word *home* had stuck in his throat like gristle.

Allegra got in first. "How often will you be coming back here? Is that what you're asking? Depends on our family schedule. Clifford is under immense pressure at work, so it's highly unlikely we'll see you at half term. The Easter holidays would be my best guess. Don't worry about your dog. He'll cope just as our rottweilers do. Eddie or the guards can walk him."

The twins had hardly had a chance to say goodbye. When Jude had arrived at the house for breakfast the next morning, Jess's bags were already in the hall. Her eyes were red with crying. He'd had to hug her goodbye under Clifford's flat, black gaze, with Allegra mysteriously absent and Caspian watching from the top of the stairs.

The following week, Jude threw up twice on the drive to Dragon Ridge School in Wales. On boats, he was famous for his cast-iron stomach, but cars on twisty roads had never been his friends.

He'd known it was a mistake to eat the service-station curried vegetable pasty. It had been frozen on the inside. Sadly, the chauffeur had urged him to finish every crumb.

"Might be your last tasty meal for a while. Dragon Ridge has a reputation for austerity. It'll be a jolt to your system after the comforts of Blakeney Park."

Comfort wasn't the first word that popped into Jude's head when he thought of the last couple of weeks at Blakeney Park, but he kept that to himself.

"I don't understand. Mrs. Blakeney told me Dragon Ridge is one of the most prestigious schools in the country."

"Oh, it's pricey all right, but there's different types of posh school. Eton, where Caspian goes, is the kind that produces prime ministers and captains of industry such as Clifford.

Then there's Dragon Ridge, which has more of a military flavor. Greville Wallingford, the head, is a former army officer. Has ambitions to turn the place into a British West Point. You'd be familiar with that, no doubt? Legendary US military academy?"

Jude had watched movies about West Point. The comparison didn't fill him with confidence. Were Dragon Ridge "cadets" bullied and forced to do push-ups till they cried?

"No tolerance for weakness, Wallingford," the chauffeur was saying with relish. "That's why Clifford likes him. He'll be hoping this experience will knock off some of your rough edges. Make a man of you."

Irritated, Jude turned away to watch a wind-blasted field of sheep whiz by through the car window. Sometimes it seemed as if half his short life, people had been ordering him to grow up and stop acting like a kid.

So the Godfather hoped that Dragon Ridge would "make a man" of him? That was a bit rich. Would Clifford's own "macho-manliness" have helped him survive a sea squall on a thirty-seven-foot yacht? Somehow Jude doubted it. Without an army of estate staff and media empire employees, Mr. Blakeney would probably struggle to tie his own shoelaces.

Ricardo, the Castaway kitchen hand, used to advise Jude to ignore people urging him to grow up too fast. "Boyhood is over in one swish of a shark's tail, Jude. Before you know it, you're dealing with bills, work pressure, and gray hairs. Enjoy being a kid while you can."

The Bentley swung hard around a roundabout and sped down the slip road onto the motorway. In a bid to ward off further bouts of car sickness, the chauffeur grudgingly allowed his passenger to move to the front seat. Now, Jude had an unrestricted view as the driver wove in and out of the dizzying traffic.

To quell his rebellious stomach, he swigged the last drops of water from his flask. The chauffeur's stare swiveled briefly to the still-healing cuts on Jude's knuckles. Self-conscious, Jude tugged the sleeve of his new school sweater over his bruised right hand.

"Lucky you didn't break it," was the verdict of the doctor who'd attended Blakeney Park after Jude's fight with Caspian.

"I'm very lucky and extremely grateful," Jude had responded sarcastically, prompting Allegra to accuse him of having an attitude problem.

Even now, Jude could feel his fist connecting with Caspian's smug face.

"You're a thug, just like your father," Allegra had screamed when she and Clifford arrived home to the carnage. To be fair, it had looked worse than it was. One of Caspian's front teeth was a little wobbly, and his cut lip had bled all over his T-shirt and the bathroom tiles, but otherwise, he was relatively unscathed.

Jude, who'd also punched a wall, was in worse shape.

Allegra had threatened, "Don't make us regret taking you in."

Jude wondered what Detective Trenton and the diner waitresses would say if they knew how quickly the twins' dream life in England had unraveled.

Two weeks was all it had taken.

· ● ✳ ● ·

Thinking about Sam now, lonely in his kennel and whining for walks and affection that might seldom come, made Jude feel even sicker.

And when would he next see his twin? Since the hour they were born, he and Jess had never been apart for longer than a school day. Already, he felt as if he were missing a limb.

The chauffeur braked to avoid a squirrel before swinging up yet another narrow, twisting lane. They passed a signpost framed with leaves: DRAGON RIDGE SCHOOL. Jude swallowed down another wave of nausea.

"Can you pull over?"

"Not again." The chauffeur regarded him with distaste. "Sorry, mate. There's nowhere to stop, and we have a dozen cars on our tail. We're almost there. Just hold it in."

But the driveway that wound past rugby pitches and athletics tracks was crammed with unmoving cars. Families lingered over goodbyes. Luggage was unloaded. Six boys and a master, all immaculately dressed in white shirts and blue-and-black blazers, greeted each new arrival. The fumes from idling vehicles snuck in the chauffeur's open window. Jude felt more wretched by the moment.

Eventually, it was their turn to park. As the chauffeur swung toward the entrance, an excited boy dashed in front of the Bentley. The driver slammed on his brakes.

It was the final straw for Jude, who projectile-vomited curried vegetables all over the windshield.

The chauffeur vaulted out of the car. He wrenched open the passenger door, and Jude stumbled out, pale and trembling.

The waiting boys, who'd witnessed Jude's humiliation at close range, were falling about in various stages of horror and mirth. They clutched their stomachs and howled with laughter.

As Jude approached them, a sour smell accompanied him.

The six boys reared back as if they were doing a country line dance. One word from the master and they snapped back into position, like soldiers.

"Jude Gray, I presume," the teacher said with a smirk, consulting his clipboard. He ticked the name off with a flourish.

"How about a warm welcome for our new cadet, Mr. Lord?" he prompted the tallest boy, who'd been laughing loudest.

"Pleased to meet you, Jude," said the boy with hands in his pockets. His wavy brown bangs flopped over his blue eyes. "I'm Garrick Lord."

"Manners, Garrick. Don't test my patience."

"Yes, sir. No problem, sir."

Gritting his teeth, he crushed Jude's sticky hand as he shook it. Jude had to force himself not to wince. One by one, the boys gripped Jude's hand, smiling wolfishly at him. They'd make him pay for inflicting his vomit on them, he was sure.

"Thomas, you're about the same size as Jude," said the master. "Take him to the washroom to clean up and lend him a spare shirt. It'll take him too long to unpack his own trunk before assembly."

"But, sir!"

"No buts. I'll expect you in the Churchill Hall at fourteen hundred hours. You have seventeen minutes. No excuses."

"Yes, sir, Mr. Critchlow. Step this way, Jude."

After the fastest, hottest shower of his life, Jude pulled Thomas's shirt over his damp shoulders and buttoned it up with shaking fingers.

The Churchill Hall was across the other side of the school. He and Thomas had to sprint most of the way there. Jude didn't mind. After the humiliation of his entrance, he was thankful to be clean and to have had a chance to freshen his breath with minty mouthwash.

They reached the hall as the last-year groups were filing into the auditorium from a squashed corridor. If the tittering and rib-jabbing was anything to go by, the tale of Jude's unique arrival had traveled around the school like wildfire.

Montgomery Cutter, one of the meet-and-greet crew,

grinned. "Much better, Jude, but you're still pretty pongy. Don't you agree, Garrick?"

Jude's heart sank. Had he missed a bit? He'd scrubbed himself raw.

"Don't worry, Jude," said Garrick. "Montgomery has some Calvin Klein cologne handy. Monty, any chance you can spare some for our new friend? Can't have him stinking up assembly."

"Sure, Jude. Go ahead. Knock yourself out."

An instant before the tide of boys swept him into the hall, Jude sprayed himself all over. An unseen hand snatched the bottle from him. Only then did he realize he'd been tricked.

The stench was volcanic. As he took his seat in the second row of the auditorium, a sulfurous wave cleared the first three rows. Gasping, laughing and shouting, boys stampeded for the other side of the auditorium, their teachers not far behind.

The microphone popped as Greville Wallingford, the head teacher, took to the stage. His bed-of-nails voice boomed: "Will someone tell me what the blazes is going on? Is a chair on fire? Has a member of staff had a cardiac arrest? Unless it's an emergency or some joker's released a pet viper, I don't want to hear a pin drop . . ."

Then, as the odor hit him: "Great Scott, has someone set off a stink bomb?"

Mr. Critchlow scurried to have a word in his ear.

"Ah. Yes, I see. The Blakeneys' foster boy?"

The head glowered in Jude's direction. He resembled a Special Forces soldier who'd eaten too many pies. "Mr. Gray?"

Jude shrank into his seat. "Yes, sir," he said timidly.

"I understand there was an unfortunate incident on the drive here. Illness can strike any of us, but you were given a chance to spruce yourself up and didn't. Don't let it happen again. Manners maketh the man. So does good hygiene."

"Yes, sir, Mr. Wallingford. I'm sorry, sir."

Jude wished again that Jess had abandoned him on the ocean floor at Horseshoe Reef. At least then he wouldn't have had to suffer the torment of 352 pairs of eyes on him as he sat marooned in the center of three empty rows.

In the midst of his misery, he suddenly realized that he wasn't alone. A woman was sitting one seat away from him. As she dabbed her nose with a tissue, he caught a whiff of menthol and pine needles.

"Ms. Flowers?" boomed the head teacher. "Ms. Flowers, Mr. Ross is saving a spot for you on the other side of the auditorium."

The woman waved to the teacher across the hall. "No need, Mr. Ross. I'm fine right here."

Onstage, Mr. Wallingford's eyebrows jutted like lichen on a crag.

A hush fell over the hall. Boys and staff craned to watch the silent clash of personalities. It was as if a gladiator and a lioness were squaring off.

"I appreciate that librarians have a reputation for stoicism," said the head teacher, "but there's really no need to subject yourself to a foul assembly, Ms. Flowers. Kindly change chairs so we can get on with today's agenda."

Ms. Flowers smiled but stayed seated. "Thank you for your concern, Mr. Wallingford, but I'm really quite content. From where I sit, Jude's as fresh as an ocean breeze."

CHAPTER 21

Divide and Conquer

"One more snap and we're done, Jess," said Adam Buckley, the *Daily Gazette*'s photographer, kneeling on the checkered tile steps of the Geraldine Rose School for Girls to change camera lenses. "How about we have you breathing in the scent of a camelia blossom and smiling slightly?"

Jess's cheek muscles ached from grinning. Though the photographer had been more courteous and considerate than he'd been at the hospital in the Virgin Islands in December, her embarrassment meter was off the charts.

The Blakeneys didn't seem to have considered how she might feel about being subjected to a photo shoot on the fourth day of term. All they cared about was their image and newspaper sales.

"Let's have your sunniest smile, Jess," urged Adam.

As Jess buried her nose in the petals of a velvety pink bloom, gaggles of elegantly uniformed girls watched from shining windows or through the railings of the leafy London square.

The Geraldine Rose School for Girls was everything Jess had wished for and more. From the Mr. Lincoln roses framing the entrance to the light-filled library, and from the science labs, with their NASA-worthy microscopes, to the cellos in the music rooms, it was school perfection. There were chess, drama, and gymnastics clubs. There were corridors lined with award-winning student art.

Her third-story room in the boarding wing was small and shared with one other girl, but Jess loved its *Malory Towers* atmosphere. It overlooked the school tennis courts, hockey field, and organic veggie garden.

"I can't tell you how proud and thrilled we are that the Blakeneys chose our little school for you, Jess," Anastasia Atkins, the head teacher, had told her earlier in the week, after welcoming Jess into her office. "The results of your aptitude test were outstanding. When the founders set up Geraldine Rose as a bedrock of academic excellence for girls, you're the kind of student they had in mind: intelligent, outward-looking, and dedicated. Sights firmly set on Oxford or Cambridge. Brave too. We pored over the reports about how you saved your brother after your yacht capsized."

"Jude's a brilliant sailor and swimmer," Jess had broken in defensively. "It's only because he was trying to help me and steer a course at the same time that the boat jibed. The boom knocked him overboard. Sea squalls are a nightmare even for experienced sailors."

Mrs. Atkins smiled. "I see that you're also modest and loyal.

Those are admirable traits, Jess. Tell me, are you close to your twin, or do you squabble nonstop like some I know?"

A corkscrew of pain twisted in Jess's heart. Since leaving Blakeney Park nearly a week earlier, she'd only managed to speak to her brother once. Clifford's aunt had allowed her to use the landline on the walnut table beside her chair, but insisted on staying in that chair throughout, making Jess feel self-conscious. A private conversation was impossible.

It hadn't helped that Jude, who was always hopeless on the phone, was more monosyllabic than ever, or that a maid began hoovering the Blakeney Park tearoom halfway through the call. Jess had had to strain to hear her brother's words. Even so, the sound of his voice had been like a comfort blanket to her.

"Say that again ... Sorry, what?" he'd said over the din. "Oh, yeah—I'm okay. How are you?"

"Fine. How's Sam?

"Missing you. Uh, how's London? Did you get to see the sights?"

"We went by Buckingham Palace just as they were changing the guard. It was beautiful, Jude. Amazing to think that our dad once paraded for the queen."

No answer. "Jude?"

"I guess he was a good man once, long ago."

"Don't be like that."

"I gotta say goodbye. Lizette needs her phone. Hope you like your new school, sis. Watch yourself."

"Jude, hold on."

"Yeah?"

"Remember, you gotta friend. Always."

He gave a bleak laugh. "You gotta friend too."

When Jess hung up, she felt indescribably lonely.

She'd hoped to have a chance to tell him how she'd seen the horse guards' parade only from the window of a speeding cab. Unluckily, Clifford's aunt had been in a hurry to get to Fortnum & Mason, an overheated store famous for its teas.

"Please can we stop, even if it's only for five minutes?" Jess had begged. "My dad was in the Blues and Royals. He guarded the queen."

"Oh, I don't think so, dear," said the aunt, who was kindly but had set notions about where everyone fitted into the world. "The queen only lets the best people ride her horses. We'll go another time perhaps."

Since arriving at Geraldine Rose, Jess had tried to find the evening star every night (not always easy in a wintry city) and comforted herself by thinking that Jude could see it too.

"It must be tough being apart when you've shared so many adventures and so much loss," the head teacher had observed shrewdly during their meeting.

"Jude's my best friend," Jess had told her.

"That's something to treasure," Mrs. Atkins had said with sincerity. "I'm assuming then that the Blakeneys enrolled him in our brother school, Ravilious, a short hop away in North London?"

"No, he's gone to Dragon Ridge in Wales."

"Dragon Ridge?"

Her reaction had set Jess's nerves jangling. "What's wrong?"

But Mrs. Atkins had regained her composure and smiled again. "Oh, nothing. The ethos at Dragon Ridge is very different to ours, but variety is the spice of life and education. Greville Wallingford, the head, is an ex-army officer. He gets superb results. I'm sure the Blakeneys know what they're doing, Jess. As your foster parents, they'll have your best interests at heart."

Jess hadn't shared her confidence. The memory of Jude being banished to the freezing stable on that first night at Blakeney Park was engraved on her mind. So were Allegra's words following the fight with Caspian: *Don't make us regret taking you in.*

"If your brother enjoys sport and the great outdoors, he'll thrive at Dragon Ridge," Mrs. Atkins had reassured her. "Their swimming team is famous."

"Swimming team?"

"You mentioned that your brother was an excellent swimmer. I'm assuming you are too. I'm sorry to say it's one of the few activities we don't offer at Geraldine Rose. There are riding lessons in Hyde Park once a week if you're interested. Oh, and I need to give you your iPad . . ."

She'd taken one from a steel cabinet and handed it to Jess.

"We supply every girl in the school with one of these. That way, we can control the settings. An hour of internet a day is all you're allowed. Any questions?"

Jess had a hundred.

A phrase had gone through her mind. *Divide and conquer.* Why were the Blakeneys so keen to separate her and Jude? Did they genuinely want to give the twins a first-class education, or was something more sinister at play?

Jess intended to get to the bottom of that mystery, and others. Until then, she'd been flying blind. Now she had Google. For the first time in a long time, she was in detective mode.

· ● ✳ ● ·

"All done, Jess," said Adam Buckley, knees cracking as he stood and packed away his camera. "There'll be a little piece on you in the weekend edition of the *Daily Gazette*. For security reasons, we won't identify the school, but those who know will know, if you know what I mean."

The photographer picked up his bag and tripod. "Good luck."

"Adam, are you going to Wales to photograph Jude? Will you take him a message?"

"Sorry, Jess. We'll be using a stock shot for that, or nothing at all. Dragon Ridge isn't quite as photogenic as this school."

The teacher who'd been supervising the photo session was

deep in conversation with a colleague. Jess lingered forlornly on the step, unsure what to do next.

Mrs. Atkins had told her that most girls started at Geraldine Rose aged five and continued there until they were eighteen. Clusters of them hung about in smart red uniforms nearby, chattering like starlings. They oozed contentment and poise. Jess couldn't see anyone who looked as awkward and lonely as she felt. As she scanned the happy groups, she noticed a woman in the leafy square staring in her direction. She seemed to be smiling at Jess. It was hard to be sure because the blue shadows and gold foliage of a sweet chestnut tree partially obscured her.

There was something familiar about the woman. According to the school brochure, Geraldine Rose was a favorite school with foreign royals, business moguls, and celebrities. Maybe the woman was an actress and Jess had seen her in a film or series. There'd always been some drama or show flickering on the staffroom TV at the Castaway Diner.

Before she could think about it further, a girl with madly curly hair and a smile gridlocked with old-fashioned steel braces tripped up the steps. She'd have fallen flat on her face had her long-haired friend—and Jess—not caught her.

"I knew I shouldn't have put in my contact lenses in the dark," the girl said, turning to Jess with a grin. "Thanks for the save. I heard you're good at that—saving people."

Jess flushed, but the girl was still smiling. "Hey, it was meant as a compliment. To be honest, you looked like you loathed having your photo taken, unlike some around here. They'd go

into full supermodel mode even if a snapper from *Lyme Regis
Weekly* showed up. Fame monsters. *Urgh*. But you're not like
that. Zia and I can tell."

Jess giggled. "What was your first clue?"

"I think it was your I-wish-I-was-on-a-desert-island expression," commented Zia, a sudden breeze lifting her long black
hair.

"That obvious, huh? I need to get better at acting."

"Nah. Fakery's overrated. Better to wear your heart on your
sleeve, like us," said the girl with braces. "I'm Florence—Flo
to my friends. This is Zia. We're the school nerds and resident
awkward squad. Scholarship kids from the wrong side of the
tracks. Wrong teeth. Wrong hair. Wrong clothes. But brainy.
Very brainy."

"Even if we say so ourselves," Zia chimed in. "Want to join
our gang?"

Jess laughed. "I'd love to."

As they moved inside, Jess glanced back over her shoulder.
The woman in the square had gone.

CHAPTER 22

Swimming Trials

"How's it going, Stink Bomb?"

It was lunchtime on the first Friday of term. Jude was at the extracurricular activities board trying to decide on the least-worst options. Every cadet had to choose two. It wasn't easy with Garrick and his buddy Monty buzzing around him like bluebottles.

"Don't sign up for rugby, Stink Bomb," Garrick goaded. "Nobody will wanna tackle you. Not when you smell like week-old haddock left out in the sun."

He and Monty went chortling off in the direction of the dining hall, slapping each other on the back like they'd won Joke of the Year at the Montreal Comedy Festival.

"Want a tip?" muttered the kid beside Jude. "Choose library duty or theater club. Less chance of dealing with brain-dead losers like those two." Taking his own advice, he wrote TEDDY HAMILL in neat capitals on the clipboards of each.

"I don't read, and I can't act," Jude told him.

"Can't or won't?"

Before Jude could reply, the boy had melted away. Thomas and Sebastian took his place, jostling Jude. They were part of Garrick and Monty's gang. Together, the four of them roamed the school like a pack of highly strung Doberman dogs, bored and looking for something to chew.

Jude was their new favorite tug rope.

"*Hey, Juuude, don't be afraid,*" sang Thomas, riffing on the Beatles hit to general hilarity as more boys came crowding round. "Jude, don't be sad. Don't feel bad. Why don't you try out for the swim team next week? Dragon Ridge cleaned up at the national championships last year."

"Poor little Jude can't swim," Sebastian informed him. "When he crashed his yacht, he fell in the sea and had to be rescued by his sister. Don't you remember, we read about it in the *Daily Gazette*?"

Something snapped inside Jude. He heard himself say, "No shame in that. My sister's one of the best ocean swimmers anywhere. She could beat any one of you with her hands tied behind her back. So could I. Before I came here, I was captain of our swim squad in Florida."

Sebastian scoffed. "I'd pay money to see you race Garrick. He's one of the fastest swimmers in the UK. Coach says he's a future Olympian."

Very deliberately, Jude wrote his name on the clipboards for swim team trials and running. "I'll see Garrick in the pool, then."

He strolled off casually, hands in his pockets. His legs were trembling so much he could hardly walk. What had he done? What had he been thinking?

He hadn't been thinking. That's what.

It was true that he'd captained his class swim squad in Florida, but that had been when he was nine. *Before* he'd had a panic attack at an interschool gala. Before he'd nearly drowned on Horseshoe Reef. He couldn't back out of the swim trial now though. Not after telling Sebastian he could beat Garrick with his hands tied behind his back. He'd never live it down.

It was 12:36 a.m. on Friday the fifteenth of January. The trial was on Monday the twenty-fifth. What could he do to change his destiny in ten days?

In his mind, he pictured his transformation into a future Olympian in record time in the manner of a movie montage. Rising at dawn to swim laps, pump iron, punch speedballs, and do double-unders with a speed-skipping rope. Expanding his lungs with secret breathing techniques known only to Zen masters and opera singers.

"Some folks have a saying, 'Feel the fear and do it anyway,'" Lucille, their diner waitress friend, had once told Jude. "I say: No—go with your gut. Sometimes, gut instinct's the only thing standing between you and the sixteen-wheeler truck that's about to roar around a blind bend and crush you flat." Jude's gut had been telling him that Dragon Ridge was the sixteen-wheeler truck ready to crush him flat ever since he'd first learned of the school's existence, but he was trapped here.

There wasn't a lot he could do about it. He'd have to feel the fear and face Garrick at the swim trial anyway.

What he needed was his very own Mr. Miyagi, the Okinawan martial arts master who'd changed Daniel's destiny in *The Karate Kid.*

As if by magic, Ms. Flowers, the librarian who'd stuck up for him in assembly on his first day, emerged from the staff room. Jude couldn't help smiling. If there were a Zen mentor anywhere in this Alcatraz of a school, she'd be it.

He could totally picture her saying solemnly: *"Never put passion in front of principle, Jude. Even if you win, you lose."*

Seeing her reminded him that he'd been meaning to thank her for her support. He'd put it off for days out of shyness and laziness.

As she turned into the library, Jude decided to follow. He walked in a minute after her and stared around in mystification. Ms. Flowers was nowhere to be seen. He even checked between the shelves. It was as if she'd slipped through a portal into another world.

He was halfway to the door when he noticed a shelf signposted RECOMMENDED READS behind the librarian's desk. In the top slot was *Lone Wolf.* Jess had bought him that exact novel at the Leverick Bay bookshop.

The coincidence of it was uncanny. It was as if his sister had wished it there for him to find. Jude's legs carried him directly to it. He took it off the shelf and turned the book over in his hands.

The scent of it transported him instantly to Jess's cabin on *You Gotta Friend*. The mysteries in her "book nook" had been read so many times, they were all seawater wrinkled and fragranced with sunblock and Jess's favorite pineapple juice.

When Jess had gifted him *Lone Wolf*, Jude had been annoyed. He'd felt as though she was pressuring him to read. He'd tossed the book into a locker and forgotten about it.

Now he was struck by its cover image: a wolf standing on a snowy crag. The blue ripples in the snow reminded him of the sea.

Something about the wolf brought back the feeling that had come over him when he'd glimpsed snowy Blakeney Park from the helicopter. Below, the welcome-tea guests had spilled like ants from the candy-striped tent. The more they'd jumped up and down and gestured, the more Jude had shrunk from them internally. He'd willed the helicopter to fly on past until he and Jess reached some remote island or wilderness.

"Hello, Jude."

Jude slapped the book crookedly on to the shelf. It teetered but stayed put. He kicked over the wastepaper basket in his hurry to escape from behind the desk. "Sorry. I was only . . . umm, sorry."

He bent to stuff the trash back into the container.

"Jude, it's no problem, really. The books are here to be discovered."

When he stood up, Ms. Flowers was smiling at him.

"Nice to see you again. Do you like reading?"

"My sister does," said Jude, sidestepping the question. "She's crazy about mysteries and adventures. She used to read them to me at night, when we were at sea. Sometimes she'd read me stories she'd written too. A lot of times those were my favorites."

Ms. Flowers perched on the edge of her desk. She swung her cherry-red Doc Marten boots. Jude was amazed that Greville Wallingford allowed them.

"What about you?" she said. "How do *you* feel about books?"

"I hate them," Jude admitted, startling himself.

"Hate books or hate reading?" Ms. Flowers retied her laces, as tranquil as a gardener discussing peas and carrots.

"I hate, hate, hate reading. Don't mind books. They remind me of my sister. She had a novel nook on our boat. It made her mad that Gabe—he was our guardian—would only let her keep seven books. After he died, she got a load more. Now they're on the bottom of the ocean."

"At least they're biodegradable," remarked Ms. Flowers.

Jude almost laughed but caught himself. What was wrong with him? It had been years since he'd talked so much to a stranger.

"Would you like to choose a book?" asked Ms. Flowers, as though they hadn't just had a whole conversation about him detesting reading.

"Only if there's one about how to become an Olympic-gold-medal-worthy swimmer in ten days."

"I have Michael Phelps's autobiography if that helps."

"I was kidding. I just came by to say thanks for the other day. For supporting me in assembly."

She smiled. "It was the greatest of pleasures."

This time Jude did laugh. "Yeah, right. I saw you stuffing Vicks gel up your nose."

"Oh, the smell was stomach-churning. I'd be lying if I said otherwise. No, I'm talking about standing up to bullies. I saw what those boys did to you. Saw who did it too. Usual suspects. I can't abide that sort of thing. I was bullied myself. Frankly, it's why I became a librarian."

"How do you mean?" Jude edged closer to the door to make it clear he was leaving. He had a bad feeling that Ms. Flowers really was the Mr. Miyagi of librarians. Before he knew it, she'd have him dusting shelves, filing books, and, worse, reading them, just as Mr. Miyagi had made Daniel sand his floor and wax his car in the name of karate training.

"To my mind, books of all kinds—whether they're adventures or mysteries, or books on space exploration, history, science, or climbing Everest—remind us that while bullies, like mosquitoes, have always been with us, heroism is everywhere. Kind people, brave people, and quietly extraordinary people are the ones you'll remember as you go through life. They're the ones we carry with us."

Jude was almost at the exit but didn't feel he could leave. Not with Ms. Flowers in full flow. "Excuse me, ma'am, I—"

"Belinda, I risked life and limb to save you the last three

chocolate cookies," interrupted the geography teacher, entering the library through a connecting door from the next
classroom. "Oh, sorry, I didn't mean to interrupt. It's just that
Wallingford's on a staff health drive, so sweet treats are off the
menu. I grabbed these for you before they were all gone."

Ms. Flowers laughed. "See what I mean, Jude? Kindness
stays with you always, even if it's only in the form of an extra
kilogram on the scales!"

"Cheer up, Gray. It might never happen," said Garrick.

Jude stopped rummaging in his locker but didn't trust himself to turn around. He stared fixedly at the shelf in front of
him, grappling with the emotions that rose in him like steam.

He wanted to yell: *Don't you know it's already happened? All
the worst and most painful things in the world. Everything and
everyone I love has been taken from me!*

Controlling himself with difficulty, he pulled a towel from
his locker and slung it around his neck, as if he'd been intend-
ing to do that all along.

"So you think you can beat me with your hands tied behind
your back, Stink Bomb?" teased Garrick.

In an ideal world, Jude would have responded with something clever, but he was focused on conserving oxygen. His
chest was tight, making breathing difficult. "Sure. No problem"
was all he could manage.

The *Karate Kid* montage hadn't happened. No weight training or speed skipping. No chest-expanding lessons from opera singers. No Mr. Miyagi advice from Ms. Flowers. No laps. The pool had been closed to juniors all week for special training sessions. And now it was the day of the swim trials and Jude had nowhere to hide.

Ignoring Garrick's taunts, he pushed through the swinging doors of the locker room and entered the swimming pool area.

Whatever he'd been expecting, it wasn't this. The pool was Olympic-size, with a deep section beneath a three-meter diving board. The atmosphere was charged with adrenaline and aggression.

Streamlined, hard-muscled boys in Speedos launched themselves into the water. They cleaved furious lines along the lanes, did professional turns, and powered back. Friends and competitors cheered them on from the stands.

The coach was a tanned demigod with a whistle. "Jude Gray? Four-hundred-meters freestyle? Lane six," he ordered without taking his eyes from the swimmers in the pool. "Garrick, you're in lane five." He leaned over lane one. "PETERSON, GET YOUR LAZY BUTT INTO GEAR OR YOU'RE OFF THE TEAM."

Had Jude been able to find the courage, he'd have pleaded cramps or illness. Nobody would have wanted him throwing up in the pool. But there wasn't an ounce of bravery left in his body.

Meekly, he made his way to lane six, which was positioned

directly below the high-diving board. As he took his mark, he had a flashback to Horseshoe Reef. He recalled the panic that had come over him when he'd realized he was tangled in fishing line and being dragged beneath the surface.

The whistle blew. Jude hit churned-up deep water for the first time since the sea squall.

His arms were so weak, he could have been plowing through porridge. A quarter of the way down the pool, he was gasping. By the end of the first lap, he thought he was having a cardiac arrest. Shooting pains cramped his heart.

The coach fished him out of the pool and made a show of crossing his name off the list on his clipboard. He was surprisingly tender.

"Something you ate again, huh, cadet? Don't worry. Happens to the best of us. You're welcome to try again next term. For now, I'd advise something less physical. Art, maybe?"

That night, Jude cried into his thin pillow until the corner was soaking wet. He missed Jess and Sam so much it hurt. Missed the ocean. Missed feeling free. Finally, the boy in the next bed spat, "Man up, Gray," causing Teddy Hamill to cross the dormitory to try to defend Jude.

Jude nearly bit both their heads off.

Jumping out of bed, he stalked off along the corridor barefoot and in pajamas. On impulse, he continued down the stairs to the main part of the school. He had a splitting headache.

The nurse's office was locked, but a light glowed in the library.

Jude went in. If Ms. Flowers was still up and working, she'd be sure to have a Tylenol in her box of tricks.

Once again, the library was empty.

Jude searched between shelves, in case he'd missed her like last time, but there was nobody there. Probably comparing notes on kindness with Aslan in Narnia, he thought bitterly.

He was about to leave when he noticed Jess's book *Lone Wolf* on Ms. Flowers's desk. Why did it just keep turning up? It was like it was taunting him.

Jude seized it and ripped out a few pages. It felt wrong. But it also felt good.

He tore the cover off. That felt even better.

With every tear, his hurt seemed to ease, so he carried on. He ripped up the pool disaster, the stink bomb, and everything he'd ever failed at. Ripped up missing Jess and Sam. Ripped up losing Gabe. Ripped up the Blakeneys and their strange, secret-filled mansion.

There was something satisfying about seeing the book reduced to postage-stamp-size pieces on the industrial carpet of the library.

Jude wondered what would happen if he went further. He gave a tall, thin bookcase an experimental shove. It rocked, coughing up a shelf-load of books.

Jude laughed. He gave it another shove.

It wobbled and went over, smashing into its neighbor. The crash was thunderous. Like dominoes, each bookcase toppled another, which destroyed another.

Dust choked Jude. Splinters pinged off him. Damaged books and debris piled up.

Then he heard shouts and the sound of running feet.

Jude was a boy in a nightmare, unable to move his legs.

At the last conceivable second, he flew to the connecting door. It was unlocked. Slipping into the geography room, he waited for the cavalry to pass. Cries of horror greeted the devastation in the library.

Jude ran.

CHAPTER 23

No Secret

Jess read the same paragraph five times before giving up and setting her mystery aside.

Every afternoon she had the same problem. After years of wishing for stories, she finally had access to the best school library in London and a pile of longed-for novels that would have made yacht-dwelling Jess green with envy, yet she couldn't concentrate.

The most riveting locked-room puzzle couldn't keep her attention. Whole pages blurred before her eyes. It drove her to despair. It was like finding oneself in Willie Wonka's chocolate factory with a sudden allergy to sugar.

It didn't help that Letitia Huntingdon, her roommate, was practicing her hockey dribbling technique in their room. She did that often. Her devotion to sports was religious.

Other girls had brought cuddly toys, pop-idol T-shirts, or family holiday photos to make them feel at home at Geraldine

Rose School for Girls. Letitia's bed was crowded with hockey sticks and mitts, tennis rackets, and ribbons and trophies that kept toppling off her shelf. Jess marveled nightly that she was able to find a corner to sleep in.

Before and after matches, Letitia practiced hockey and tennis in and around their room and listened to matches on her digital radio. She used headphones, but they didn't mute her melodramatic reactions to the successes and failures of her sporting heroes.

"How do you stand it?" wondered Flo, after witnessing Letitia's meltdown when her favorite tennis star double-faulted to lose a game. "You can complain to Matron, you know. It's enough to send anyone round the twist."

"Doesn't bother me," said Jess. "Five months at sea in a cramped thirty-seven-foot yacht is a brutal lesson in getting along with people. My brother's noisy and full of energy too. I used to moan that living with him was like living with an elephant. He took it as a compliment. Told me that elephants were famously quiet on the savanna."

She smiled at the memory. "That's Jude. Irrepressible. Least he *was*. I'm afraid to think how he's coping at Dragon Ridge. What kind of name is that for a school? Sounds like a boot camp. Jude's too much of a free spirit to respond well to strict rules and bossy, yelling drill-instructor teachers."

"You must miss him," sympathized Flo, who came from a large, close-knit family and pined terribly for them.

Jess didn't want to say that, after being separated from her twin for five whole weeks, she felt as if half of her heart was in a locked box she couldn't open. She felt guilty every day that the Blakeneys had enrolled her in wonderful Geraldine Rose, with its talented, generous teachers, infinite opportunities, and pretty grounds, while dispatching Jude to the next thing to a kid prison.

"Have you tried writing to him?" Flo asked.

Jess had. Two emails and a letter. All three had been met with auto replies. Something about how, in the interests of fairness and the well-being of Dragon Ridge cadets, "no outside correspondence will be entertained."

Perhaps because she was missing Jude and Sam more than ever that afternoon, Letitia's larking about with her hockey stick had started to get on Jess's nerves. She was about to say something when there was a crash.

Jess screamed.

Her only reminder of her mother—the little framed oil painting—lay in pieces on the floor.

Had Matron and a passing teacher not immediately rushed in, joining Flo, Zia, and Letitia, who were all talking over one another while trying to placate Jess as she sobbed, someone might have noticed the corner of an envelope poking out from beneath the bedside table where it had slid when the picture broke.

Unluckily, Flo kicked the envelope farther under the table in her eagerness to console Jess.

The next day, the boardinghouse cleaner, who was mostly

very thorough, but had long since been defeated by Letitia's sporting accessories, failed to pull out the bedside table to vacuum beneath it. Jess and Letitia's room received only the lightest of dustings.

As a consequence, the letter that would have altered the twins' destiny in an instant lay undiscovered, noticed only by a mouse.

* • ✳ • *

It was Mrs. Atkins who suggested that Jess take her picture to the art teacher for repair.

As it turned out, it could be easily fixed. When Jess returned to collect it a week later, it was as good as new. Better, if truth be told.

"Good thing it's an oil painting, not a watercolor," said Ms. Gregory, smiling at Jess's rapturous reaction. "Oils are almost never framed with glass, which might have broken and slashed the picture. I've replaced the mount with museum-quality cream board and touched up the gold on the frame. Nice piece. Who's the artist?"

"I was hoping *you* could tell *me*. I wish I knew more about it. My mom lived in New Zealand, England, and the US. Apparently, she traveled a lot. She could have bought it anywhere."

"Hmm, an art mystery. How intriguing. The artist's style is familiar, but I can't think where I've seen it before. Have you tried googling the title on the back, *Dolphin Dreams*?"

Jess didn't tell her that googling *Dolphin Dreams* was the first search she'd done on her iPad after arriving at the school in January. Her screen had filled with images of dolphins leaping through tangerine sunsets, Reiki practitioners, and marine biology courses.

She'd also done a search for HOPEFLI, the reference on Gabe's bank statement, in the hope of finding who had been gifting Gabe thousands of dollars. That had gone nowhere too.

"What about the cottage or the landscape?" Jess asked the art teacher now. "I'm sure it's a real place. I've always had this sense that it's somewhere that was special to my mom because the painting was one of the only things she saved when she, uh, left the UK. Any idea where it could be?"

"Hard to say. Could be Cornwall, the Outer Hebrides, Northumberland, New Zealand, somewhere in Scandinavia. The painting itself looks valuable, but the frame is cheap. It's possible your mum bought it at a yard sale or flea market. I did notice one thing—an indent and a strip of yellowing tape on the inside of the backboard I threw away. Was anything stuck to it when it broke? People often keep secrets hidden in paintings."

Jess stared at her. "What kind of secrets?"

"Photos of loved ones, notes, secret maps . . . But there was nothing?"

Jess thought of the crowd in her room. "Not that I saw."

"I'll help you investigate the mystery of *Dolphin Dreams*,"

Ms. Gregory said with a smile. "I fancy myself as a bit of an art sleuth. I'm sure I've seen a similar picture. I just have to remember where."

She picked up a brush. "If you enjoy art so much, why don't you join my watercolor class? I'll teach you to paint seascapes. I've done some sailing myself. You must long for the ocean, here in landlocked London."

Jess almost burst into tears again. In one deft phrase, the teacher had identified why she felt so empty. At night, she tossed and turned and itched and sweated, the way Jude did if he felt claustrophobic. Aside from missing her brother and their dog, she'd been unable to work out why she was so unhappy. Now she knew. She was lost without the ocean.

She missed the sound of the sea and the mineral tang of salt in her nostrils. She missed the snap of the sails and the creaking of the mast. She missed freedom.

Perhaps because Ms. Gregory loved sailing too, she correctly intuited Jess's thoughts.

"I've always had the eccentric notion that it's possible to paint dreams into being," she said with a smile. "I'll give you an example. When I was your age, I wanted a Border collie puppy more than anything. I'd lost my mum, and my dad couldn't afford a puppy. I decided that if I couldn't have the real thing, I'd draw my dream puppy.

"So I did. I painted, doodled, and sketched that puppy everywhere. I visualized him sitting on our front step wearing a red bow, with one ear flopping. I did that for eight months.

One day, my dad collected me from school. We'd both had awful days and we were quiet on the way home, missing Mum and feeling down, but there, on our front step, was a Border collie with a red bow and one ear flopping. We never did find out who gave us that puppy."

She laughed. "Jess, the moral of the story is, paint the dog you want, the yacht you want, and your dream home on the ocean. You might just paint them into existence."

Up in her room, Jess comforted Letitia once more and reassured her that, yes, she forgave her, and that the restored painting was better than new. Letitia in turn promised to never again use their room as a hockey pitch.

After Letitia left to take a shower, Jess did a fingertip search of the floor. She even braved the area under her roomie's bed. She didn't check beneath the bedside table because Letitia's hockey boots were in the way, and Jess was keen to avoid a verruca.

Jess went to sleep satisfied that she had done all the investigating she could for one day. As far as she could tell, the painting had concealed no secret.

CHAPTER 24

Lone Wolf

"*Carpentry?*" repeated Jude in bewilderment.

Greville Wallingford regarded him with intense dislike. "Yes, carpentry. You know, the art of working with wood? For reasons that escape me, Ms. Flowers has this theory that, growing up in a boatyard, you might have developed some talent for it."

Jude was having difficulty processing this latest turn of events. When a senior had hauled him out of history mid lesson and ordered him to the head teacher's lair, he'd anticipated being given a Dragon Ridge–style punishment for trashing the library. Solitary confinement in a dank, rat-filled cellar, perhaps? Three thousand burpees in the rain? Afterward he'd be sent "home" to Blakeney Park in disgrace, barely a fortnight after leaving it.

Fearing the worst, he'd arrived to find Ms. Flowers sipping coffee in an armchair by the toasty fire. So far, Wallingford hadn't even mentioned the library. Bizarrely, he had opened their "chat" by asking about Jude's woodworking skills.

Jude couldn't even look at the librarian. The fact that she was here meant she knew he was the culprit who'd destroyed her library.

He felt ill with shame. She'd been his only ally at the school, and he'd repaid her by ripping up and smashing everything she loved and believed in.

"Belinda—Ms. Flowers—and I don't always see eye to eye . . ." Wallingford told him.

"Next to never," the librarian agreed tartly.

"But she came to me this morning with a radical and, dare I say it, visionary proposal. I'll get straight to the point, Gray. Last night, we had an unfortunate incident in the library. The contractor who built the bookcases before our time was, it turns out, a woodwork and engineering dunce. A bookcase collapsed, triggering a domino effect that took out its neighbors. All of them. The devastation is quite something. On combat duty, I patrolled tidier bomb sites."

He focused on Jude like a sniper lining up a target. "Personally, I find it a stretch to believe that that level of destruction could have happened without human interference. Additionally, a security guard and two teachers reported hearing someone running from the scene—"

"You were telling Jude about my radical and visionary plan," interjected the librarian.

"Ah, yes. Ms. Flowers thought that, rather than hiring an

outside contractor, we could task one or two cadets with reimagining the Dragon Ridge library by building new bookcases. For the chosen cadets, it would be an immense but rewarding challenge."

"I can do it, sir," Jude said immediately.

"You *can*?"

"Yes, sir. I love woodwork. From when I was small, I used to help my guardian—he was a shipwright—build and repair boats or loose boards in the jetty or whatever. And at the boatyard diner, if the manager needed shelves put up or a broken chair fixed, me and Al—"

"Al and I," said Ms. Flowers.

"Sorry, Al and I would fix them for her. Mainly Al, but I watched and learned."

"Ms. Flowers, what are your thoughts? Shall we give Gray a trial run at this? See if he can come up with a design that suits and then build some bookcases for you?"

"I think Jude deserves a chance," said Ms. Flowers, leaving Jude in no doubt that it would be his last one. "I'd suggest we ask Teddy to work side by side with Jude on the project. It's a huge amount of work, and there are books to repair and catalog too."

Wallingford snorted. "Edward Hamill? That boy is a total waste of space."

"I beg to disagree, Mr. Wallingford. Teddy is the best library assistant I've ever had."

The head glowered but resisted comment. "Like you say,

everyone deserves a chance. *One* chance. Don't waste yours, Gray. You won't get another. Rebuilding the library will be tough physical labor, so I'll excuse you and Hamill from all sports and extracurricular activities until your work is done. No need to look so pleased about it, Gray."

"No, sir. I mean, yes, sir."

"Oh—and Gray, we'll keep the library project between us for the moment. Just until it's completed. I'm not sure that building bookshelves was quite what Blakeney had in mind when he enrolled you at Dragon Ridge."

In the cold light of day, the wreckage of the library was as grim a sight as the wreckage of the twins' yacht. Somehow Jude had been responsible for both.

He picked his way through the rubble to the librarian's desk, stricken with guilt.

"Good afternoon, Jude."

"How did you know it was me, Ms. Flowers?"

"You made the mistake of shredding the book you were transfixed by when you first came into my library."

"I didn't mean to do what I did," Jude said miserably. "I'm so ashamed and so sorry. I don't know what came over me. Everything got to be too much. I just sort of boiled over."

"You can say that again," put in Teddy, standing up from behind a broken bookcase. He'd been leaning against it, restoring a damaged adventure novel. He was another person who'd been kind to Jude and been blasted halfway to space for his trouble.

Jude was mortified. "Sorry for yelling at you last night, Teddy, especially when you were only trying to stand up for me. I'm an idiot. I didn't mean to take it out on you."

"Apology accepted." Teddy shuffled his feet and stared awkwardly at the floor.

"Well done, boys," said Ms. Flowers, smiling at their embarrassed attempts to bond. "I accept your apology too, Jude, although only as a down payment on the many weeks of hard work that lie ahead for you. I suggest that the three of us shake hands on it. If we're to create the finest library in the land as a partnership, we need to turn a page on what's happened and start afresh."

They did as she asked and grinned at one another. But just as Jude was heaving a relieved sigh at getting away with his crime relatively lightly, Ms. Flowers opened a drawer in her desk. She took out a pristine copy of the book Jude had destroyed. Turned out, she had a spare.

Jude stared at it in resigned disbelief. *Lone Wolf* was like a phoenix. Forever rising from the ashes, or the depths of Horseshoe Reef.

"What was it about this particular book that made you 'boil over'?" asked Ms. Flowers. She was staring at him intently.

"Jess gave it to me when we were in the Virgin Islands."

"Your sister? I thought you were close. Was there something in the story that upset you?"

"No—I never even opened the book. We had a fight about it right before the sea squall. I still feel bad about it."

"Would Jess want you to feel bad about it?"

"No, she's not like that. She forgives really easily. If we argue about something, she's over it in about a minute. She's not perfect, but she has the biggest heart of anyone. It makes me happy to make her happy."

"Would she be happy if you read more books?"

Jude's blood began to simmer again. As he'd suspected, the "library project" was a trap to get him reading. "Yeah, she would, but *I* wouldn't be happy, so what's the point of that? I don't want to read any book, but *Lone Wolf* most of all. It's like it's following me. It's spooky."

Ms. Flowers was looking fierce again. She'd been playing nice, like a lioness lazily watching a baby zebra, but now her metaphorical tail was swishing.

One wrong move and he'd be brisket.

"Jude, don't go mistaking me for a doormat. You have two choices here. You can be part of something special, creating and crafting a library that will inspire and thrill other young people long after you've left this school. You can hone your carpentry skills and carry those with you always. Teddy will teach you how to bind and mend books, and I'll show you how to shelve them.

"You can do all of this in the warmth and comfort of the library, in the unrivaled company of Teddy and me—*or* you can spend every afternoon for the rest of term being shouted at on the track or getting your face mashed into the mud on the rugby pitch."

"Gee, let me think," Jude said with a grin. "Hmm . . . I choose the cozy library and your unrivaled company."

"Fabulous. I have one condition. You're to read two pages of *Lone Wolf* tonight and describe them to me tomorrow. If, after that, you still feel strongly that reading's not for you, I'll free you from all future library commitments. I'll tell Mr. Wallingford that I've changed my mind and we'll be hiring a professional carpenter."

She pressed the book into his unresisting hands and put a postcard on top of it.

"This came for you earlier. As you're aware, Dragon Ridge cadets are strictly forbidden from receiving outside correspondence, but somebody kind left it in my staff room pigeonhole. They clearly intended that I should pass it on to you."

Jude's heart began to thump. The postcard was a photo of a boy on an old jetty with weathered boards, looking out over a blue bay. Printed on the sky was a quote:

YOU CAN'T GO BACK AND CHANGE THE BEGINNING, BUT YOU CAN START WHERE YOU ARE AND CHANGE THE ENDING . . .

The postcard was addressed to Jude but unsigned. The anonymous sender had written just two words: *God speed*.

Jude stared at them. Was it a coincidence that those precise words had been the sign-off to the email the twins had found in Gabe's cabin? Could this postcard have been sent by the same person? Instinct told Jude that it had. That could only mean that Gabe's friend or enemy had tracked Jude all the way to Dragon Ridge in Wales.

It was unnerving to say the least, but he tried to keep his voice casual. "Ms. Flowers, did this arrive in an envelope? There's no stamp or postmark on it."

"If it did, it's been recycled. Is there a problem? I assumed the card was from the Blakeneys . . . ?"

"I guess," Jude murmured vaguely. "Okay, I promise I'll read two pages of *Lone Wolf* tonight. And I'll build your bookcases if you'll let me. I'm not going to pass up a chance to be warm and dry in"—he grinned at Teddy—"unrivaled company."

That night, Jude finally opened The Book. *Lone Wolf* was a story about Markus, a troubled boy who stows away on a plane carrying supplies to the Arctic. When it crashes in the Swedish wilderness, Markus has to form a bond with the wolf that starts hunting him—or die trying.

Jude was gripped by the third line. He was on page five when the prefect came to turn off the lights.

He lay in the dark, thinking about the boy in the story. How would Markus tame the savage wolf? Would the pair survive the coming snowstorm?

He leaned toward the next bed. "Torquil? Torquil, are you awake?"

"I am now. Gray, has anyone ever told you you're a royal pain in the butt?"

"Too many to count. Please can I borrow your flashlight? I'm at an exciting bit in my book. I need to know what happens next."

There was a smothered laugh. "Yeah, it's full of cliffhangers, that one. If you like it, I have a zombie-invasion book I can lend you."

"Thanks. Uh, good night."

"Night, Jude."

CHAPTER 25

Sacred Ground

Jude did three fruitless searches of his locker and the changing room before accepting the inevitable: Someone had stolen his sneakers.

He knew they'd been taken, because he'd spent the previous evening cleaning them and changing a broken lace in preparation for the Explorer's Challenge.

It didn't surprise him they were gone. Outside of the library and the classes of a few caring teachers, Dragon Ridge was a jungle. The majority of boys were in survival mode. It wasn't quite "kill or be killed," but toughness and a cutting wit were highly prized among the lords of Dragon Ridge.

Jude thanked his lucky stars daily that his library-building job kept him out of the clutches of some of the bigger, rougher boys on the rugby pitch and in cadet training. It had even earned him the respect of those boys who did want to study and read.

But the endless struggle to keep his head down without reacting to vicious jibes and spirit-sapping pranks—the swiping of his sneakers was just the latest of many—was exhausting.

That day, though, Jude's mind was on something more important than missing shoes. He was thinking about the article Ms. Flowers had read to him when he'd swung by the library first thing:

BLAKENEY SET TO REAP MILLIONS IN SALE OF ANCIENT FOREST TO DEVELOPERS
Fury at Plan to Build 250 Apartments in Woodland Idyll by the River Severn

According to the *Guardian* newspaper, hundreds of oaks and pines were set to be "razed to the ground."

"How do you raise something to the ground?" Jude had asked the librarian.

"Not *raise* with an *i*—*raze* with a *z*," replied Ms. Flowers. "It means to destroy."

"Kind of like what happened to your library?"

Her lips twitched, but she'd stayed looking at the newspaper article. "Indeed. Not so easy to put right, however. You can't restore a three-hundred-year-old oak the way you can shove up some shelves."

"*Shove up some shelves?*" Jude said in mock outrage.

"Naturally, I didn't mean *your* bookshelves, which are, of

course, an architectural masterpiece," Ms. Flowers had joked, and they'd both laughed.

Rebuilding the library had been a mammoth job. Some nights Jude had fallen into bed with his muscles on fire from the sheer physical effort of it. But it was worth it to see Ms. Flowers walking between oak shelves that she, Jude, and Teddy had codesigned, chatting to boys lolling on bean bags or studying in book nooks. The library had gone from being mostly empty to mostly full.

That morning it had been quiet again because half the school had been out competing at a sports event, and the rest had been preparing for the Explorer's Challenge.

Jude, who should have been getting ready himself, had instead been reading the article over Ms. Flowers's shoulder. "Go on."

"It says here that if the sale goes ahead on May third, the developer plans to chop down the trees and replace them with landscaped gardens, luxury apartments, shops, and cafés."

Jude had been distraught. He'd never forgotten that day in the forest with Jess. The cathedral calm of it had been a balm to his soul. There had been something so soothing about the rustling and tweeting of the woodland creatures going about their daily lives as the winter light filtered through the leaves.

The forest had felt like home in a way that the Blakeneys' museum house never would. It had felt sacred.

"What about the rare owls, woodpeckers, and roe deer?" Jude had asked Ms. Flowers. "What about the foxes? Where are they supposed to go if there's no forest? And what about the three-hundred-year-old oaks? I thought that Robbie Blakeney bought the estate to preserve those things forever. Clifford might not give a hoot about the owls and oaks, but you'd think he'd honor his father's wishes."

"I'll venture that you're cut from different cloth, Jude," said Ms. Flowers. "You'll always value love and nature over money. But these are difficult times in the media world. Many newspaper owners are in trouble. The millions Clifford Blakeney expects to make from the sale of the forest land might be needed to prop up Daybreak Media.

"As for being loyal to his dad's wishes, it's well known that they had a rocky relationship. It's possible that he doesn't have any sentimental feelings toward the forest. Or maybe he does care, but is more concerned with saving the business his father built than a few oak trees and birds."

Jude doubted that. He remembered Jess telling him about the documentary she'd watched on the plane. How Clifford's mom had run off with a concrete millionaire when he was nine. How he'd fallen out with his dad after Robbie had reneged on his promise to buy him a Rolls-Royce for his eighteenth birthday.

As Daybreak Media grew, had there been some kind of power struggle between them?

"If only we could tell the Water Rats about the forest being sold to greedy developers," Jude had said to Ms. Flowers. "Apparently, they're eco warriors. Jess and I helped them stop a foxhunt. Maybe they could hold a protest or tie themselves to trees or something."

"If they have a website or a contact email, what's stopping us from letting them know about the rare owls and wood-peckers?" Ms. Flowers had replied. "Leave it to me, Jude. If I can find a way to send them the article, I will. They might not be aware of it."

She glanced at the clock and gasped. "Aren't you meant to be competing in the Explorer's Challenge this morning, Jude? Run like the wind or we'll both be in trouble with Mr. Vesper!"

Jude had sprinted from the library, smiling. Ms. Flowers had a way of making him feel they were in things together. Like Jess, she was always in his corner.

Now, as he sat beside his locker wondering whether he could run the Explorer's Challenge in his school shoes, a familiar feeling of defeat was creeping through him. With minutes to go until the bus left for the Brecon Beacons, his sneakers were still missing.

"What's up, Gray?" asked Garrick, smoothing his hair in the mirror on his way through the changing room. "Need any help?"

Jude was taken aback. He couldn't remember the last time Garrick had called him anything but Stink Bomb.

"I've lost my sneakers."

"Hard luck. Hope you find them." Garrick turned to go, then paused. "What size are you, dude?"

"Nine."

"I have a spare pair if that's any use. They're trail runners, better suited to hilly terrain than sneakers. You'll be less likely to twist an ankle in them."

Jude hesitated, sensing a trap. "Seriously?"

"Seriously. Look, I know I gave you a rough time for a while after you got here. I've always felt bad about the swimming trials. This is my way of saying sorry." He opened his locker and handed Jude a box of shoes. "I've worn them once. Try them. They're cutting-edge tech. Bouncy as slippers."

They looked brand-new. Jude put them on. They were as bouncy as slippers. Tight slippers.

"Cadets, what's the holdup?" demanded the PE teacher from the doorway. "If you're not on the bus in the next three minutes, we're leaving without you."

Garrick grinned. "Just helping Gray out with some running shoes, sir. His have been mislaid."

Mr. Vesper, bouncing on his own top-flight trail runners, grinned back. "Helping the competition? That's the spirit, Lord. Come on then, boys. Let's move."

CHAPTER 26

Tombstone

The Explorer's Challenge combined running, hiking, and orienteering. Teams of six competed in different sections of the Brecon Beacons National Park for the most prized trophy in Dragon Ridge history.

"Remember, cadets, this is more about teamwork than speed," Mr. Vesper told the boys as the bus rattled through the narrow sunlit lanes. "A unit is only as good as its weakest link. The forecast is for a March seventh high of twenty-two degrees Celsius today. That's climate change for you. Keep hydrated. If you feel faint or otherwise incapacitated, stop where you are. We'll collect stragglers later. In an emergency, your team lead will call my mobile."

Before Jude had reached the top of the first hill, his left heel had been rubbed to a pulp by Garrick's "cutting-edge" shoes. Ten minutes on, he was limping so badly that he had to quit the race. He hobbled to a patch of shade and painfully peeled off the pinching trail shoes.

Two of his toes were bleeding. Three had been reduced to bloated, blistered piglets. His teammates went on without him.

Mr. Vesper, who came by soon afterward, was unimpressed.

"You're pathetic, Gray. Truly," he said pityingly, jogging on the spot as if to prove that he was three times as fit as Jude, despite being three and a half times his age.

Jude lifted a bloody foot. "It's Garrick's shoes, sir. They're a size and a half smaller than he said they were."

"Don't try to shift the blame to a boy who's done you a kindness," barked Mr. Vesper. "It was your responsibility to check they were the right size. Now you're going to have a long, boring wait until I can send someone on a quad bike to collect you. Two hours minimum, I'd say. Put on sunblock and keep your fluids up. Don't add heatstroke to your problems."

He shook a finger at Jude. "And don't you dare move or talk to strangers. A person can vanish in a heartbeat out on these hills. Mr. Blakeney will have a fit if you're on the front page of the *Daily Gazette* for all the wrong reasons."

After the teacher had gone, Jude made himself comfortable on a bed of heather. A slow grin spread across his face. He wasn't angry with Garrick for pranking him yet again. He could not have cared less about the Explorer's Challenge.

Garrick had actually done him a favor. Sore toes were a small price to pay for a few hours of freedom and the chance to lie in the sunshine drawing in a lungful of sweet, herby Welsh air.

To Jude's irritation, Explorer's Challenge competitors and instructors kept stopping to ask if he was okay, so he relocated to a better position 150 feet off the trail. From there, he could see without being seen. When the quad bike came, he'd hear it.

Until then, nobody would bother him.

Relaxing in a heathery hollow, he had a roof-of-the-world vista of hazy blue mountains and a patchwork quilt of farmlands in the valley below. He made out the crest of a dried-up waterfall and, beneath it, a silver lake like something out of the legend of King Arthur and his knights. Jude could imagine himself pulling an Excalibur-style sword out of it.

The landscape reminded him of the characters in *Lone Wolf*, a story he'd fallen in love with. The Brecon Beacons were hardly the Swedish wilderness, yet hikers, campers, and the army recruits who trained on the moors were frequently caught out and even killed by the fickle Welsh weather.

It occurred to Jude that what happened in fiction could happen to him in real life. He could soon be the star of his own high-stakes adventure. If Mr. Vesper forgot to send a quad bike, and a snowstorm moved in, would Jude survive if he wasn't found for days?

Could he build a shelter like Markus in his book? Could he start a fire and find water to drink? Could he eke out his sandwiches?

Jude thought he probably could. He understood now where Jess's inner confidence came from. She was armored by the detectives in her books. Lost in a snowstorm, Jude would choose to be armored by the adventurers he'd read about, both fictional and real. If they could survive polar temperatures and gales, attacks by savage beasts, and hunger so extreme that they ate their own shoe leather and were thankful for it, surely Jude could cope with a little Brecon Beacons' blizzard?

He squinted up at the blue sky. For the time being, there was approximately a 0.0001 percent chance of snow. Unzipping his backpack, he took out the mysterious postcard and studied it for the hundredth time.

YOU CAN'T GO BACK AND CHANGE THE BEGINNING, BUT YOU CAN START WHERE YOU ARE AND CHANGE THE ENDING...

GOD SPEED.

Whoever had sent the postcard cared about him, Jude was sure of it. That ruled out the Blakeneys. And Jess had flowy, artistic handwriting, so it wasn't her.

Who then?

Out of nowhere, he was struck by a thought. His mom had told Gabe that her husband had died saving his best friend. When the twins moved to Blakeney Park—where Jim had once been a humble groom, and their mom had been a carer changing sheets and bedpans—they'd assumed that the best-friend story she'd told Gabe was an invention, like her name, Ana. But what if it wasn't? What if Jim and Robbie Blakeney really *had* been best friends?

How would Clifford have felt about Jim, a mere servant, replacing him in his dad's affections?

Jealous enough to send Jim's widow packing the moment he passed away?

Spiteful enough to accuse Joanna of stealing a ring?

It was worth investigating when he returned to Gloucestershire for the Easter holidays, but Jude put away the thought for now. It was too glorious a day to waste thinking about the Blakeneys. He was about to tuck into a sandwich when he noticed a band of wild ponies on the slope below.

Jude couldn't resist going to see them. After getting a fix on his position—lining up a twisted tree, a sharp boulder, and a gap in the hills—he picked his way carefully down a steep path, wincing when the prickly undergrowth came into contact with his injured toes.

He'd almost reached the horses when he heard Monty's plummy tones. "Trust me, it'll be fine. I've scoped out every angle. From the trail, it's impossible to see us."

Jude had a split second to avoid being seen. He belly flopped behind a boulder, landing heavily in a clump of bracken and gorse. He had to bite his fist to stop from crying out when a wicked thorn pierced a blistered toe. By the time the pain had receded, the boys were so close he could hear one of them burp as they clomped past.

"What could go wrong?" Garrick was saying cheerfully. "At least fifteen boys I know have done it. That's why I told you to bring microfiber towels. We'll dry off, take the shortcut, and be at the rendezvous point on schedule to meet the bus."

"Why do they call it tombstoning?" asked a boy whose voice Jude didn't recognize. "The name creeps me out a bit."

Jude was shocked. Teddy had told him that tombstoning was a craze in the area around Dragon Ridge. Kids risked death and broken necks jumping off cliffs, piers, and waterfalls.

He peeked around the boulder. His worst fears were confirmed. Garrick and his pals were headed to the ledge of the old waterfall that Jude had seen from his vantage point earlier.

"No one forced you to come, JJ," Monty was saying. "If you were scared, you could have stayed behind. If it makes you feel better, it's called tombstoning because you jump in feetfirst, not because you wind up needing a tombstone."

"Right. Cool. Can't wait," said JJ.

"Won't it be freezing?" said Thomas. He sounded nervous too.

"What's got into you both? It's March, so, yes, it'll be a trifle chilly," Garrick said impatiently. "If you're a baby about cold water, you shouldn't be on the swim team. And if you're worried about dying or getting paralyzed, don't be. There are no rocks in the landing area. It's quite safe. We'll be in and out in five minutes. Everyone I've talked to tells me this is much more of a rush than Dead Man's Cove."

"Count me in," said Monty as they reached the edge.

Jude had to strain to hear them now.

JJ gasped. "Whoa. How high is it?"

Garrick laughed. "Twenty-five meters."

"Ace! I'll practice my reverse four-and-a-half somersault in pike position and still have time for a nap and a curry," joshed Sebastian. "Who's going first?"

"I'll go," said Garrick. "It was my idea."

He stripped down to his boxer shorts and stood like a sculpture on the flat rocks, poised to jump.

Jude felt a panic attack coming on. His chest was tight, his breathing ragged. Every time he looked down at the still, silver lake, all he could think about was what could go wrong. He wanted to yell at the boys to stop. Tell them it wasn't worth it. That jumping into icy water on an unseasonably hot day could bring on shock that could be fatal.

But Jude's limbs refused to obey him. He couldn't move so much as a finger. And when he tried to shout, all he managed was a croak.

Garrick and Monty were arguing about something. In the end, it was Monty who jumped first. He whooped and hollered as he surfaced in the lake, shaking a triumphant fist. "It's f-f-f-freezing, but what a rush," he yelled up at them. "That was the best feeling ever. I want to go again."

"Incoming," shouted Garrick. He took a running leap, hit the water at an angle, and sank in a whirlpool of bubbles.

"I'm next!" shouted Sebastian.

"Wait, you idiot." Thomas wrenched him back. "Let Garrick reappear. You don't want to land on him while he's underwater."

Sebastian snapped at him, but did as he was told. "Garrick's such a joker," he said, beginning to shiver in his boxers. "He's pranking us by holding his breath underwater."

JJ was leaning over the edge in a frenzy of anxiety. "Monty, you need to find him quickly!" he called down. "He's been under too long. Can you see anything? Bubbles? A shadow?"

"Hey, Garrick, don't fool around," shouted Monty, treading water. He ducked beneath the surface. The boys on the ledge watched him circle, sharklike.

When Monty surfaced, his skin was yellow with fear. "I can't find him," he yelled. "He's gone. Garrick's gone."

Thomas grabbed his shoes. "I'll run down and help search."

"Coach always says 'Four minutes without oxygen and it's all over,'" Sebastian told him, a note of hysteria in his voice. "It'll be quicker if we jump."

"Are you insane?" cried Thomas. "What if Garrick hit his head on a rock and we do the same? Fat lot of use we'll be if we're drowned too."

Behind the boulder, Jude found his voice. "I'll do it!" he shouted, stumbling from his hiding place on bleeding feet. "I've had lifesaving training."

"Stink Bomb!" Sebastian said in astonishment. "What are *you* doing here?"

"Trying to help, which is more than you're doing," JJ barked at him.

Jude pulled off his shirt as he ran. "Call an air ambulance!" he yelled. "Send up a flare! Garrick's going to need all the help he can get. Watch out, Monty. I'm coming down."

The boys parted like a wave, mouths open. Jude leaped before he could think about it. Leaped before he was paralyzed with terror. He armored himself with the spirit of his dad, who'd given everything to rescue Robbie Blakeney—and Jess, who'd braved the sea squall to save her brother.

As he hit its rippled silver surface, the lake closed over his head like a tomb. The water was shockingly, burningly cold. Jude was sure his heart would seize up if fright didn't kill him first.

He fought his way free of it, gasping for air. Getting his bearings, he dived again. He'd seen where Garrick had entered the water. He could visualize the exact spot.

When he came up again, Garrick was in his arms. Between them, he and Monty dragged the unconscious boy to the shore.

Thomas and JJ had rushed down to the shore with their backpacks and were waiting with fleeces and thermals. The boys lifted Garrick onto an impromptu bed of heather and wrapped him in their clothes. Shivering in their boxers, the dry boys worked to keep Jude, Monty, and Garrick warm as Jude performed CPR.

The air ambulance flew in six minutes later. A school rescue party came roaring over the moors just as the paramedics were lifting Garrick onto a stretcher. Jude expected Mr. Vesper to be furious that he and the others had broken the rules and risked their lives, but the master seemed shaken to the core that a boy had almost died on his watch.

Back at Dragon Ridge, he, personally, brought Jude hot

cocoa and saw to it that Jude's sore feet were treated too. He didn't quite apologize, but he did grip Jude's shoulder and say, "There are grown men, soldiers even, who couldn't have done what you did today. As an act of selfless bravery, I've never known its equal. Well done, lad. Well done."

· · ✳ · ·

Garrick spent two nights in the hospital but made a full recovery. He was almost more upset about being suspended from the swim team than he was about his near-death experience. In many ways, he was the same Garrick, just a little more humble, and a lot less arrogant.

For Jude, the most noticeable difference was that he was suddenly and completely left alone—not only by Garrick's gang but by every other mean-spirited prefect, brat, or prankster. He got the feeling that Garrick had put the word out. *Harm Jude and you'll have me to deal with.*

And when term ended with a surprisingly moving prizegiving ceremony, it was Garrick who presented Jude with the Dragon Ridge Medal of Courage Award and told the story of the day Jude had saved his life.

"It was a team effort," Jude told Ms. Flowers afterward. "I couldn't have rescued Garrick without the help of Monty and the other boys. I especially couldn't have done it if I hadn't been inspired by the stories I've read, especially the one about Markus and his wolf. I wouldn't have even known about Markus if you hadn't believed in me and got me liking books."

"Oh, I think you have your sister to thank for that particular spark," the librarian observed with a smile. "I simply added some kindling. Wherever life takes them, you've taught Garrick and Co. a lesson they'll carry with them always: Don't judge a book by its cover."

CHAPTER 27

Storm Tactics

Never in her wildest dreams had Jess imagined that she might one day compete in a transatlantic yacht race, and yet here she was, bracing herself as the north-northeasterly gusted to thirty-five knots. Ahead was a Himalayan mountain range of waves, each steeper and more violent than the last.

Decision time loomed, but Jess was torn between storm tactics.

She could "heave to" on a close reach with the jib jammed to windward. That way, the boat could be "parked" on a safeish line while she retreated below deck. Or she could "run off" before the storm winds, under bare masts, keeping the stern toward the overtaking waves.

Jess made the wrong call. She chose running-off downwind. As the yacht tipped over the next peak and raced down the other side at high speed, she lost control of the steering.

The boat went over, flinging Jess into the ocean. Had she

clipped on her safety line? Yes, she had—but she'd forgotten to use a storm drogue. The special sea anchor would have slowed the boat and prevented the hull from turning side-on to the waves. A reproachful message scrolled across her screen:

Oh no! You did not succeed. Let's try again.

Jess groaned. She hit the Play button on the sailing simulator. Ms. Gregory had installed it on her iPad after Jess confided that (a) she was pining for the ocean, and (b) she wished that Geraldine Rose offered sailing courses.

"Everyone always blames Jude for what happened to our yacht," she'd told the teacher, "but it was *my* fault that we wrecked *You Gotta Friend*. He left the helm to help me. If I'd been a better sailor, it might never have happened."

"My dear girl, how can you say such a thing?" cried Ms. Gregory. "You were two grieving children alone at sea in a deadly storm. You're heroes for coping as well as you did. Now, if it's brushing up your sailing technique you're after, I can help. Sailing simulators are the best. You can design your own boat and work your way through the Royal Yachting Association syllabus. It's as if you're sailing for real, only warmer and drier."

On Jess's bedside table, mysteries had been replaced by a new book: *Sailing a Serious Ocean*. Jess liked to read random pages. Its author, John Kretschmer, had a knack for pithy quotes such as "Fatigue is a stealthy enemy at sea."

As Jess prepared once again to tackle the Atlantic on her iPad, she tried to keep a flexible attitude, as advised by John

Kretschmer. If she capsized, pitchpoled, or fell overboard, she got up and did it again. If she learned one new thing a week, that was progress.

"You're obsessed with that game," remarked Letitia, who sat across from Jess, cross-legged on her bed, reading a tennis biography. "It seems fun, but why do you play it as if your life depends on it?"

"I want to be ready," said Jess.

"Ready for what?"

"Just ready."

"What exactly am I preparing for?" was a question Jess asked herself night after night as she tossed and turned in the darkness.

It was a question without an answer. She only knew that as the end of term drew nearer, the prospect of returning to Blakeney Park filled her with dread.

Don't make us regret taking you in . . .

Jess's hopes of using her hour of internet access a day to investigate the Blakeneys had ended just ten days after she'd started at the Geraldine Rose School for Girls. By then, she'd learned two key things:

1) The Blakeneys did a lot for charity. *So they must be kind*, Jess had thought, scrolling through glossy shots

of Allegra and Clifford attending endless balls and gallery openings in aid of refugees, guide-dog training, and local causes.

2) Oddly, their big hearts weren't large enough to include their own employees. Clifford was being sued by several who claimed they'd been fired after disagreeing with him or falling ill. Overnight, each had found their work sabotaged. Vital documents went missing from their computers. Briefcases, phones, or business credit cards disappeared from their desks or homes, and they were sometimes accused of stealing them. Eventually, each individual was fired for slacking on the job or incompetence.

"Clifford's the sort of man who'd have considered his own father weak for being in a wheelchair," snarked one sacked manager, who'd lost his job after breaking both arms falling off his bicycle.

When the *Daily Gazette* ran a story poking fun at these disgruntled employees, arguing that their claims were hardly likely to be true when everyone knew that the Blakeneys gave millions to worthy causes, an anonymous fired staff member told a rival paper that Clifford specialized in "never getting his hands dirty. He has an enforcer who does his dirty work for him."

A spokesman for Daybreak Media dismissed the comments

as the rantings of an employee "caught red-handed" fiddling her expenses.

The day after Jess discovered the "enforcer" story, Allegra had shown up at her school looking impossibly glamorous. She presented Jess with a new tennis racket and Mrs. Atkins with enough cupcakes for Jess's entire year group.

"I was passing and couldn't resist popping in to see my best girl," she'd cooed at Jess in the head teacher's office.

She lost no time in getting to the real reason for her presence. "Darling, Mrs. Atkins rang me to ask if everything was okay at home. Apparently, you've been doing internet searches on our family. I confess to finding that a teensy bit worrying. Is there anything you'd like to ask me, Jess? Anything on your mind?"

Jess knew that Mrs. Atkins had only acted out of concern, but it was difficult not to feel betrayed. In the future, she'd have to be more careful to cover her tracks. She wondered how Allegra would have responded if she'd asked: *Is it true that your husband uses an enforcer to do his dirty work?*

"I hope you know that Clifford and I only wish the very best for you," Allegra had purred. "That's why we enrolled you here at the finest school in London."

That, at least, Jess could be honest about.

"Oh, I love it here!" she'd responded without hesitation. "The teachers and girls are so lovely. I was only curious about Daybreak Media because I'm considering becoming a journalist when I leave school. While I was reading up on your amazing company, I learned that you and Mr. Blakeney are even more generous than I thought. You help so many people."

"It's kind of you to say so, dear Jess," Allegra had said, preening. "We do what little we can. How marvelous that you're interested in becoming a reporter. Clifford can certainly advise you. But this episode has been a lesson to me. Too much computer time can be unhealthy for a young mind. I've asked Mrs. Atkins to restrict your internet privileges for the time being. I want you to settle in and concentrate on your school-work free from any distractions."

With her Wi-Fi access canceled, Jess's detective efforts had been put on ice for the entire term. Now, just days before the holidays, she still had no idea who had sent money to Gabe, or why the Blakeneys had fostered the children of a groom they barely knew.

She'd begun to wonder if she and Jude had been mistaken in believing that the email in Gabe's cabin was about them. In the nearly four months since their guardian's death, the only hint that anyone might be "hunting" them was the sketchy man in mirror glasses who Jude claimed had been trying to photograph him that day at the ATM in Leverick Bay.

Even Detective Jack Trenton had believed that their guardian's death was an accident, pure and simple. After the twins had told him they suspected foul play, he'd had a toxicology report done on Gabe's remains. That, like the autopsy, had been inconclusive.

As March slipped by, Jess began to fear that she and

Jude had learned as much about their past as they were ever likely to.

The Mystery of Us, as Jess thought of it, *would remain a mystery*.

"You must be over the moon about going home to Blakeney Park," said Flo, using a wire broom to sweep out the greenhouse in the school vegetable garden. "In photos, it looks impossibly grand."

"I'll be over the moon to see my brother and our dog," Jess replied truthfully. She was preparing plant pots for spring seedlings. Gardening duty was compulsory for every girl at Geraldine Rose, and she'd grown to love it. "Sam will go berserk with happiness when he sees us."

"How about the Blakeneys?" asked Flo. "Will you be happy to see them too?"

Jess was saved from replying when Ned "Gruff" Griffiths, the gardener, stuck his head around the door. "Apologies for interruptin', Miss Gray. Any chance I could have a minute of your time?"

Jess was surprised. He'd never previously uttered a word to her. "Uh, sure."

Flo propped the broom against the glass door. "Jess, I'm done, but I can wait for you if you like."

"Thanks, Flo—but don't worry. You go on ahead." After her friend had gone, Jess smiled at the gardener. "How can I help you, Gruff?" she asked, rinsing her hands under the garden tap.

"No, miss, it's t'other way round. I think *I* can help you."

Jess straightened. "I'm not sure I understand."

"Miss, forgive me, I've never been one for social media."

"Okayyy?"

"All that tweeting and retweeting when you could have actual tweeting from real birds. All that 'liking' or blocking. Who cares? As for the Kashardians—I wouldn't know one if I fell over 'em."

"I think it's the Kardashians," said Jess.

"Still wouldn't know 'em."

"I'm the wrong person to ask about social media." Jess took a firm step toward a group creating a tomato bed with their teacher, in case things got any weirder. "I've never used it."

"I'm just trying to explain why I didn't make the connection. I'm the sort who'd rather deadhead roses than watch some lying, blustering politician on the news. Also, you were introduced by your first name."

Jess was getting nervous. In mysteries, seemingly innocuous gardeners often turned out to be serial killers who'd been burying bodies beneath the dahlias for years.

"Gruff, I need to go. I have a meeting with my art teacher."

"I knew your mum and dad," he blurted out.

The ground swayed beneath Jess's feet. She had to sit down on a rickety garden chair before she fainted. "That's impossible."

"I assure you it's not," he said gently. "I apologize if this comes as a shock. I only found out who you were just yesterday when someone brought me seeds in an old newspaper. I recognized your photo on an article about your rags-to-riches story. It mentioned your parents were Jim and Joanna Gray, Robbie Blakeney's groom and carer."

"What of it?" Jess said defensively.

"Miss, in case it's any comfort, I wanted to tell you that, although I only worked with Jim and Joanna for a few months—"

"You worked with them?"

"Yes, I was head gardener at Blakeney Park back in the day. Miss, they were two of the finest people I've ever had the privilege of meeting."

Jess's eyes filled with tears. Since leaving Blakeney Park, she'd been haunted by Caspian's cruel taunts about her mom being a thief and her father a killer driver. To hear someone who'd worked alongside her parents speak about them in the highest terms was overwhelming.

"What were they like? Oh, please, if there's anything you can remember, the smallest detail, I'd love to hear it. Start with my mom. Tell me about her."

He smiled. "A steel magnolia is how I thought of her. Beautiful and always so smiley and kind, but fiercely strong too. She needed to be to stand up to Clifford."

"Clifford? Why? He said he hardly knew my parents."

"To put it bluntly, that's a lie. He knew them well. Unlike Allegra, who rarely left London. Looking back, Clifford probably feels guilty. Joanna was his father's nurse in his later years, and back then, Clifford cared about nothing but money. Your mum was always trying to persuade him to spend more time with his dad and be more patient with him. Fell on deaf ears. He was more interested in buying the latest flashy car or gadget.

"He and your own father were opposites. Jim was a hard worker, down-to-earth, animal-mad, and always laughing. 'Irrepressible,' your mum called him."

"That's what my brother's like," Jess said with a giggle.

"That so? Is he audacious too? That's how I got to know your dad so well—we were partners in crime."

Jess stared at him in horror. "What kind of crime?"

Gruff shook his head. "Forgive me, miss. Poor choice of words. Jim and I teamed up to do something that some would consider dishonest. I don't happen to be among them. There are times when one has to do the wrong thing in order to do the right thing, if you catch my drift."

Jess folded her arms and said coldly, "No, I don't."

"Let me explain. Clifford had a champion racehorse called Sun Queen, stabled at Cheltenham. She won a string of trophies before injury cut short her career. Clifford ordered Jim to take her to the knacker's yard for slaughter. Robbie Blakeney, his father, loved horses as much as your own dad did. He was furious. Tried to talk his son out of it. But not even he could change his son's mind. Clifford said he didn't want the horse in the barn, eating money.

"Jim and I came up with a plan. We moved Sun Queen to a friend's field for three months. She had a nice rest, recovered from her injury, grew out her mane and tail, and Jim worked his horse-whispering magic on her. We renamed her Autumn.

"Luckily, she had a gentle, easygoing nature. With Robbie's help, we brought her back to Blakeney Park as a perfect ride for visitors. Clifford couldn't tell one end of a horse from another, so it's not like he was going to recognize her, and none of the staff had ever seen her in the flesh. Last I heard, she was still there. Worshipped your dad, that horse. Seemed to understand he'd saved her."

Gruff smiled at the memory. "I quit Blakeney Park a month later. Couldn't get along with the foreman. But I never forgot your mum and dad. That's all I wanted to say. They were good people, your folks. Don't let anyone tell you different."

He lifted his coat from a hook outside the greenhouse.

Jess said tentatively, "What about the accident? Do you know anything about that?"

The gardener glanced toward the teacher. "Don't upset yourself thinking about that. What's past is past."

"Please, Gruff. I can handle it. It's so long ago. I just want the truth, that's all."

He returned his coat to the greenhouse hook. "It was after my time, but I heard about it. Terrible tragedy. Accidents happen, but he shouldn't have been driving. Not in wild weather."

"My dad? Why not?"

"Oh, it wasn't your father at the wheel. They were in Robbie's car. It had been specially adapted for his disability. Jim couldn't have driven it if he'd wanted to. It wasn't the old man's fault. A corner of the bridge gave way. Could have happened to anyone. The car went into the river. Jim managed to get them both out and lift Robbie onto the shore, but he was swept away by the current himself. The newspapers made out that Mr. Blakeney died of pneumonia. They didn't want to call it what it was: a broken heart."

"You're saying that Robbie died of a heart attack, not pneumonia?"

"No, miss—I'm saying he blamed himself for the death of the man he considered a son. He was devastated."

"I don't understand. I know that my dad was his employee but—"

"Oh, miss, your father was much more than just a groom to Robbie. Old Mr. Blakeney cared for him like a son. They were best friends. Kindred spirits. Over the years, Robbie had come to hate his wealth. To him, money had only brought misery. When Jim and Joanna came to work at the estate, their love of nature reminded him of life's simple joys. A robin's song. The ancient energy of an oak tree. The innocence of a newborn lamb."

Purposefully, Gruff reached for his coat. He seemed anxious, as if belatedly regretting his candor. "Like I said, I left Blakeney Park a long time ago. No doubt losing his father changed Clifford as it would change anyone. From what I read in that rag, he and Allegra are practically ready for sainthoods now. They rescued you and your brother, didn't they?"

Jess returned to the main building like a sleepwalker. "You're late," scolded Ms. Gregory, jingling the keys to the art room. "I was about to give up on you. Wait—you're very pale. Are you coming down with a cold?"

"I have a headache," said Jess. "Sorry, I was held up. The gardener wanted to explain something to me."

"Gruff? How interesting. I've only ever heard him grumble."

Ms. Gregory unlocked the door to the art room and went over to her desk. She fired up her laptop.

"I thought you might like to know that my art sleuthing finally paid off. In the middle of last night, I remembered where I'd seen a painting similar to that little oil of yours. It was in the Dulwich Picture Gallery. The artist is Amelia Starr. The way you can tell for sure is that she never signs her name, just paints a little star. Look, here's her website."

Ms. Gregory read aloud: "'Originally from Tasmania, Amelia has worked all over the world. The Scottish Islands, Ireland, Nantucket in the US . . .'"

Jess stared in wonder as Amelia Starr's gallery unfolded on the screen before her. Most of her paintings were seascapes. Otters paddling in the shallows. Seabirds wheeling over cliffs. A lighthouse in a storm.

"Still doesn't tell us where your mum bought the painting," said Ms. Gregory, "but it's a start. From here, you can try to find out more. It may not be easy. From the little I've learned, Amelia's become a recluse in recent years."

"Where does she live now?" asked Jess.

"I'm still working on that."

"Are there any photos of her?"

"I've only found one. Going on her age, this was taken ten or more years ago."

Ms. Gregory clicked on Amelia's biography, and the picture sharpened into focus.

Jess blinked.

It was the woman she'd seen watching her the week she'd started at Geraldine Rose. The woman from the leafy London square.

CHAPTER 28

Spies and Lies

The Dragon Ridge Medal of Courage earned Jude a helicopter ride back to Blakeney Park for the holidays, sparing him a repeat of the grim drive to Wales. All Clifford had asked for in return was a shot of Jude with the trophy for Saturday's *Daily Gazette*. Jude had happily agreed. Anything was better than a repeat of the motion sickness episode.

The best part about the flight was that Jess was on it too. The pilot, who was based in London, had collected her earlier that morning before setting off for Dragon Ridge.

Jude, who'd counted the hours until he and his twin were reunited, found himself strangely shy when he stepped into the helicopter. To begin with, Jess was just as tongue-tied. But it didn't take long for them to start teasing each other again.

"Did the drill instructors force you to play rugby and pump iron?" Jess asked Jude when they hugged. She squeezed his bicep and raised an eyebrow.

"Nah, I just built a library," he said with a grin. "I have so much to tell you, sis. Believe it or not, you and Ms. Flowers—she's the world's coolest librarian—finally got me reading!"

"She *must* be the world's coolest librarian if she's got you liking books," said Jess, laughing. "Oh, Jude, I've missed you so much. I can't wait to hear your news and to tell you mine. I can feather a mainsail and trim the jib in my sleep now! My art teacher got me into e-sailing!"

They smiled almost all the way back to Gloucestershire.

It was the pilot who brought them crashing down to earth. Not with an actual crash, but with a brusque remark as they zoomed across the River Severn: "The old man must be spinning in his grave."

Jess exchanged glances with Jude. The dragonfly shadow of the helicopter shivered over the coppery water and crossed the northern boundary of Blakeney Park.

"Why would Robbie be spinning in his grave?" Jess said into her headset.

"Haven't you seen the newspaper reports?" growled the pilot, who was temporarily filling in for the Blakeneys' regular man. "The ancient forest beneath us is being flogged off to developers. If the sale goes ahead on May third, Robbie Blakeney's paradise will be paved over with apartments and a parking lot."

The helicopter zoomed so low over the forest that the tree-tops swished like palms in a cyclone.

"I had the privilege of flying him a couple of times," said

the pilot. "A true gent. He understood that some things are more valuable than gold."

Jude glimpsed a ribbon of silver through the leaves. Something quivered near the inlet that cut into the forest. He tried to focus on it, but the chopper had turned and was approaching the golden house before he could be sure that he'd seen what he thought he had.

Jess gave her brother a questioning look, as if to say: "What's the pilot going on about? Who's paving over paradise?"

"Tell you later," Jude mouthed back.

It was surreal landing at Blakeney Park after everything they'd been through. On the one hand, it seemed as if mere days had passed since they'd left under a cloud after the fight with Caspian and his parents. On the other, so much had happened.

As the helicopter rocked to a standstill, the twins' eyes met. The journey had reconnected them. Whatever fate had in store for them from now on, they'd face it together.

For weeks, Jude had promised himself that the first thing he'd do once he got back to Blakeney Park was tear down to the kennels with Jess to cuddle Sam.

That plan went out the window when Clifford, Allegra, and Caspian greeted the twins like long-lost friends beneath the hallway chandelier.

Assembled behind them stood a crescent of beaming staff. Only Lizette was missing. Later, the twins learned that the au pair had been "let go" after an undisclosed "incident."

"She probably got fed up with Caspian ordering her around as if she were his personal assistant," Jess said to Jude.

She wondered again if the newspaper story about the Blakeneys' shady "enforcer" was true. Could such a character exist? Had Lizette complained to Allegra about Caspian, then suddenly found herself being accused of laziness, or "mislaying" something belonging to mother or son?

Much to the twins' disappointment, there was no time to see Sam before lunch. They barely had a minute to freshen up before they were ushered into the main dining room. There, too, the Blakeneys were niceness personified.

Caspian had had a major attitude adjustment. He smiled and nodded and even congratulated them both on their awards: Jude on his Dragon Ridge medal, and Jess on her art and English prizes.

"I almost preferred it when he was behaving like a beast," Jess whispered to Jude when they had thirty seconds to themselves between courses. "What have they done with the real Caspian?"

After a maddeningly slow lunch, the family moved to the drawing room for coffee and cake. Some visitors arrived and talked about the media world and golf until Jude thought his head might explode.

Even after the visitors left, the twins weren't free because

Allegra insisted on personally showing Jude his new room. "It's finally ready. Sorry it took so long, Jude. I hope it meets with your approval."

The room was hard to fault. It was the ideal teenage den, as envisioned by an expensive interior designer. Jude felt bad for wishing he could be in the stable room instead. He'd been looking forward to being within breathing distance of Autumn again.

"It's amazing! Thank you so much," said Jude with what he hoped was the right degree of enthusiasm.

Jess was happy at first because their rooms were linked by a connecting door, but it turned out that the key was missing.

"I'm sure it'll show up," Allegra said, in the tone of someone aiming to make quite sure it never would.

Jude was unable to contain himself any longer. "Please may we be excused to go and see Sam?"

Allegra seemed perplexed. "Who's Sam?"

Jess struggled to conceal her irritation. After all this time, how could the woman not know the name of their Swiss shepherd?

"Sam's our dog."

"Ah, the dog." Guilt flitted across Allegra's flawless face.

Jess paled. "What's wrong?"

"You can explain, can't you, darling?" Allegra said to Clifford, who'd entered the room like a dark star in his thousand-dollar suit. "About the dog?"

"What dog? Oh, *that* dog. Couldn't be helped, I'm afraid. Slipped his lead and got in with the sheep. Cost us a king's ransom in vet's bills getting a lamb stitched up. We couldn't have a dangerous animal like that around the farm. Some of our rams are worth their weight in gold."

Jude felt a freezing rage seep into his bones. "I don't believe it. Sam has never wriggled out of his collar, not once in his whole life. And he's not a killer. There were kittens and chickens around the diner and he never touched them. Where is he?" His voice rose. "What have you done to our dog?"

"When did this happen, Mr. Blakeney?" asked Jess, as softly as if she were asking about the weather.

Had Clifford known her better, he'd have been worried.

"Not long after you left," snapped Allegra. "Eddie dealt with it. Obviously, we didn't want to distract you from your schoolwork by telling you we'd been forced to send Sam to the local shelter. The good news is, he was adopted within days and has gone to a good home. If you love him, you'll be happy that he's happy. It's a win-win situation."

"How is it a win-win for me and my sister?" demanded Jude with cold fury. "Sam's our family. Our *only* family."

"ENOUGH!" Clifford shook slightly, as if he were struggling to control his own temper. "He's a dog. We'll get you another someday. For now, I'll have no more of this fuss."

"We can't stay here till we're eighteen," Jess ranted to Jude the next morning. "We'll go nuts. These people are like pantomime villains come to life."

The twins were at the stables, stroking Autumn. Neither of them had slept. They were too devastated and too angry. Walking down to the stables, they'd taken a detour to Sam's former kennel, hoping that the Blakeneys had relented overnight and sent Eddie to retrieve their dog from his new home. But he wasn't there. A vicious young rottweiler had taken his place.

Jude had been so enraged that Jess had done everything she could to distract him. She'd told him all about Letitia and the painting. Now, as they bonded with Autumn in the stables, she made him laugh with the story about Gruff and their father conspiring to defy Clifford by saving the racehorse from the slaughterhouse.

"I can't believe they rebranded Sun Queen the ex-racehorse as Autumn, a beginner's ride," Jude said with a grin. "That's hilarious. If Clifford can't even recognize his own racehorse, he's not as smart as he thinks he is. Neither is Allegra. Our parents stood up to them. We can too. We just have to figure out a plan."

The horse in the next stall shifted. A groom they didn't recognize ducked under its neck and grinned at them. "Don't mind me. Just checking for ticks."

"Everywhere we turn at Blakeney Park, there are spies and lies," despaired Jess as the twins walked off up the lane ten minutes later, anxious about how much the man had overheard. "I'm starting to believe that our mom fled this place for a reason. Not because she was grieving, or had stolen Allegra's ruby ring, but because she was afraid. Jude, what are we going to do? Without money, where do we run to?"

"Why did they even foster us?" Jude said. "That's what I don't understand. They've never wanted us here. Do you think they felt guilty about falsely accusing our mother of theft or something—?"

Right then, an SUV with blacked-out windows came hurtling around the bend, its engine purring so quietly that the twins only just had time to flatten themselves against a yew hedge.

As it whipped by, all the hairs stood up on Jess's neck. There was no apparent cause. It's not as if she could see anyone in the vehicle.

The twins were almost back at the house when the post van came rattling down the lane. That, too, almost mowed them down.

The postman pulled up beside the SUV and jumped out. "Sorry, kids," he said as they walked up. "I didn't mean to give you a fright. My fault for driving too fast. An overturned tractor held me up for ages, and now I'm running behind."

He took a stack of mail from a bag. "Would you mind calling Terence, the valet?"

Jess was about to answer when she spotted the Geraldine Rose School for Girls logo on the top letter. She said sweetly, "We'll take the post."

"I have strict instructions to only hand it to Terence or Allegra."

"We'll take it to Allegra. No problem at all."

The postman looked at his watch. "I s'pose that's okay. Mind you carry it directly to Her Majesty."

"Oh, you can count on it," said Jess, crossing her fingers behind her back.

The minute the post van roared away, she slipped the Geraldine Rose letter into her pocket. If, as she suspected, it was her school report, she didn't want any lectures on trying harder from Allegra.

Jude was flicking through the rest of the mail. "Hey, Jess, this one's for us. And here's another that looks the same, only addressed to the Blakeneys."

He handed her a blue envelope with a curlew stamp on the front.

Jess recalled seeing a similar letter soon after they'd arrived in England. With a glance at the house, she ripped open the envelope addressed to her and her brother and read aloud:

DEAR JESS AND JUDE,

I HOPE THIS FINDS YOU IN THE BEST OF SPIRITS AND HEALTH. THIS IS THE LAST TIME I WILL WRITE IN HOPE OF HEARING FROM YOU. I UNDERSTAND THAT YOUR SUPERB NEW SCHOOLS AND WONDERFUL NEW LIFE AT BLAKENEY PARK MUST BE KEEPING YOU BUSY. FORGIVE ME IF MY CORRESPONDENCE IS UNWELCOME. AS YOUR GODMOTHER, I WOULD SO LOVE

TO MEET YOU, EVEN IF IT'S ONLY ONCE. YOUR MOTHER
ENTRUSTED ME—

"How dare you!" Allegra swooped on Jess and snatched away the letter. "How dare you read my private mail, you monstrous child."

Terence, the valet, grabbed the other letters, including the second blue envelope, with a poisonous look at Jude.

"Why am *I* the monstrous one?" cried Jess. "We have a godmother we didn't even know about who's been desperately wanting to meet us. Why have you been keeping her a secret? Please give us that letter. It's addressed to me and my brother."

"I refuse to discuss this in the driveway like a common peasant," snarled Allegra, swiveling on her Jimmy Choos and stalking up the steps into the house.

The twins ran after her. There was a brief tussle in the hall with Terence, who tried to prevent them from following Allegra into the drawing room. By the time they'd wriggled past him, it was too late. The final lines of the unread letters were being swallowed up by flames.

Jess watched their only link to their godmother, to hope, burn to ash in the fireplace. Her eyes were dry. "Why would you stop us seeing our godmother? She says she's written many times before. Where are the other letters? What's her name?"

When Allegra set down the poker, her face had resumed the mask she'd adopted in the Virgin Island hospital: warm, sympathetic, and beguiling. With the envelopes disposed of, she was composed again. "My dear children—"

"We're *not* your dear children," Jude said angrily.

"Oh, but you are. I can't tell you how sorry I am about this. It was a shock, that's all, seeing you reading the deranged musings of a woman claiming to be your godmother. You're right. She has written before. Each letter more concerning than the last."

Jess glared at her. "What are you talking about?"

"If you'll only allow me to explain. As you can imagine, my husband's high profile in the media business means he's attracted many enemies over the years. Add in wealth and, sad to say, the number of crazies increases exponentially. Death threats. Ransom demands. You name it, we get it. I regret to say that, thanks to your newfound fame and the fact that you're living at Blakeney Park now, you've become the subject of loony letters too."

"I don't believe you," said Jude. "Why would someone pretend to be our godmother? She didn't threaten us. She just asked to meet us."

"Don't believe me?" Allegra opened a drawer in a writing desk. "I wouldn't normally show this to a child, but if you need proof of what our security have to deal with on a daily basis, here it is."

She handed the twins a printout of an email from Scotland Yard, thanking Clifford's head of security for his help with foiling a kidnap threat against Caspian.

"*That's* why we sent a helicopter to fetch Caspian from school and another to fetch both of you. We were worried about you traveling by road until this maniac was arrested."

It was a disturbing revelation and went some way to explaining Caspian's subdued manner at lunch the previous day. But Jess wasn't about to let go of the issue of their godmother.

"But *who* is she?" Jess demanded. "Why won't you tell us?"

Allegra sighed. "As I explained, she's not your godmother. She's simply a batty old crone—"

"That's a big fat lie," said Jess. "And I don't believe our mother stole your ring either. I bet if I went upstairs right now, it would be sitting in your jewelry box or your husband's safe. You lied to us about our dad too. He wasn't driving the night of the accident. Robbie was. Our dad saved his life and lost his own in the process. Your old gardener told me that Robbie and our father were best friends. He said that Robbie died of a broken heart."

Allegra was looking at Jess as if she were speaking Latin. "I—we—uh—what gardener? There have been so many."

Somehow Clifford materialized by her side. "Don't distress yourself, darling. I'll deal with this. These children are out of control. I'll speak to Mr. Riker. We may have to move to plan B."

After that, things had escalated rapidly. The twins were sent to their rooms and told to stay there until further notice. A tray of leftovers was sent up at 8 p.m.

At 10:20 p.m., just as Jess was dozing off, there was a knock at the door. Astrid let herself in.

"You need to put on some warm clothes and come with me, Jess," she said. "I hear that you and your brother have been very hurtful to poor Allegra. Clifford's very upset with you. He's decided that a night in the stable accommodation might make you both reflect on your behavior and realize how fortunate you are."

She flipped open Jess's school trunk, which had not yet been unpacked, and pulled out leggings, socks, a sweater, and a rain jacket. "These will do. I'll meet you in the corridor in five minutes. If there's anything else you think you might need, bring it in your backpack."

Once dressed, Jess ventured out with trepidation. Astrid was tapping a message into her phone. She favored Jess with a brilliant smile and took her arm, just as Jude, accompanied by a short man in a black Stetson, emerged scowling from his own room.

Neither twin objected to being marched down to the barn. They were relieved to be out of the house. It was only when Astrid unlocked the door to the windowless storeroom that they started to feel alarmed. Why weren't they being put into the stable bedroom? The storeroom was perishingly cold.

"I'd advise you to think long and hard about how rude and unpleasant you've been to a family who have only ever shown you kindness," said Astrid. "If you're genuinely sorry in the morning, you'll be out in time for breakfast. If you're not, Mr. Riker here will have to have a chat with you."

The man in the Stetson gave a barely perceptible nod, then

turned away without a word. He'd been silent since they had left the house.

In the split second before the door slammed shut behind him, Riker took off his hat. His shadow was thrown into sharp relief on the opposite wall. Jess bit back a scream as his silhouette loomed large on the limewashed plasterboard.

With a dungeon-like screech, the key turned in the lock.

CHAPTER 29

Water Rats

"It's him."

Jess was shaking as if she had hypothermia. "Jude, it's him. The man I saw behind the sail at the boatyard in Tortola. The one who was fighting with Gabe. I'd recognize that silhouette anywhere. As soon as I saw Mr. Riker without his hat, I remembered his spiky hair."

Wary of eavesdroppers, Jude steered his sister away from the door and sat her down on a sack of horse feed. Ripping open a box of sodas, he made her sip one to quell her nerves.

He didn't ask how she was so sure when she'd only ever seen the man once, through a dinghy sail, the previous November. He believed her.

The soda revived Jess in double-quick time, and she began to update Jude on her detective work in London.

"The fact that Allegra showed up in person to cancel my Wi-Fi privileges just twenty-four hours after I found that story online about their 'enforcer' tells me that I was potentially onto something huge."

"You think Mr. Riker and their enforcer are one and the same person?" asked Jude. "That maybe he travels the world doing the Blakeneys' dirty work?"

"It's a stretch, but it's not impossible. Let's suppose it's true. If an employee takes too much sick leave or starts asking difficult questions about the business, Mr. Riker flies in like a dark knight and manufactures false evidence about them slacking on the job or stealing company stuff. That way, it's much easier for Clifford to fire them. To me, a man capable of being so cruel wouldn't think twice about tracking down Gabe or paying somebody to put a tranquilizer in his drink."

"That's the part I'm having trouble with," Jude told her. "Where does Gabe fit into the picture? He was so easygoing. Everyone liked him. Why would the Blakeneys want to harm a shipwright from a backwoods Florida boatyard? I don't get the connection."

"What if *we're* the connection?" said Jess. "Remember the email we found in Gabe's cabin? 'A long time ago, you promised that you'd go to the ends of the earth to keep them safe. Circumstances have changed, and I'm afraid that is now necessary.'"

Jude was impressed that his sister remembered the words by heart.

Jess paced the storeroom as she tried to piece together the clues. "We know that our mom left Blakeney Park in a rush within days of Robbie Blakeney's death. She must have been in pieces losing both Dad and her dear friend. It would have been understandable if she'd wanted to escape the memories by returning to New Zealand or going to stay with a friend. Perhaps even our godmother, if she exists."

"She does," said Jude. "Allegra was lying, I'm sure of it . . . Go on."

"Well, Mom didn't do anything you'd think she'd do if she was grieving and expecting twins. She crossed an ocean to the US, took a Greyhound bus to the middle of nowhere, and pitched up in Bantry Creek in a raging hurricane with only the clothes on her back. No suitcase. No identity papers. A made-up name. Nothing but the little oil painting and that horseshoe."

"Probably Autumn's," said Jude. "And now we're back at the estate where everything started, and we still don't know what Mom was running from. When we first got to Blakeney Park, I thought we'd be safe. I thought that if anyone really was hunting us, the guards, dogs, and razor wire would keep the bad people out. But what if they're in here with us? What if the Blakeneys brought us here so they could lock us up and *control* us? What if they think we know some secret they're trying to hide? We don't, but maybe they're scared that we do."

Jess took another swallow of soda. "Jude, I think you're onto something. It could be that, before he died, Robbie Blakeney told our mother about some scandal involving the family or Daybreak Media. It wouldn't surprise me if Clifford's done something criminally corrupt. Something that would ruin the Blakeneys if it ever got out. Maybe Clifford discovered Mom knew about it and threatened her life or got his enforcer to do it."

She looked anxiously at her brother. "Jude, what do you reckon Clifford meant about moving to plan B?"

"I guess they're going to send us to some hideous orphanage after all, escorted by Mr. Riker. Or maybe they're planning to get rid of us in some other way. Personally, I really don't think we should hang around to find out."

Jess gave a sad laugh. "What choice do we have? We're in a locked room, surrounded by guards, dogs, and razor wire, as you just mentioned."

Jude hopped onto a chair and took a tin down from a high shelf. He rattled it. "Seth showed me where he stashed his spare key. He got locked in the storeroom by mistake once and didn't want it happening to me."

"Great start!" cried his sister. "Now, how do we get past security, and where do we go if we do manage to escape? If we don't catch pneumonia in this room and die in the meantime. Maybe that's plan B: Turn the twins to icicles."

Rubbing the goose bumps on her arms, Jess went over to a heap of laundered horse blankets. As she rummaged through it, the pile toppled over, exposing a shiny cardboard box.

"Jude, look!"

Her brother rushed over. He flung open the box. Inside was a military-type drone. Unlike Caspian's, this was no toy.

Jude gave a low whistle. "So Caspian *was* telling the truth when he said that it wasn't his drone that frightened Tempest that day she threw you. Looking at this one, I'm ninety-nine percent sure that the drone that buzzed you was army-green and silver, like this one. Whoever owns it intended to hurt you that day. We both know you could have been killed."

Jess shuddered at the memory. "Jude, do you think Mr. Riker could have been behind the drone attack too?"

Jude was tense, poised for flight. "I don't think we should wait around to find out. Jess, these people aren't playing games. We need to get out of here."

"I agree," said Jess. "The Blakeneys want us out of the picture, dead or alive. Jude, what about the river? If we could make it there without being devoured by the dogs, maybe we could swim across and escape through the fields."

"Yeah, but we'd die of hypothermia along the way. It's cold enough in here." He grabbed a rug and wrapped it around Jess's shoulders. "I have a better idea. How about we try calling in that favor from Sirius. Remember the hunt sab? We trusted him once, and it worked out pretty well. We saved those foxes. Maybe this time, Sirius will save us."

"Genius plan," Jess said wryly. "Or it would be if we had the faintest idea how to locate a stranger we met in the woods in January on a pitch-dark night in March."

As she spoke, she had a light bulb moment. "Jude, I don't suppose you still have Sirius's map."

Jude grinned. He hopped up. Borrowing a hoof pick from

a grooming kit, he used it to lever a crack in the plasterboard wall. The map was in the cavity beneath. "Before I went to Dragon Ridge, I hid this. I was afraid it might get confiscated."

He retrieved the map and spread it out on the floor. "You know how I told you that Ms. Flowers emailed the Water Rats about the forest development? Well, while she was trying to track down a contact, she found a Cornish blog with a map like this one. Apparently, the Water Rats use a water-taxi system for their volunteers."

He pointed at the symbols dotted along the River Severn.

"See these pen marks? The Water Rats restore old boats and leave them moored in different places. One volunteer will take a kayak upriver to a tree protest, say, and someone else will drive a fishing boat somewhere else. Basically, if we can get to the river and find this boat marked right here, we have a chance of escape."

"Riding bareback isn't all it's cracked up to be in the movies," said Jess, gritting her teeth as Autumn's bony spine jutted through the saddle pad and bumped against a nerve in her coccyx. She leaned forward and clung more tightly to Jude's waist.

"Shhh, we're almost there."

At night, the atmosphere in the forest was more cemetery

than cathedral. Blue mist hung between the trees. The ghost wings of a fleeting owl startled Autumn. She shied and almost threw them. To be on the safe side, the twins dismounted.

Before they could get their bearings, an engine revved. A searchlight strobed the trees. Jude dropped Autumn's lead rope in fright. The mare wheeled around with a whinny and was gone.

"Stop where you are!" ordered a guard over a megaphone.

"Run, Jess!" yelled Jude.

They sprinted into the undergrowth but couldn't keep up the pace. Jude's feet were still recovering from the Explorer's Challenge, and Jess was unfit after spending too many afternoons e-sailing on her iPad.

Soon, a stitch skewered her side.

"Release the dogs!" someone shouted in the distance.

"How much farther?" Jess whispered between gasps.

"It's around here, I think."

Panting and wheezing, the twins slithered down a steep bank to the water's edge. Jess's heart leaped with hope when she saw the kayak. The rottweilers were baying somewhere behind them, invisible in the darkness.

"Where are the oars?" groaned Jude, looking around frantically. "What use is a kayak without oars?"

Before he could take another step, a man materialized out of the shadows and seized Jude's arms, twisting them behind his back. A young woman in a scarf rushed down the bank and barred Jess's escape route with an oar. "Identify yourselves."

Terror ripped through Jess. She was torn between saving Jude and flinging herself into the water to try to swim for help. At the last second, she glimpsed the woman's sweatshirt logo: KEEP THE SEA PLASTIC FREE.

"You're Water Rats, not guards," she cried with relief. "We're looking for Sirius. We need his help to get to our godmother."

The man regarded her with extreme suspicion. "How do you know Sirius?"

The woman flicked on her flashlight. "Blake, these must be the kids who helped with the foxes. Thanks to them, the vixen has six healthy cubs."

"That's ace for the foxes, but what's with the midnight flit? If we're caught aiding and abetting two runaways, it'll stir up a whole hornet's nest of trouble for us."

Blake released Jude. "Sorry, kid, but if you've had a row with your new foster parents, the best we can do is call social services and ask them to check on you. Olive, let's go before we're shot or arrested by the Blakeneys' guards."

"You're going to abandon us after we risked our necks to help Sirius?" accused Jude. "He promised he'd be there for us if we ever needed help—and now we do!"

He pulled the map from his pocket. "Sirius gave us his word that if we could get to his narrowboat, right here"—he put a finger on the X—"he'd return the favor."

Jess was a nervous wreck, watching the guards' powerful searchlights rake the trees. The dogs sounded frighteningly close now.

"I don't like this," the man said stubbornly. "The last thing we need is the law breathing down our necks. We'll help you call social services, kids, but that's as far as it goes."

"Blake, have you forgotten the Water Rats code of honor?" demanded Olive. "I'll take the twins to Sirius, even if I have to row."

Suddenly, a rottweiler bounded onto the bank—Jess recognized it as Gnasher, the security guards' biggest dog. Blake now had two choices: abandon the children to a grisly fate, or save them. He flew into action.

"We're going to need a bigger boat!" he shouted to Olive and the twins. "Follow me!"

It was nearly too late. As Jude scrambled into a cleverly concealed RIBCRAFT, stashed three hundred feet away beneath a willow—Gnasher sprang at him, ripping his jacket sleeve. Olive wrenched him to safety as Blake pressed the Start button and eased the boat into gear.

Had the engine on the camouflaged boat been any more powerful, and had the dogs not been baying so hysterically, the guards would have heard it.

But by the time the men reached the river, the twins and their rescuers were gone. The RIBCRAFT left barely a ripple in its wake. All that remained was a circling otter.

CHAPTER 30

Firebird

Whenever Jess thought back to the planet-aligning miracles of that night, she saw them in numbers: *one* ex-racehorse, *two* grumpy Water Rats, *two* stars, and *one Firebird* had helped the twins escape *two* rottweilers, *three* menacing guards, *one* apoplectic enforcer, *one* hapless police constable, and a *trio* of livid Blakeneys.

She wasn't there to witness the grimacing and wailing of the Blakeney Park mob, obviously. Nor did she have a psychic hotline into the local police station. She had no clue how many constables were summoned to the house, or whether they were hapless or as sharp as Detective Jack Trenton.

It made no difference. Forever afterward, that's how Jess would picture them all, like amateur actors who'd forgotten their lines.

The first star was Sirius.

Blake, the RIBCRAFT owner, drove the twins many nautical miles along the River Severn without complaint. But when it emerged that the *X* on Sirius's map marked an area where about a hundred boats were anchored in near darkness, he lost his cool. "What do you mean, you've no idea what his boat's called?"

In the nick of time, Jess recalled Sirius telling them that the clue to the narrowboat's name was his own.

Minutes later, they found his narrowboat, *Brightest Star*—Sirius being the brightest star in the night sky. By now, it was 2 a.m. Their dreadlocked friend was remarkably sanguine about being woken from a dead sleep and asked to repay a fox-saving favor.

Once the twins had explained their dilemma, he set about preparing them a feast of veggie sausages, onions, and ketchup on white bread.

It was Sirius who solved a puzzle that had defeated Jess's art-sleuth teacher, Ms. Gregory. Willa, his Jack Russell, lent a helping paw.

Meeting Willa reminded the twins that their own dog had been stolen from them. There were tears as they told Sirius about the heartless Blakeneys sending Sam to a shelter.

"As soon as we're settled somewhere, we're going to track down his new owners and beg them to let us have him back," Jude said.

"What a family of charmers those Blakeneys have turned out to be," Sirius said, grimacing. "That makes me even more determined to help you. I'll put the word out in case anyone hears of a recently adopted Swiss shepherd. Do you have a photo of him?"

"I have a painting." Jess pulled a padded folder out of her backpack. "My art teacher says that if you visualize your dreams in a picture, they might come true. She calls them 'wish fulfillment' paintings. That's what this is. I copied the oil painting our mom left us. The orginal's at my boarding school because I thought I'd be returning after the holidays. I've added in me and Jude on the beach with Sam, our dog."

"Who's that at the window?"

"I'm not sure," said Jess, feeling a pang. "Maybe our godmother. We think we have one, but we're not sure."

"You're very gifted, you can be sure about that." Sirius took the painting and held it up to the lamp. "Hey—I know that cove."

"Everyone knows that cove," Jess said resignedly. "Don't tell me. It's the Isle of Arran. No, it's Northumberland or Norway. Everyone thinks they've seen it before."

"Maybe so, but I've actually been there. I anchored in that bay many times when I was volunteering on a seabird project on that coastline. See that seal-shaped rock? I've dived off it. And there's the viewing point where I watched a pod of dolphins jump at sunset. I remember the white cottage too. Its name stuck in my head: Hope Flies."

"Hope Flies?" Jess gasped. "Did you say 'Hope Flies'? Oh, my gosh, Jude—is it really possible? It can't be a coincidence, surely?"

Jude had already made the leap. "The reference on Gabe's bank statement—HOPEFLI? Short for HOPE FLIES. But how? Why? I don't understand."

Sirius was studying Jess's painting. "What's this mark? A star?"

"I copied it from the original," said Jess. "The star's actually the artist's signature. Her name's Amelia Starr."

Jude said impatiently, "Sorry to interrupt, guys. This is riveting and all, but I can't wait a second longer. Where is this bay and how do we get there?"

Sirius laughed. "Apologies, Jude. I got carried away reminiscing. I'm ninety-nine percent sure it's Bluey's Cove in West Cork . . . Ireland."

"No!"

"Yes," insisted Sirius. "I can even show you the chart."

Jude pulled a scrap of blue paper from his pocket. "After Allegra burned our godmother's letter, I found this on the rug. It only has one word on it, but I kept it in case it was a clue."

He handed it to Jess. It was charred at the edges, but there was no mistaking the word in bold, clear print: *BLUEY'S.*

"Be warned, it can get pretty hairy out there," Sirius said as he led the twins aboard *Firebird*, a thirty-seven-foot Moody yacht, shortly before dawn the next day.

"Once you've negotiated the shipping lanes and tides of the Bristol Channel, you'll be dealing with the Atlantic swell. On the Irish Sea, the southwesterly feels gale force even when it isn't. I'm praying that the *Daily Gazette* didn't exaggerate your sailing skills. The ones you had prior to crashing your yacht, that is! I wouldn't want to be responsible for two twelve-year-olds capsizing on the crossing like those tragic Fastnet Race sailors who got caught in a massive storm."

"We're not going to capsize," said Jude, with more confidence than he felt. "But are you sure we're not going to get *you* into trouble? Isn't this technically stealing?"

Sirius laughed. "More like poetic justice. In Russian folk tales, the firebird steals golden apples or pearls from the rich in order to help the poor. Think of it as a metaphor. I've been caretaking *Firebird* for five years for a wealthy man who sails her once or twice a year with his wealthy friends. Last year, he didn't visit her at all. To me, yachts are like wild horses. Every now and then, they need to run free on the prairie."

He tossed a dry pack onto the deck. "Salopettes, extra thermals, gloves, hats, and enough supplies for three days. Weather permitting, that's how long your voyage will take."

"Sirius, you've thought of everything," Jess said in amazement as she unpacked hot chocolate, frozen pizza, pasta, soup, cheese, and ginger cookies in the galley.

He shrugged. "You've had a rough time. I thought you might need a few treats. Now remember, it can get Siberian real fast out there. Keep warm and drink plenty of hot fluids. Rest when you can."

"Sirius, we're going to owe you forever for what you've done for us," Jude told him, as the twins prepared to cast off.

"Call it even. If you're not back from Ireland in a week, I'll send a friend to pick up *Firebird*. Hope things work out with your godmother. You're good kids. You deserve a home like the one in Jess's painting, with a dog waiting on the shore."

· • ✳ • ·

The twins took to the ocean as if they'd never left it. As if the yacht and the sea were family. They felt as free as dolphins.

Jude took the helm. Jess raised the headsail and checked the lines. Once they were underway, she took up her favorite position at the starboard shroud, breathing in deep as the waves turned from pink to indigo, then dove-gray, steel-green, and ultramarine. The salt spray stung her cheeks and brought out the roses in them.

Jude, guiding *Firebird* as if she were an extension of himself, felt whole again.

Much later, a storm blew in out of nowhere. Violent crosswinds and a turbulent sea pulled *Firebird* beam-on—sideways—to the waves. A mini tsunami sloshed across the deck.

There was one adrenaline-fueled moment when the angle at which the boat could stay upright without capsizing—the angle of vanishing stability—became vanishingly small. *Firebird* heeled but somehow righted herself.

Throughout, the twins worked as a seamless team. "Shall we run off or heave to?" yelled Jess, battling to stay upright on the slippery deck.

"Your call," shouted Jude from the helm.

Jess decided. "Let's heave to and ride out the weather."

After she'd trimmed the main, Jude turned the bow of the boat through the wind to back the headsail. Quick as he could, he lashed the helm while Jess deployed the sea anchor. Then they ducked into the living quarters for a much-needed rest.

Once they'd peeled off their wet salopettes, the twins curled up on a squashy seat, warming their bellies with hot chocolate and toasting their toes on the heater.

It was only then that Jess remembered the school letter in her pocket.

She tore it open, expecting to see her school report. Instead, she found a note to Allegra Blakeney, asking her to pass the enclosed letter to "Jess and Jude Gray" and apologizing that it hadn't been found sooner. It had been discovered beneath the bedside table in Jess's boardinghouse room.

In a flash, Jess realized that this must be the secret document that had been taped to the back of her mom's painting. It must have fallen out when the picture broke. Written on the yellowing envelope were five words the twins would never forget:

Letter to My Beloved Children

With shaking fingers, Jess took out three thin pieces of paper inside and began to read.

Dearest Jess and Jude,

If you're reading this letter, I am no longer with you. It's too much to hope that my passing brings you no pain. I know how lost and heartbroken I was and am without your father, and I wish I was there to wrap you in my arms. As your mum, I wish I could spare you all suffering always. But that's not how life works. Perhaps that's as it should be. Adversity teaches empathy, and with empathy comes compassion. When those qualities are absent in a person, it can lead to the sort of situation I'm about to outline in this letter.

I'm painfully aware that if your dad and I are gone, your lives will not be easy, but I have taken care to ensure that some of the best people I've ever known are watching over you. They will do everything in their power to protect you, guide you, and equip you with the necessary skills and qualities you will need if you ever cross paths with the powerful forces I am about to describe. If all else fails, trust in your own moral compass. If you're anything like your father, it will see you through.

I wish you could have known your dad. Jim was courageous, humble, and always laughing. Most of all, he was kind. I think that's why our employer, Mr. Robert Blakeney, was so fond of him. They shared the same values. Within months of us moving to Blakeney Park in Gloucestershire, England, where Jim was head groom and I was a personal assistant and, later, carer to Robbie, the men were best friends.

You need to know that the accident that took the lives of Robbie and your dad was just that—an accident. Robbie was driving, but it was not his fault. If anyone was to blame, it was the council for not repairing the bridge that collapsed. Jim jumped into the raging river and managed to save Robbie, losing his own life in the process. In truth, I think Robbie wished he hadn't. He loved Jim like a son and blamed himself for your dad's death.

Robbie passed away a week after the accident. The doctors put it down to pneumonia. I believe he died of a broken heart.

It's hard to explain how devastating it was to lose the two men I cared about most in the space of a week. Days later, as I reeled from these terrible blows, a nurse confirmed what I suspected: that I was pregnant. With twins! In the midst of such profound sorrow, the joy and hope of that news lifted me like nothing else. It felt miraculous.

The first person I rang was my own best friend—my cousin Amelia Starr. She lives by the sea in Ireland. I asked her to be your godmother. She has always been my safe harbor, and I knew that she'd be yours too.

The following day, I was tidying away some of Robbie's effects in his study when I came across his will and testament. He had recently altered it, leaving Blakeney Park—every blade of grass, tree, horse, and painting—to Jim. With my husband gone, the estate, house and everything in it was mine. Clifford would still inherit a small fortune, but I knew it wouldn't be enough. To a man like Clifford, it was

Blakeney Park—worth tens of millions if broken up and sold to developers—that was the real prize.

Before I could take in this stunning development, a floorboard creaked. Some instinct made me hide. It was lucky I did. Clifford and Mr. Riker came into the room. Riker was Clifford's right-hand man. A practitioner of the darkest arts of human imagining. All the staff were terrified of him. Not for nothing was he called the Enforcer.

From behind the curtain, I heard the men discussing the will. Clifford was raging. He declared that Robbie was of unsound mind, that Jim and I had manipulated him, and that I should be got rid of. Eliminated was the word he used. I felt in my bones that this was no idle threat. Fearing for the two of you, my unborn babies, I resolved to hand in my notice without delay, using the excuse that I was grieving too much to do a good job.

I'll always regret leaving my hiding place too soon. As I stepped out from behind the curtain, Mr. Riker returned to the room. He'd forgotten something. He realized immediately that I'd overheard everything. Sheer terror lent me wings. Somehow, I evaded him as he lunged at me. It wasn't hard to lose him in the maze of corridors and staircases. I fled down to a seldom-used cellar and exited via a storm drain on the grounds.

From there, I risked a quick detour to my cottage to grab cash, your father's lucky horseshoe, and Amelia's painting, given to us on our wedding day. Then I ran for my life.

I made it on to a train and away, with Riker hot on my heels.

Amelia saved my life. She organized a fake passport and money. I flew to New York City, took the first Greyhound leaving the Port Authority bus station, and traveled as far south as I could go. I knew those men would never rest until they'd hunted me down and destroyed me or finished me off.

They didn't want any chance of Jim's wife contesting their right to Blakeney Park, which was worth tens of millions if sold to greedy developers. The one saving grace is that the Blakeneys never found out that I was expecting, not just one but two babies. That is the secret I am so desperate to keep. I know that if they discover the truth, they will do anything to prevent the two of you growing up to claim Blakeney Park. Your lives will always be in danger.

That's the real reason I fled Blakeney Park—to make sure Clifford and Mr. Riker never find out about you. To keep you safe.

I'll always believe that some guiding star led me to meet Gabe and the good people of the Castaway Diner that night. Only time will tell if I made the right choice entrusting you to their care. Whatever happens, I know that Amelia will watch over you from afar.

As for Robbie's will, I managed to take a photo of it on my phone right before Mr. Riker returned to the room. A copy is held in the office of a respected London solicitor.

Amelia has the details. Blakeney Park is yours if you want it: I'm bequeathing the estate to you, just as Robbie left it to your father.

With the guidance of your godmother, my will's executor, I have the utmost faith that you'll make the decision that's best for you and the estate. I have faith, too, that you'll find this letter—and Amelia—when you most need them.

Know this, darling Jess and Jude, wherever life takes you and however life shapes you, your dad and I will always be proud of you. We will love you to the stars and back until the end of time.

Your Mum xxx

CHAPTER 31

Homecoming

Amelia Starr was waiting on the beach at Bluey's Cove. Even from a distance, they were certain it was her. A dog was at her side, his creamy-white fur rippling in the breeze.

The moment the twins had anchored the yacht and hopped into the dinghy to row to the shore, Sam was in the sea, swimming toward them.

"Tell me I'm not dreaming, Jude?" cried Jess in wonder, reaching down to haul their friend aboard and getting drenched in the process.

Delirious with joy, Sam washed their faces and scrambled all over them, nearly upending the little rubber boat.

As they stepped onto the pale lilac beach, the sandy, wet dog leaped out of the dinghy and raced back and forth between the twins and Amelia Starr, barking wildly.

"*You* did this," Jude said to Jess, laughing. "You wished upon a painting, and Sam and our godmother came true."

"*We* did this," Jess told him, slinging an arm around her brother's shoulders as they walked up the beach. "It was you who spotted the Water Rats' kayak from the helicopter and deciphered the symbols on Sirius's map. You're the one who skippered us here."

"And you crewed the yacht and made the right call about heaving-to," said Jude. "Without that, we'd probably have capsized. We sailed through the storm together. And, thanks to Sirius, our godmother knew we were on our way."

Amelia Starr was smiling when they reached her. "So you made it across the Irish Sea, Jess and Jude? That's no mean feat, but it doesn't surprise me in the least. Nice yacht. Good name too, *Firebird*. Appropriate, under the circumstances."

"We thought so," Jess answered with a giggle. "A Water Rat lent it to us because we helped him save some foxes." She grinned. "Long story."

"Well, of course you saved some foxes! I wouldn't expect anything less."

Amelia clasped their hands. "Oh, my beautiful godchildren. I've waited for this moment, *dreamed* of it, for almost your whole lives. And you look so like your wonderful parents!"

"Are we allowed to hug you?" Jess asked shyly.

Amelia put out her arms and the twins stepped into the circle of them. She was soft and warm and felt like home. In a way, she was. The moment they saw her up close, they realized that they'd known her for as long as they could remember.

Once a year, every year, from the day they were born, she'd found a way to be near them. She was the woman who'd lingered over pancakes in the Castaway Diner, reading a novel. The artist they'd seen painting fishermen hauling in nets on a trip to Key West. The tourist who'd left a box of adventure stories for Jess on the porch of Gabe's cabin one birthday, on the exact same day that Jude found a sailing T-shirt and fishing rod on a near-deserted beach. Looking back, he recalled passing her as he and Gabe strolled onto the sand.

"Did you and Gabe ever meet?" he asked her now.

"Never. Before your mother passed away, she and I worked out every detail of how her babies would be taken care of if the worst should happen. I often wonder if she had a premonition that she was not long for this world, because the day before you were born, Joanna—Ana—told Gabe that your lives would be in danger if anyone from her previous life ever found you.

"She also informed him that you had a secret godmother who'd ensure that you were provided for until you were at least eighteen and made him promise that, if anything ever happened to her, he'd take care of you as if you were his own. She told him my first name but nothing else. For everyone's safety, it was agreed that the less he knew, the better.

"In twelve years, Gabe and I spoke just once, on a pay phone, soon after your mother died. He gave me his word that he'd go to the ends of the earth to protect you. I believed him. After that, we only ever communicated a couple of times a year, using a special email address created for that purpose alone.

"When we did correspond, it was usually to discuss money and update his exit strategy in case it ever became necessary for him to walk away from his life and job to keep you safe.

"Meantime, I had my own spies at Blakeney Park and Daybreak Media: a cleaner and a mailroom worker. When I learned that a friend of the Blakeneys had seen a photo of a waitress bearing a striking resemblance to their ex-employee, Joanna Gray, at a Florida diner, and that Clifford seemed very agitated about it, I was sure that his notorious enforcer, Mr. Riker, would leave no stone unturned checking out the lead.

"I emailed Gabe asking him to put our escape plan into action. I sent him money. I was relieved when the plan seemed to be working—or at least it was, until Mr. Riker somehow traced your yacht to the Virgin Islands and confronted Gabe. Imagine my distress when Gabe, having sent me an emergency email about the encounter, went silent and didn't return my own increasingly frantic messages.

"The first I knew of the cruel hand fate had dealt you was when I read about it in the *Daily Gazette*. Before I could act, you were in the clutches of Clifford and Allegra and on your way to Blakeney Park. From then on, I had to be incredibly careful. I needed to extricate you from a deadly situation, but I had to do it without endangering you further. Two and a half days ago, Bridget, my cleaner spy at Blakeney Park, discovered that you'd escaped by boat. The Water Rats were accused of helping you.

"By chance, I knew a member of the Water Rats. Before I could call her, Sirius contacted me via my website. He said that you were sailing to Bluey's Cove *at that very moment*. I was stunned and so deliriously happy that I hardly dared hope his message was real. I was also afraid. A storm was forecast, and I was terrified that the Blakeneys would somehow hunt you down in the Irish Sea and spirit you away before the coast guard or anyone else could reach you. I couldn't sleep I was so anxious. Finally, Sirius sent me a link to a boat-tracking app. I stopped worrying when the app showed *Firebird* making steady progress despite the storm."

She smiled at them both. "Gabe would be so proud of his young sailors. He taught you well."

"It probably helped that the Blakeneys didn't know what yacht we were on," said Jude. "They'd have sent Mr. Riker after us on a powerboat."

"According to Bridget the maid, the Blakeneys waited almost twenty-four hours before they reported you missing," Amelia told him. "I have to admit, I let them sweat. This afternoon, when I was sure that you were almost here, *almost home*, I rang Allegra Blakeney and informed her that I was your godmother, and that you'd be living with me from now on. I strongly advised her to tell her husband and Mr. Riker to leave you well alone if they didn't want me going to a rival newspaper with everything I knew."

Jude was impressed. "How did Allegra react?"

"There was a long, calculating silence, then she said tersely: 'As you wish,' and hung up."

"What about Sam?" asked Jess. "How did he find you before we did?"

"That, too, was down to Bridget. She rang to say that the

Blakeneys had sent him to a shelter the day after dispatching you to separate boarding schools. I called the shelter right away. After the usual medical tests and background checks, Sam was brought to Bluey's Cove. He's been with me, safe and loved, ever since. We've been waiting for you."

"It was you who sent me that postcard, wasn't it?" Jude said later that evening, as they sat around a worn oak table, eating delicious homemade leek-and-potato soup with crusty bread and butter.

Amelia smiled. "I had a sense you might be in need of some cheer. I think of those words often, and I believe them with all my heart. We can't go back and change the beginning. Nor would I want to. It's the voyages we embark on and the storms that we endure that make us and shape us. But the three of us—"

Sam, sprawled in front of the fire, twitched in his dreams, chasing seabirds.

"Four of us," Jude reminded her, and they all laughed.

"Four of us," agreed Amelia, "can start from where we are and change the way our story ends."

"Can we request a happy ending?" asked Jess.

Her godmother's eyes sparkled as brightly as the bay. "Oh, I think a happy ending's exactly what's needed here. Don't you?"

EPILOGUE

THE MORNING TRIBUNE

The High Court at London's Old Bailey today ruled that fifteen-year-old twins, Jess and Jude Gray, are the legal owners of Blakeney Park, Gloucestershire, denying the last appeal of media baron Clifford Blakeney and his wife, Allegra.

In a joint statement issued by their godmother, artist Amelia Starr, the twins said: "We're grateful that the court has honored the wishes of Robbie Blakeney and our parents, Jim and Joanna Gray. We intend to continue transforming Blakeney Park into a sanctuary for wildlife. Going forward, the estate will be managed by the National Trust, as it has been for the past three years. It will be held in trust for the nation for generations to come.

"In addition, permanent mooring rights have been granted to five narrowboats on the River Severn, including one owned by our friend Sirius Emerson, who helped us when we needed it most."

The Grays sailed to England on their new Rustler yacht, *Dolphin Dreams*, bought with the insurance payout received after their previous boat, *You Gotta Friend*, was wrecked in a storm. The twins wanted to be at the Old Bailey for the verdict. They declined to press fraud charges against Clifford and Allegra Blakeney.

"That chapter of our life is closed," the twins said.

Tomorrow, Jess and Jude Gray will sail home to Ireland, where they live beside the sea with their godmother, Amelia, their dog, Sam, and their horse, Autumn.

AUTHOR'S NOTE

Wave Riders was written during the COVID-19 lockdown of 2020, which was both a blessing and, well, a challenge.

To be truthful, writing a novel during a pandemic was one of the hardest things I've ever done. But it was also a glorious escape. I love the ocean as much as I love telling stories. As the months passed and the UK lockdown stretched on and on, and separations became harder and more painful, and the global news ever more dire, *Wave Riders* became my sanctuary.

As every writer and reader, young and old, knows, imagination lends you wings. In the real world, I was constrained by COVID rules and confined to four walls, but every single day, as I sat down to write with my Bengal cat, Max, beside me, I had the freedom to swim in turquoise lagoons and sail the wild waves with Jess and Jude.

By sheer chance, I'd done the sailing part of the research

for *Wave Riders* the previous year, when it was originally going to be published.

Before I became a children's author, I wrote sports and music books and was a journalist for London's *Sunday Times*. Almost the best part about my job was traveling the world, seeing extraordinary places and wildlife, and interviewing extraordinary people. When I started writing children's novels, I saw no reason to research fiction differently.

For *Dolphin Song*, for instance, I went all the way to the exquisite Bazaruto Archipelago in Mozambique. I swam in lagoons and climbed the crumbling steps of the eerie but curiously magical abandoned lighthouse that later became Martine and Ben's fictional shelter in the second of my White Giraffe series.

For *The Glory*, my YA novel about an endurance horse race across the American West, I drove 1,120 miles from Boulder, Colorado, to Hood River, Oregon—in winter. When I wasn't driving through blizzards, I rode through the snowy mountains of Wyoming on a palomino mustang called Kicker. He later became the inspiration for Scout in my book.

When it came to researching *Wave Riders*, I was determined to learn to sail. There was only one problem. A big one. The few times I'd ever been on a boat on the ocean, I'd been seasick. Seasickness, as anyone who's had it will tell you, is no joke.

I started slowly, and nervously. I signed up for a Royal Yachting Association (RYA) first aid course and proudly earned my certificate.

The next bit was harder. To learn to sail—really sail—I needed to do an RYA Competent Crew course with Nomad Sailing. That meant five whole days on a yacht with five strangers. Once we left shore, there'd be no turning back.

I went prepared. To ward off seasickness, I bought ginger cookies, crystalized ginger, and acupressure point Sea-Bands. Then I set out to find the gear.

I learned very quickly that sailing in the UK at the tail end of winter is bone-numbingly cold. I'd bought and/or packed thermal vests, leggings, sailing gloves, hats, fleeces, technical offshore salopettes, and deck boots.

Sound like a lot? Some days I was so freezing that I wore two pairs of gloves, two thermal hats, a thermal vest and leggings, a T-shirt, fleece, the special salopettes, and a borrowed sailing jacket, and I was still cold. I just didn't have actual hypothermia.

My berth beneath the deck was so low and snug that I had to slide into my sleeping bag from the door. But all of it—every waking minute of it—was an adventure. And I adore adventures. Most important, I experienced sailing and close-quarter yacht living in a way I'd never have understood if I'd studied a thousand DVDs and books.

Just like Jess, I lay in my sleeping bag and heard the whining of the wind, the clanking of the halyard, and the *slap-slap* of waves against the hull. Through the salt-splattered hatch of the galley, the sky at night was panther-black.

Thanks to my industrial supplies of ginger, I never felt

unwell once during the week, not even on the second day when we woke to force 6 winds that later reached force 7. That's near gale-force on the Beaufort scale, the wind-force scale used by sailors.

It was an unforgettable experience. I learned, as the twins do, that sailing is hard, risky, physical work; that it takes courage and immense skill. It's an unrivaled test of character. Decks are slippery. Waves are unpredictable. Conditions can change in a moment. Mistakes can cost lives.

My absolute favorite part of the "Comp Crew" course was our night sailing lesson in force 6 winds—not a sentence I ever thought I'd write! Each of us took a turn at the helm. The memory of oil-black waves coming at the yacht from every angle, and the knife-sharp wind wolf-howling through the lines and sheets, will stay with me always.

Throughout the surreal and icy hours, my crewmates Gabriella and John kept me laughing, and I did my best to repay them with frequent coffees. It wasn't the sailing fairy tale that I'd envisioned, but it was pure magic.

All stories start, for me, with a feeling or an atmosphere. At the end of that night, as I crawled—exhausted but very happy—into my sleeping bag, I knew I'd found it.

ACKNOWLEDGMENTS

There were two types of writers during the 2020 pandemic lockdowns: those who found writing easy, and those who found it hard. I freely admit that I fell into the second category.

There's not a chance that this book would have been finished without the support, patience, and utter loveliness of my agent, Catherine Clarke, and my editors, Venetia Gosling at Gosling Editorial, and Wesley Adams at Farrar, Straus and Giroux, three of the most wonderful people I've ever known.

I'm indebted also to Melissa Warton, Ilana Worrell, Kat Kopit, Claire Maby, Erica Ferguson, and Veronica Mang at FSG, and Lucy Pearse, Sam Smith, Belinda Rasmussen, Jo Hardacre, Cheyney Smith, and Sarah Clarke at Macmillan Children's Books. Thank you is inadequate but meant with all my heart.

Special thanks to Rachael Dean, who created *Wave Riders'* showstopping cover in the UK, and to Matt Rockefeller, for the equally brilliant American cover.

For the technical, sailing parts of this book, I'm hugely grateful to my sailing instructor, Lou Barden of Nomad Sailing. Any mistakes in this book are mine alone. Massive thanks to Anne Tudor for putting me in touch with Arthur Hicks in the Virgin Islands, and to Arthur for sharing his extensive expertise in ocean sailing, instructing young people to sail, and local Virgin Island currents and weather systems.

For the Horseshoe Reef storm scenes, I was helped enormously by Phil Aspinall, director of operations at Virgin Island Search and Rescue (VISAR), and for the Irish Sea crossing, I'm beyond grateful to Sarah Webb for both local knowledge and technical advice.

Lockdown living has proved—if it were ever in doubt—that friends, family, and nature are as vital to our happiness and well-being as oxygen.

Thanks to Virginia McKenna, Jenny Seagrove, and Ruth Wilson, whose grace, humor, and kindness were points of light for me throughout the past year.

I'm grateful every day to be part of the children's book community, which is filled with wonderful, supportive booksellers, publishing folk, and writers. Thanks especially to Abi Elphinstone, Katherine Rundell, Piers Torday, Hilary McKay, and Gill Lewis for keeping me smiling and hopeful through the darkest of days.

Last, thanks to my family and friends, especially Merina McInnes, my niece, Alex, my sister, Lisa, my mom and dad, and my godsons, Matis and Francis. This book, about the importance and specialness of loved ones and home, is for you.

A LETTER FROM THE
FAMILY OF LUCIA, TO WHOM
WAVE RIDERS IS DEDICATED

Dear Reader,

A few words about Lucia, who loved Lauren's stories and to whom *Wave Riders* is kindly dedicated. She was the brightest, bubbliest, most fun and most loyal friend you could have. There when you needed someone, wise beyond her years, more than ready to party, dance all night, and then finish it off with a dawn dip in a freezing sea. Lucia was packed with life but knew it couldn't be taken for granted.

When she was eight, she suddenly became extremely ill. A liver transplant was her only hope. Lucia was lucky, and deeply grateful for her medical team. Even more so for the organ donor whose liver was now keeping her alive, and whose family agreed to that selfless gift.

Lucia needed a second transplant a year later and, when she was sixteen, a third. By then, the decision to accept another transplant was Lucia's. It wasn't easy. She spent lots of time at the beach, her place of energy and solace. One evening, watching the sun set over the waves, Lucia made her decision. "It was the moment I knew I could go through with it, and I wouldn't look back."

Not knowing when, or if, a transplant would become possible, Lucia had two goals.

The first was to make a difference. She knew her life had already been saved twice by people she didn't know. She would use her story to help others think about organ donation, encouraging them to talk with family and friends and share their decisions.

Lucia launched her campaign, **Live Loudly Donate Proudly**, writing amazing blogs full of energy, humor, fun, and courage. You'll find plenty there about organ donation, and lots of encouragement to enjoy life, to find what matters most to you, and how to make a difference yourself.

Her second goal was to compete in the 2017 Transplant Games in Málaga, Spain. Lucia was introduced to Transplant Sport UK (TSUK) after her first transplant, to help her recover and stay fit.

Each year, the UK Transplant Games bring together over 1,000 competing transplant recipients and many more families, friends, and donor families in a festival of life and sport. It was always the highlight of Lucia's year. She was a swimmer and competed in nine UK Games for her hospital team and three World Games (including Málaga) for her national team, fundraising for TSUK whenever she could.

In the Games, Lucia found a unique circle of understanding friends; another family, with whom she could continue to laugh loudly, dance wildly, and live fully, knowing everyone else knew how precarious and precious the gift of new life is, made possible by the kindness of strangers. "The feeling I get when I am racing alongside others who have been through similar experiences to me, is second to nothing I have ever experienced." Every medal she won was in honor of her donors.

At the end of 2019, Lucia needed a rare fourth transplant. The transplant worked, but recovery slipped away. Lucia died in May 2020, just a few days before her twenty-first birthday.

She left us her passion for life and for the Transplant Games. She left us her campaign, **Live Loudly Donate Proudly**, and her encouragement to open conversations about organ donation. Maybe one day we, or someone we love, may need that gift of life. Or perhaps we may give that gift to someone else, maybe someone like Lucia, who will go on to show us how precious life is and how to live it fully, gratefully, loudly, and proudly . . .

With love,
David, Rachel, and Alice